I0772154

WE *Fell in Love* IN OCTOBER

A Pineridge Novel

STARLA DEKRUYF

This book is a work of fiction. Names, characters, places, and incidents either are products of the author's imagination or are used fictitiously. Any resemblance to actual events or, places, living or dead, is entirely coincidental and not intended by the author.

WE FELL IN LOVE IN OCTOBER: A Small Town Friends to Lovers Romance—Pineridge Series-Book 2

STARLA DEKRUYF

This book has been modified from its original version, (Tricked in October) and has been independently rereleased under this new title.

Copyright © 2024 by Starla DeKruyf

Cover character art by: Stephanie Henigen @stephsbooktherapy

Cover design by: Starla DeKruyf

All rights reserved. No part of this book may be reproduced, distributed, or transmitted in any form or by any means, including information storage and retrieval systems, without prior consent and written permission from the author, except for the use of brief quotations in a book review.

Second Edition

Print Edition ISBN: 979-8-9856269-8-8

Digital ISBN: 979-8-9856269-9-5

WE
Fell in Love
IN
OCTOBER

A Pineridge Novel

BOOK 2

STARLA DEKRUYF

*To the women who are strong even when they don't want to be,
who keep going when they want to quit, and who attempt a
chance at love after loss.
This one's for you.*

Content/Trigger Warnings

This book is intended for readers who are 17+. Please note that there may be content in this book that may be triggering for some readers. This list is not exclusive, so please proceed with caution.

- Open door w/o graphic details
- Mild explicit language/cursing
- Alcohol consumption
- Death, (in the past/off page)
- Grief
- Alcoholism

Kelsey

Kelsey O'Henry didn't believe in the traditional five stages of grief. She had her own way of dealing. Push through. No matter what. She was many things—but being a quitter wasn't one of them.

Her bestie, Isabella often called her bullheaded. She wasn't wrong. But the thing was, Kelsey wasn't only bullheaded, she was short on time.

Who had time to go through the five stages of grief when they had three kids to take care of, a bar to run, and an alcoholic mama to babysit? Denial, anger, bargaining, depression, and acceptance would have to take a backseat.

With a crying baby on her hip, Kelsey filled a pint glass of beer from the tap. A local brewery had just sent over a keg of their newest seasonal brew—an autumn IPA with touches of peach and tangerine. Kelsey hoped it would be a welcomed addition to O'Henry's growing fall menu of beer and hard ciders.

She slid the glass across the smooth bar top to one of her favorite awaiting customers to try. Isabella smiled at Kelsey as she picked up the glass and took a sniff before taking a sip. Typically a wine drinker, Izzy was picky when it came to her beer selection.

Isabella pursed her lips and took another drink before setting her glass down.

"So?" Kelsey's brows lifted, bouncing the still fussing baby Charlotte on her hip.

Isabella propped an elbow on the bar top. "It's good. Really good. I'm impressed."

The music in the bar was loud tonight, making it hard to hear her bestie's response. A fall playlist the O'Henry's server, Sophie picked out full of cozy and angsty vibes reverberated through the bar's old speakers.

"You actually like it?" Kelsey leaned in.

"Yeah, I mean what's not to like? A citrus IPA...in autumn? Where do I sign up?" Isabella stood from the stool she'd been perched on and adjusted the hem of her dark green sweater.

The tension in Kelsey's shoulders loosened, but only slightly. Satisfied customers of the new beer meant she could cross one thing off her mental to-do list. Now she wouldn't have to cancel the recurring shipments of the IPA kegs from Tapp's Brewery.

That was, if she could afford the recurring shipments. The unpaid bills piled on the back desk haunted her like the Grim Reaper. Outwardly she pretended as if she had it all together, but her worry over the possibility of losing everything threatened to unveil itself.

Isabella reached her hands out for Charlotte who was still crying. Kelsey hesitated before handing her over. Charlotte was a difficult baby to console. She only favored a handful of people and Izzy usually wasn't one of them.

"If you wanna try, be my guest," Kelsey said.

"Shh," Isabella shushed in Charlotte's ear while she

bounced her, but the baby continued to fuss. "Where's your mom? I thought she was keeping the kids tonight?"

The tension returned tenfold, and Kelsey's shoulders tightened. "Do you even have to ask?"

Rita, Kelsey's mama was currently passed out on the small sofa in the back office of O'Henry's Bar and Grill. After years living with the disease, Rita was generally a functioning alcoholic. Meaning, she could be drunk without anyone knowing and a hangover rarely fazed her. But occasionally she went on a binger and Kelsey was reminded what life was like in those first few years after her dad left and the horror began.

Kelsey pushed up the rolled sleeves of her flannel and then filled more pint glasses two at a time now that she had both hands free.

"Why didn't you call me? You know I'd take the kids," Isabella said.

Kelsey snorted a laugh as she set the overfilled glasses onto a tray. "Sorry." She cleared her throat, trying to recover. "I love you, Izz. But you're not exactly Mary Poppins."

Isabella gasped in mock offense and pressed a hand to her chest. "I should be insulted."

Nudging her chin at Sophie as she approached, Kelsey slid the full tray across the bar. Sophie lifted it with a natural ease and carried it to a table of awaiting customers.

Kelsey returned her attention to Isabella. She tugged on the sleeve of Isabella's sweater. "I appreciate you offering, but I need to come up with a more permanent solution. I can't keep bringing them here." She gestured at her two other children who sat at a nearby bar height table stacking salt and pepper shakers into a pyramid.

Her heart pinched in her chest. They didn't deserve this. The two of them used to enjoy coming to the bar and seeing their daddy working. Ricky would make them Shirley Temples with extra cherries. He'd been such a proud father. He always introduced them to everyone who came into the bar.

Charlotte wailed even louder.

Kelsey exhaled a drawn-out sigh. She was so tired. She was pretty sure even the black hair on her head was tired. Taking Charlotte from Isabella, Kelsey pressed a kiss to the ten-month old's head of soft strawberry blonde curls. Out of the three kids, Charlotte resembled Ricky the most. She had his green eyes and red hair. The other two, June and Zach, took after her with dark hair and blue eyes.

"It doesn't help that Charlotte hates everyone."

"She likes my mom. Call her next time," Isabella said.

"Your mama is a saint. She's already watched the kids once this week."

"And she'd be glad to do it again." Isabella smiled.

Kelsey kissed Charlotte on the head. "Thankfully, my in-laws are coming to my rescue—once again." These days, Ricky's parents spent nearly as much time with the kids as she did.

"You better plan ahead and ask them early to babysit on Halloween," Isabella said.

"Already done. While the grandparents take the kids trick-or-treating, I'll be working."

The signs posted around the bar were an annoying reminder of the O'Henry's Halloween Couples Costume Party in a few weeks. Last year she and Ricky dressed as Jim and Pam from The Office. This year, she'd planned on dressing in her usual wardrobe of a flannel and jeans.

Isabella pouted her lips. "Kels, no. Please at least dress up."

"What am I gonna wear? Who am I gonna get to dress up with me? The only person other than Ricky I've gone to a couple's costume party with was Davis, and that was so many years ago."

A spark twinkled in Izzy's eyes, and Kelsey shut her down

before she could even speak. "No. Davis and I are friends. Best friends. It's not gonna happen."

She and Davis Vance hadn't worn those costumes since before there was a '*Kelsey and Ricky*'.

Nearly ten years ago on Halloween, the two of them had shared an *almost* kiss. It was still her biggest regret. It had nearly ruined their friendship.

"Hey, I thought I was your best friend?"

"You're my bestie." Kelsey flashed her a smile.

Leo shuffled up behind Izzy, wrapping his arms around her waist and pulling her in close.

Seeing Isabella happy caused a flutter in her chest.

"Hey, Kels," Leo said, releasing his hold on Isabella.

"Don't stop groping my bestie on my account," Kelsey teased.

Leo hunched his shoulders. "Can you blame me?"

"Not even a little. She *is* the hottest woman in the bar tonight." Kelsey set a beer in front of Leo with a smile. "You better take her out on that dance floor."

"You know I don't dance." Leo chugged his beer.

"That's a great idea. Please, Leo," Isabella coaxed, dragging him away and toward the dance floor.

Leo gave Kelsey a strained look, pushing a hand through his hair.

"Hey, if you don't, I will. And you can watch the three hellions." Kelsey held out Charlotte who hadn't stopped sobbing. The little girl had tears and snot streaming down her red, blotchy face.

"Uhh...on second thought, dancing doesn't sound so bad."

Kelsey smirked and returned Charlotte to her hip, squeezing her closer. She knew that would do the trick.

"We'll be back." Isabella dragged a still reluctant Leo toward the dance floor.

"Hey, Kelsey?" Julian, the bar's chef called from the kitchen. "The water is still leaking."

A crowd of customers huddled at the bar, signaling her. Even with a baby on her hip, she filled glasses of hard cider and beer one by one as if on autopilot.

"Yeah, yeah. It's on my list," she said, pinching at her flannel shirt to find some relief to her overheated body in between serving the customers.

Igniting the gas fireplace in the corner of the bar to ward off the crisp temperature outside felt like a horrible mistake now as her skin sweltered. The thousands of glowing fairy lights she and Isabella had strung across the ceiling to create a cozy fall vibe seemed like a good idea at the time, too. Now though, they only made her feel feverish.

Sophie approached the bar and slammed down her tray. "Miss Kelsey, there's a tourist at table six who needs to be cut off."

Kelsey shuffled to the computer screen and frowned. "But he's only had one beer."

"Well, I don't know. Maybe he was already drunk before he came in. He's making crude comments and I swear, if he touches me, my jujitsu training might make an appearance."

Ricky always handled the drunk and disorderly customers. It was just another reminder of the things Kelsey had to take care of now that he was gone. But with Charlotte screaming in her ear, the packed bar, and the leaking sink, she felt near the breaking point.

She pinched her eyes shut and swiped the back of her arm across her forehead. She absolutely hated asking for help.

"Hey, Kels. Everything okay?"

At the sound of the soft and rumbling voice, Kelsey's muscles relaxed, and tears nearly welled behind her eyelids. Her throat thickened as her eyes flew open. The sight of the familiar and kind face of her best guy friend, filled her with relief.

Davis.

Despite his over six-foot-tall frame, she felt like tackling him with a hug.

"Thank, God you're here," she said, breathing out a lengthy sigh.

As shocking as his presence was—because he rarely came into O'Henry's—she was grateful. People who didn't know him, might find him intimidating. But to the ones who did, they knew the introverted, shy, Vance twin was down to earth.

When Davis smiled, his lips practically disappeared and his glassy, blue eyes crinkled at the corners. He kept his facial hair at a permanent three-day stubble that drove Kelsey crazy. Was he growing out a beard or was he just being lazy?

Ugh.

His dark brown hair was unruly, not quite curly but not straight either. He was soft-spoken and often dressed in flannels and oversized sweaters and sweatshirts, hiding the fit physique that would make any woman swoon.

Any woman but Kelsey.

Tonight, Davis had on a light blue sweater and his wild hair was tucked beneath a Tapp's Brewery hat.

"What's going on?" he asked, brows furrowed and concern streaking across his face.

"What's not going on? I've got a drunken tourist at table six, a leaky sink in the kitchen, and a crying baby in a bar." She gestured at her hip where the youngster clung on.

Charlotte's crying had turned to a whimper, and she kicked her legs. Charlotte loved Davis. He crouched and leaned in toward her, tickling her tummy. She didn't react with a full-blown belly laugh, but she did let out a squeal, which felt like progress.

Davis put his hands out for Charlotte, and she went to him easily.

Kelsey's heart shifted in her chest, shoving against her rib cage as Charlotte stopped crying nearly instantly. The girl reached up and tugged on the bill of Davis's baseball hat before yanking it off completely and she giggled.

"Ha, you're a little thief," he teased, his eyes sparkling.

Charlotte smiled wide; her rosy cheeks still dampened with tears.

"You gotta stop giving your mama such a hard time. You hear me?" Davis pressed his finger to the tip of Charlotte's nose.

Charlotte clutched Davis's hat to her chest and giggled.

"Kelsey?" Julian hollered from the open door of the kitchen.

"I'm coming," she called, agitation building in her chest.

"You take care of the leaking sink. Let me go take care of table six," Davis suggested, handing Charlotte back to her.

"You sure?"

A blush swept across Davis's unshaven face as he nodded and chewed a bruised thumbnail, the oversized sleeves of his blue sweater tugged over his knuckles. "What? You don't think I can handle an irate tourist?"

Charlotte began to whine again in between fits of fresh sobs.

"I know you can handle it, it's just that you don't usually like confrontation."

"Doesn't mean I won't handle it. For you." He returned his hat to his head before shuffling backward toward table six.

Kelsey's chest heaved and her words caught in her throat. She honestly didn't know how she would've survived the last nine months without Davis's friendship.

"Kels?" Julian called again, impatience in his tone.

"Coming," she replied.

Rushing into the kitchen, it didn't take Kelsey long to see the problem Julian had warned her about. Water gushed from the shut off under the sink. He had placed a bucket there to catch the water but that was only a temporary fix. Especially by the looks of the wet towels laying on the floor surrounding the bucket.

This was not good. All she could envision was dollar signs flashing in her brain. It would cost money she didn't have.

Julian ran a hand over his tired face. "It's the cold water shut off valve."

She knelt to get a closer look. "You sure?"

"Yeah, pretty sure. I need a wrench to tighten it and I can't find one in Ricky's office. And Kelsey, besides the fact that I don't have time for this, I'm not a plumber. I'm a line cook."

She dropped her head. "I know, I know."

"I told you last week it was leaking. And then I reminded you this morning."

"Damn it, Julian, I know." She folded her lips in between her teeth.

Charlotte stopped crying and sniffed, staring at her mom wide-eyed.

Kelsey wasn't typically a stressed-out person. Where had the cheerful, easygoing woman she used to be gone? If that woman could come back soon, it would be much appreciated.

"I'm sorry," she mumbled.

Julian sighed, pushing both of his hands through his greasy hair. "I know you're overwhelmed. But you don't have to do everything on your own. You need to ask for help. Or hire someone."

Hiring a plumber would be costly. She knew how to use a wrench. How hard could it be to tighten the shut-off?

"I don't need help. I've got this. I will find a wrench and do it myself."

Julian threw his hands up and cursed under his breath. "Fine. You take care of it. I'll go back to cooking. Or did you want to do that too?"

"Don't be silly. I'm not a cook."

"You're no plumber either," Julian replied.

"Tonight, I guess I am."

Julian backed away, shaking his head but smirking. "Smart ass," he mumbled.

Kelsey rushed to the back office she'd now claimed as her own. She flipped on the light and set Charlotte down on the floor. While she'd left Ricky's posters of monster trucks and 90's grunge bands on the walls, current pictures of the kids now sat in frames on the desk. Orange and white faux pumpkins lined the windowsill and black, hairy spider toys perched in a fake web in the corner of the office.

Kelsey's mama, Rita stirred on the worn-out leather sofa. She wiped at her raccoon eyes where the black mascara and eyeliner had in smudged circles.

"Be a good daughter, and turn off the light, will ya, love bug?" Rita muttered.

Kelsey ignored her and yanked open the closet door. She rummaged around inside, perching on her hands and knees until she finally located Ricky's tool bag in the back on the floor. She lifted it and straightened, tossing the heavy bag onto the desk. The faded green, thick fabric had seen better days. It, along with the tools had been passed down from Ricky's grand-dad. She'd given him a hard time about not replacing the old tools, telling him they were rusty. But there were few things Ricky treasured in life, and these tools were one of them.

She dug inside the bag until she found a wrench set. She set it aside before lifting the bag in a hurry, but it was heavier than she'd expected, and she lost her grip. The bag slid off the desk, toppling to the floor with a loud *crash*, spilling an assortment of tools and taking a stack of papers with it.

Her mom, Rita, groaned. "Kelsey, what is all that racket?"

Kelsey exhaled and pressed a hand to her chest upon finding Charlotte out of harm's way. "It's fine, mama. Just go back to sleep."

Grumbling under her breath, she crouched amongst the fallen tools. She didn't have time for this. There was not only a leaking sink to tend to, but she had a bar packed full of customers and her kids to keep an eye on until reinforcements arrived.

Quickly, Kelsey shoved each tool back into the bag before gathering the papers into a stack and trying not to allow them to distract her. She sat back on her heels, about to push herself up to her feet when something on the top sheet caught her eye. The logo of the bank O'Henry's Bar and Grill had their loan with was reflected in the corner. Bright red words stamped on the page: PAST DUE.

Her heart skidded behind her ribcage. There was a silent roaring in her ears, and a rumble in her chest as she felt herself losing control of everything. As much as she'd been trying to push this information to the back of her mind, the reality of her financial situation sat staring her in the face. The contents of this letter, and all the rest in the stack, meant things were about to change.

And she hated change.

Forcing herself to focus on the letter again, the date in bold letters caught her attention. If she didn't come up with a solution, in less than forty-five days, O'Henry's would have a new owner.

After Ricky's snowmobile accident the winter before resulting in his death, Kelsey had taken over the responsibilities of the business. Including handling the finances and managing the bar. In all honesty, it had been a lot to take on. Juggling the bar and the kids the past year had been exhausting.

Yet, she'd found herself taking to her new role as O'Henry's manager easily. She enjoyed serving the customers, chatting with the Pineridge locals, and connecting with vendors from breweries all around Colorado.

O'Henry's Bar and Grill wasn't just a bar or a livelihood. And it wasn't only a part of Ricky and his legacy.

It was a part of *her*.

It was a part of Pineridge.

After the accident, she'd closed the bar for a full month which caused her to get behind. And the bills had piled up. She'd had to take a second loan against the business to be able to afford to keep it going. Even though the bar was frequently busy, there was more money going out than what was coming in.

Kelsey wasn't sure how she would fix this, but she had to. She couldn't let this happen. She'd already lost Ricky; she couldn't lose the bar too.

CHAPTER 2
Davis

Swiping a thumb at the condensation on his glass, Davis Vance contemplated leaving the bar. Coming into O'Henry's on a Friday night had been a mistake. It was loud and crowded. The only exceptions he made for putting up with either of those things was for a concert. And it had better be a damn good one.

The drunk customer grew louder, and Davis groaned. He took a long, satisfying drink of his beer before setting the glass on the bar and pulling himself off the stool. Kelsey wasn't wrong, he typically shied away from confrontation. But he'd told Kelsey he would handle the drunk guy and he didn't want to let her down.

As he lowered his head, and yanked the brim of his hat down, someone bumped into his shoulder. When he glanced up, he spotted a familiar face.

"Leo, hey."

Davis and Leo Hoffman shook hands.

"Hey, Davis?"

Davis nodded, confirming his identity and Leo hadn't just mistaken him for his twin brother.

"It's good to see ya. How've you been?" Leo asked.

"I'm good. And you?"

"Can't complain. Hey, how's the show going? Izzy and I don't miss an episode."

"It's moving along. Looking forward to filming wrapping up for the season honestly and getting a break." Davis rubbed a hand at the back of his neck.

Looking forward to the break was putting it mildly. If Davis truly wanted to be honest with Leo, he'd tell him the show sucked and he missed the old days. Back when it was just him and his twin brother, Garrett working job to job, never really sure when a paycheck would come. They'd help friends and the residents of Pineridge, sometimes taking trade work instead of payment. That's how he'd ended up with an old snowmobile and a tattered sailboat. Both sports he'd never been into.

"It's pretty cool having celebrities in our own town." *Celebrities.*

He'd hardly refer to himself as a celebrity. Though Garrett didn't mind the title. Even let it go to his head.

When Garrett's fiancée died in a helicopter crash while vacationing in Hawaii with her parents a year ago, he was lost. Davis would've agreed to just about anything to help his brother out of his depression. And apparently, he had. Because he signed a contract with HGTV he'd never been thrilled about.

"That renovation you did on the Lopez's kitchen was amazing."

Davis tried to shrug off the compliment. "Thanks."

"Hey, Garrett." Ashley, one of the elite and rich girls he'd gone to school with shimmied up next to him, smiling wide. In school, she'd never given him the time of day. And not much had changed since then. Unfortunately, this was your typical twin mistaken identity situation Davis had grown used to.

He cleared his throat, and fidgeted with the sleeves of his sweater, yanking them over his knuckles further. "Sorry, but you got the wrong twin...again."

The *again* part was the kicker.

Ashley cupped a hand over her mouth and giggled into it before saying, "Oops, sorry."

"Not a problem," he replied.

She sauntered away, but not without giving him the once over first and grinning.

Hmm...that was new.

"Oof. How often does that happen?" Leo asked.

"More often than you might think."

He supposed he should take it as a compliment. Lately, more and more, women especially, were mistaking him for his more attractive twin brother, Garrett. He hadn't given Garrett that label, it had been attached to him at a young age while Davis was labeled studious.

The brothers had the same six-foot, muscular frame, but Davis hid his beneath bulky flannels and sweaters while Garrett wore workout clothing and tailored suits. They styled their similar shade of dark brown hair differently as well. Davis preferred his hair longer and messy and he kept some facial stubble. Garrett had his hair short and his face clean-shaven.

Commotion sounded out from rowdy table six, and Davis exhaled a deep sigh. "Any chance you wanna help me get that drunk tourist an Uber?"

Leo glanced over his shoulder. "Ha! Are you kidding? A chance to kick out a tourist—I'm your guy."

Relief expanded in Davis's chest. He had every intention of following Leo, ready to handle the situation like he'd told Kelsey he would, but the screams that sounded from behind the

Employees Only swinging door didn't give him the opportunity. Instead, they prompted his feet to propel in that direction, a nod over his shoulder to Leo on his way.

Davis pushed through the swinging kitchen door, and he frantically searched the space.

"Kelsey? Where are you?" Davis hollered.

"I'm back here," she called out.

Davis tore off toward the back, he scanned the space to the left where the office was and then to the right where the sinks were. There, he finally spotted Kelsey kneeling on the floor near the sink. With her clothes soaking wet, and a wrench in her hand, water continued to spray at her.

For a fraction of a second, he was at a loss for words, his gaze fixated on—dare he say it—the sexy woman standing before him. He shook away the thought. "You okay?"

"I'm fine. Just trying to fix the leaky shut-off."

"Here, let me help you." He reached for her, and she slipped her hand into his awaiting one.

The water sprayed at his face and chest as he helped Kelsey off the floor where she was perched underneath the sink. As her feet slipped against the slick, wet floor, he gripped her hand tighter and yanked her up, causing her chest to collide with his. Instinctively, his gaze moved over her, finding her soaked white t-shirt transparent and accentuating her breasts as she pressed against him.

Swallowing hard, he jerked his attention to her face. "Sorry...I...you okay?" he asked again.

What the hell was he doing?

This was Kelsey. His best friend. He didn't check her out. Even if lately, there'd been this faint, sort of weird ache in his chest each time she was in his presence.

Kelsey lifted her chin, her wet lashes sweeping up until her eyes stilled on his. Water droplets ran down the bridge of her nose and over her full lips. She drew her lower lip in between her teeth, and he unconsciously did the same, biting his firmly and holding his breath. The alluring way she looked in that moment, so fascinating and inviting tempted him, making him feel reckless. Like he might do something foolish. Like kiss her.

Which was incredibly idiotic.

"I'm fine. Just a bit of a mess." Kelsey exhaled a laugh, breaking him from his animalistic trance when she took a small step backward.

Davis cleared his throat. The sensual moment they'd just shared could've derailed their friendship, damaging it beyond repair if he'd followed through with his unfamiliar urge. He needed to get things back on track.

Fast.

"Just a *little*?" Davis chuckled, running a hand through his wet hair.

"I thought you came back here to help. Because cracking jokes isn't helpful."

He rolled his eyes, snatching the wrench from her hand and crouching underneath the large triple sink, getting sprayed once again with the cold water. "You become a journeyman plumber since the last time we talked, or what?" he teased.

"Okay, now who's being the smart ass?"

The best thing about Kelsey was that she razzed him right back. And thankfully, re-aligned their friendship with one comment.

With the cold wet wrench in his hand, Davis tightened the cold water shut-off. As he did, the water went from a spray to a trickle within a few seconds.

"Finally! Thank you," Kelsey said.

Davis straightened, pushing his damp hair back and catching sight of Kelsey as she wrestled out of the unbuttoned drenched flannel. Water droplets slid down the sleek column of her neck, gliding to her already soaked t-shirt. He tore his eyes away.

Nope. He wasn't going there again.

"It was nothing," he said.

"No, seriously. Look at this mess." She gestured at the water covering the tiled floor. "And look at me," she said.

Oh, he was looking. And he needed to stop.

"And look at you," she added. "Your sweater is soaked. I'm so sorry."

Davis shrugged. "It's fine. It'll dry."

He gathered his damp sweater at the hem and yanked it over his head, tossing it onto the floor. He dared another look at her and caught her peeking at him. Her vision grazed over his chest where his fitted white tank top remained, luckily still dry. He sucked in a breath.

It made no sense—her checking him out. Not when they'd never been attracted to one another. Not really.

He shook his head, willing himself to think with his brain and nothing else. "I wish I could say your problem here is solved. But unfortunately, tightening the stop isn't enough. The shut-off is old and it needs to be replaced."

"Of course it does," Kelsey muttered, throwing her hands up.

"I might have a replacement in my truck. Should take me less than an hour to replace both the hot and cold shut off. But that will mean closing O'Henry's early because I'll need to turn off the water until I'm done."

Kelsey nodded slowly, but then her lower lip trembled and tears at the corners of her eyes formed. An ache pulsed in his throat and a heaviness throbbed in his chest. He'd rarely witnessed Kelsey cry. She was the toughest woman he knew. Something like a plumbing issue normally wouldn't faze her this much.

"I can't afford to close early," she finally said quietly, crossing her arms.

The action accentuated her see-through t-shirt, and he flicked his attention away, running a hand down his face. He groaned. *What was he doing?*

"Well, you can't really afford to have the restaurant flood either."

"You've got a point."

"Tightening the shut-off was only a Band-Aid. It won't last long before the water starts leaking again. And next time, it could be gushing."

Kelsey chewed on her lip while she slid her phone from the back pocket of her jeans, checking the screen. "Mrs. O'Henry will be here soon to pick up the kids. I'll ask Julian to help me close the bar early."

Davis nodded. "I'll check my truck to make sure I have the part."

Sighing, she said, "You're the best, thank you."

She stepped around him, but before she made it far, he stopped her.

"Wait. You shouldn't go out there dressed like that." He hurried and pulled his tank top off, handing it to her. Her eyes danced over his bare chest, and an immediate fire ignited below his belt, arousing him. And he wished with all his strength that it hadn't.

That invisible line of their friendship had blurred, and now, he had a feeling there'd be no turning back.

FIFTEEN MINUTES LATER, HE WAS CRUMPLED UNDERNEATH the disgusting restaurant sink, dressed in an old t-shirt he found in his truck, and replacing the shut-off valve. His hair was still damp, and it flopped in his face. Both Garrett and the producers of Renovation Dudes had been harassing him to get a haircut. Now, he wasn't positive if he was putting it off because he hated making small talk with barbers or out of spite. Probably the latter.

Davis tried not to think about how Kelsey looked only moments before—hair disheveled, beads of water on her face, shirt soaked through. But it was practically impossible because it was the only image that flickered into his brain each time he closed his eyes.

In the beginning of their friendship, he had an inkling she might have feelings for him. But Davis was awkward and inexperienced with women. And even though there'd been a spark of interest on his end as well, by the time he was ready to act on it, she was with Ricky. And for the last ten years, he'd been content with their relationship—just friends.

So what was happening now? Had the increased time together caused prior nonexistent feelings to slowly develop? Davis had been at Kelsey's house more often as of late. He'd replaced her garbage disposal, changed the oil on her minivan, and re-watched every Jim Carrey movie with her after the kids had gone to bed. He was happy to help her out, even if she was too proud to ask for it.

"Hey, how's it going?" Kelsey came in and crouched next to him.

He glanced away from his work momentarily, and instantly regretted it. The sight of her dressed in his tank top caused a slight pain to pinch in his chest. She bit at her lower lip, concern creasing her forehead. Seeing her worry was becoming one of his least favorite sights.

"Looks like you had the part," she continued when he didn't speak.

"Yeah, we got lucky. Err...you got lucky."

We. They were a *we* when people referred to them and their friendship. But why did it suddenly feel weird to say aloud?

"That's a relief." She laid towels onto the wet floor, before dropping down onto her knees and handing a dry one to him.

"The kids get picked up okay?"

"Yep. And Leo and Izzy took my mama home."

"I could've taken her when I finished up here. You know I don't mind."

She shrugged. "I know. But she's on their way home. Besides, you're doing enough to help. I'm already gonna owe you free beer for life."

He chuckled, returning to his job underneath the sink. "Definitely not for life. But I'll take it as long as you're running this place."

He cranked the wrench a few times until it was tight, but then noticed she was silent behind him. Glancing over his shoulder, he found her eyes watering. His chest tightened.

"Hey, what's going on?"

"Just a funny choice of words is all," she muttered.

"Why's that?"

"Turns out, I may not be running this place for much longer."

The wrench nearly slipped from his grip. "What? Why?"

"There's a stack of bills on the desk that I can't afford to pay."

The air in the room thickened, and his heart felt heavy. "What about another loan?"

"Already did that. And now I can't afford to pay those." She dropped her chin to her chest.

A lump slid up his throat. He swallowed it down. "Why didn't you tell me?"

"Too proud." She shrugged a shoulder, trying to play it off as nothing.

"What about the O'Henry's? Have you asked them for help?" Even before he said the words out loud, he knew how ridiculous of a question it was. If Kelsey hadn't even told him, there was no way she'd gone to her in-laws for help.

"Not yet. But now that I've let the payments on the second business loan lapse, I have no choice. The bank is threatening to put a lean against the house. I have forty-five days to either come up with the money or..." she stopped speaking and her lower lip trembled.

Davis gasped. *Forty-five days?*

"Davis," she whispered. "What if they can't help? What if I lose this place?"

Losing Ricky and becoming a single mother had been incredibly difficult for her to adapt to. Learning how to manage the restaurant took her months. But she'd found her way, found her groove. And it suited her. It had him seeing her in a new way. The thought of her giving it up and losing more than she already had, left him feeling troubled.

"Have you thought about selling? Maybe if you found an investor, someone who bought the place but let you continue to manage it?"

She shook her head. "I don't know. What if they wanted to change the name? Or change the vibe of this place? What if some big shot investor bought it and changed everything?"

He hated the idea of that almost as much as she did. The only reason Davis ever went to O'Henry's Bar and Grill was because Kelsey owned it, but even if she didn't, he wouldn't want some out-of-town investor swooping in and buying it. There was nothing worse than people coming from Denver, trying to *big-city* their small town.

"I doubt the O'Henry's would let that happen, they're

locals. I can't imagine them wanting O'Henry's to change either."

"Probably not." Kelsey handed him a dry towel.

Davis wanted to help Kelsey in any way he could. But if she hated change, she hated asking for help even more. And what could he do anyway? Buy O'Henry's to assure nothing would change with the bar?

Wait. Could he actually do that?

His skin tingled and his pulse kicked up. Kelsey would never agree to it. She'd assume he was only doing it for her. But what if this idea was exactly what he needed as well? A way to get out of renewing his contract with HGTV.

After toweling her own hair, she sat back on her hands and shrugged. "I have to hold onto hope the O'Henry's will want to buy back the bar. Or at the very least, help me get back on track until I can afford to take over the payments again."

Had she just admitted to needing help?

Davis gazed at her. She rarely looked exposed like she did in that moment, not only with her dampened hair and dressed in his fitted tank-top, but in her demeanor. She appeared abnormally shy, and it did something in his gut. Lately she'd been opening herself up to him in a different way, this vulnerable side to her caused an unwanted hunger to build. For her, of all people. And it made absolutely zero sense.

Maybe it was a combination of empathy for her and her situation. Or maybe it was his lack of food intake that day. He and Garrison had skipped lunch because they'd been too busy trying to get their latest job ready for filming the next day. They'd argued over their wardrobe of all the hellish things they could've possibly argued over. The producers were trying to change things. Change *him*. And he wasn't about to stand for it. This new prospect of possibly buying out the O'Henry's could be exactly what he needed.

Or maybe, this ache he was feeling was because he'd caught her checking him out—for the first time in, well, forever. And the idea of that not only scared the hell out of him, but it excited him.

Kelsey kept her eyes fixated on him as this weird sort of desire expanded within him. He fidgeted with the towel in his lap, resisting the urge to pull her in close and embrace her. They were friends, sure. But they'd always been better at bantering with one another rather than touchy-feely side of their friendship.

The silence had grown uncomfortable, and it sat between them for too long.

Say something.

"Kelsey O'Henry, did you really just say you're gonna ask for help?" he teased.

Her lips curved into a delicious smile until she rolled her eyes and came after him with a decent punch to the shoulder.

He chuckled, rubbing at the now tender spot before standing and reaching a hand to her.

"Thank you, as always, for lightening the mood," she said as he hiked her to her feet.

"That's what I'm here for. And to be your handyman, apparently," he added with a smirk.

"I knew there was a reason I kept you around."

She hadn't let go of his hand yet, and he was so focused on the detail of that fact that he nearly missed her fixed stare on his face, specifically on his lips. Impulsively his mouth pulled in a smile, and he sucked in a breath. With trembling fingers, he tightened his grip, and pulled her closer, his face drawing near hers. For a brief wild moment, he considered kissing her.

But she yanked her hand away, taking a step back and giving him a sheepish smile, before saying, "I should probably finish closing up."

He cleared his throat. "Right. Yeah...I need to go. Early day tomorrow."

"Thank you...again."

"Anytime."

And then he left the bar, his mind cloudy and his hormones on overload.

CHAPTER 3
Kelsey

On the rare occasion Kelsey was ever alone, she screamed curses into the void. She chalked it up as a form of self-care. Great for her mental health. And if it was up to her, these screaming sessions would happen more often.

Most of the time she either had the kids with her or she was surrounded by noisy customers at the bar. And then there was Isabella, who wouldn't allow Kelsey to be alone for more than an hour at a time since losing Ricky. It was sweet of her bestie to worry about her, but she didn't need to be babysat. She did, however, need a regular babysitter for her children.

When Kelsey picked up the kids that morning, she was running late getting the older two, June and Zach to their ice-skating lesson and she still had to drop Charlotte off at her in-laws. There hadn't been time to talk to them about the bar. Besides, she wanted to be prepared to be sure she said the right things without growing emotional. And she'd had zero time to prepare.

After she'd closed the bar the night before, said an awkward as hell goodbye to Davis—*what was up with that by the way?*—and then she'd crawled into bed, it was after 1:00 a.m. To say she was exhausted would've been an understatement.

Today was one of those rare days where she had alone time. She should be using these ninety kid-free minutes to take a nap. But how could she nap when she had so much buzzing through her mind? Besides the concern over losing the bar and the past-due statements, things between her and Davis were awkward. And things were never awkward between them.

She was now alone while her thousand and one thoughts battled in her mind, all her worries striving for first place on her to-do list. Instead of going inside and watching her children's session like the other parents, she sat in her minivan in the parking lot. She synced her phone to the radio and cranked the music. While The Chainsmokers' blared through the speakers, the bass making the minivan's door rattle, Kelsey sang-shouted the lyrics.

About halfway through the second verse, there was a knock against Kelsey's window. She shrieked, clutching at her chest, and letting out an even louder expletive as she whipped her attention to the window.

Davis stood on the other side of the glass, an intrigued, crooked smile on his chiseled face. Warmth pooled into her cheeks. An unexpected flutter in her chest caused her pause. A glimmer of an image of a shirtless Davis from the night before flickered into her mind. She'd seen him without a shirt count-less of times. But had his muscles on his chest and abs always been that defined?

Cooper, Davis's golden retriever sat obediently at his side wagging his tail.

Once Kelsey had caught her breath, she lowered the music

before opening the window. "Davis! What the heck? Are you trying to give me a heart attack?"

"Sorry." He laughed so hard into his fist, and she honestly didn't find the humor. He cleared his throat. "No, I'm serious. I'm sorry."

"Yeah, right. You sound really sorry." She crossed her arms. It was a good thing he was fully dressed today in a jacket and a pair of dark Carhartt's. Because if he was shirtless again, she might've had a difficult time being annoyed with him.

"Well, if you're embarrassed, then maybe you shouldn't be singing at the top of your lungs in public," he shot back, raising a brow.

"I'm not embarrassed," she replied.

Okay, so she was a little embarrassed. Typically, she wouldn't be. It took a lot to rattle her. So why was she now?

"Fine, if you say so," he said, putting his hands up in surrender.

"And technically, I'm not in public. I'm in my car," she muttered and glanced down at the dog who had been waiting patiently for a personalized greeting. "Hey, Cooper." She opened the door and climbed out of the minivan to give him a proper *hello*.

Cooper wagged his tail with even more enthusiasm. She bent and scratched both his ears and buried her face in the top of his head. Cooper was nearing a decade old. Kelsey had gone with Davis when he adopted the puppy all those years ago. It was hard to believe she'd known him almost his entire life.

"I think he missed you," Davis said.

"Aww, I've missed you too, Coop." She straightened and petted him on the head. "You should bring him with you next time you come into O'Henry's."

"Um...sure. Next time."

She heard the falter in his voice, caught the roughness in it. His hesitation of not wanting to come into O'Henry's would normally grate on her, but instead she was aware of this new awkwardness between them.

The history she and Davis shared sat heavy on her mind. These new and raw feelings or attractions—whatever they were —if acted upon could threaten to ruin the relationship they'd built. The perimeters set years ago had been easy to maintain. The common denominator always in position in between them —Ricky and her sacred vows. But now, with those elements gone, she could feel the barriers weakening.

When the silent pause between them sat too long, she swung her attention back to Davis, the reflection from the autumn sun ricocheting off his crystal blue eyes. Her cheeks warmed and something stirred in her depths. An awakening of a craving she'd pushed away months ago and had assumed she would never feel again. And yet here she was—feeling it. Just slightly. But enough for her to notice. Enough she couldn't push it away or ignore it.

Did he feel it too? Or notice her unusual behavior? The idea was ludicrous. Her and Davis. Her and *anyone* other than Ricky. But last night, when Davis had looked at her, his eyes darker than usual, it had set fire to her skin, and she felt a shift in their relationship.

Before Ricky, Kelsey had a crush on Davis. But because of their friendship, she'd never acted on it. And she'd never told a soul either.

"Well...we should get going." Davis tugged on Cooper's leash.

"Thanks," she blurted before he could take a step away. "For last night...for fixing the leaky shut-off."

He shrugged, shuffling his feet back and forth, Cooper's

leash loose in his hand. The action was both adorable and childlike. "It was nothing."

She waved him off. "You know me, I hate asking for help."

The corner of his lips pulled into a crooked smile. "Don't I know it."

And he did know her well enough. Enough to see through her BS. Which meant he had to know exactly what she was feeling.

She felt exposed. And suddenly the cool, fall breeze didn't feel quite cool enough. She pushed up the sleeves of her sweater.

"But I'm grateful you were there. Last night," she confirmed her meaning. "I don't know what I would've done if you hadn't been."

"I'm just glad you needed me."

At his words, her skin buzzed. She shielded the early morning sun with a hand to her forehead. She would always need him. In that moment, her body was suddenly betraying her, making her feel a different kind of need for him. A desire so unexpected it caused her head to spin.

She swallowed. "Anyway...thanks again."

He nodded, though he couldn't quite meet her eyes when he finally said, "Well, I'm heading into The Daily Grind. Picking up coffee for Garrett and I and taking it to the Larson house."

"When will the episode air?"

"Sometime this winter, most likely."

A woman in her late twenties passed Kelsey's minivan on her way out of the coffee shop. The woman waggled her fingers as she called an overly friendly *hello* to Davis, as if Kelsey didn't exist. But Kelsey couldn't help but notice the woman didn't specify which twin she was ogling. If she had to guess—the woman had no idea. Identical twins could sometimes be difficult to decipher if you didn't know them well enough.

Davis waved to the woman, hardly giving her a second look, never mind a first.

In Pineridge Davis might as well have been a movie star. The way the locals swooned over him and Garrett lately was beyond irritating, but it didn't take much for people around town to get excited. Everyone was always up in each other's business. After Ricky died, they didn't stop gossiping about Kelsey for months. Not until word had gotten around that Landon Hoffman was cheating on his wife, Norah.

"She's cute," Kelsey said, nudging her chin toward the pretty woman swishing her hips as she strolled down the sidewalk.

"Eh, she's all right."

"*All right?* She practically sexed you with her eyes."

Davis's face turned a bright shade of red. He blushed so easily, making it more fun to tease him. But it was also a dead giveaway that he'd so obviously noticed the pretty girl. Without permission, her chest burned. *She was not jealous.*

"That's not a thing," he muttered.

"I bet it happens to you more often than you know."

He pushed his hand through his hair, causing it to stick straight up before it flopped back over. An action she'd seen him do probably fifty thousand times and yet, this time it made her fingers ache to touch it herself.

"Pft. Probably because they think I'm Garrett."

Oof. His comment hit her in the gut. He'd said what she had already been wondering. It wasn't as if Davis looked much different than Garrett. But they did have different styles and personalities.

She wanted to ease his mind. "Shut up, you know you're the better twin."

He gave her a half smile but remained silent while he scratched Cooper's ear.

To Kelsey, Davis had always been the better twin. His love of indie rock music, of woodworking, and craft beer were just a few things she loved about him. Sure, Garrett was attractive, but he was also conceited. He strutted around town as if he were God's gift to women. That arrogant personality had never really done it for Kelsey.

With his focus still on Cooper, Davis said, "I think you're the only one who might share in that opinion."

"Well, I'm the only one whose opinion matters." When he didn't say anything, her nerves got the better of her and she blurted, "You planning on going to the Halloween costume party?" *Why'd she ask that?* She was only going to be there by default—she'd be working.

"I don't know. You know how packed the bar gets on those nights." He rubbed at the back of his neck before adjusting the collar of his jacket. "I'm assuming you'll be there?"

"Don't really have a choice. I'll be working that night. The in-laws are taking the kids trick-or-treating."

He nodded, the wind blowing through his hair.

She needed to somehow get them back on track, to be free from this awkward tension. "C'mon, please just say you'll come. You don't even have to dress in costume. Please, I don't want to be stuck talking to the other single losers."

His features softened, and he chuckled. The sound of it scraped against her skin, causing a tingle to wriggle through her body.

"Like me, you mean?"

"What? No," she corrected. "Not like you. You're different. You're always the exception." What was she saying? Okay, normally she would say something like that. But after their heated encounter the night before, her comment sounded strange. *Say something else.* "I owe you a beer anyway."

"You don't owe me anything." Davis backed away, tugging on Cooper's leash who wagged his tail. "But you know going to the bar on a holiday, when it'll be packed full of locals and tourists is really pushing it for me," he teased.

"I think you can make the sacrifice, especially for me."

"Anything for you," he said, his voice trembling.

He flashed her that familiar smile over his shoulder, but this time there was a timidness to it, and it was enough to cause her heart to flutter.

What was happening?

She watched him as he strode away, Cooper stepping in time with him.

Before last night, that comment combined with that smile would've done nothing to her. But now, *after* last night, the combination set her skin ablaze. It baffled her and she wasn't sure how to process this foreign reaction.

Having these feelings was not only unexpected but it was unwanted. She had no desire of being in a relationship. After Ricky passed, she swore she'd be fine being single for the rest of her life. She didn't need a man. Besides that, what other man would accept her as she was. All her quirks and bad habits.

A relationship could screw up her plans. She needed to focus on paying back the loans and saving the bar. And besides that, she wasn't sure how her kids would handle her being in a relationship. She wanted to make things as easy as possible on them. If that meant being single until they were out of the house—so be it. She'd sacrifice anything for them.

But that decision didn't help these uninvited feelings that had suddenly appeared from left field and that she had absolutely zero time for. Typically, when she had a problem, she went to Davis for advice. But this time she couldn't. And as much as she didn't want to expose these feelings to anyone, she needed to talk them out with someone in hopes they'd make sense. She needed Izzy.

Kelsey climbed back into her minivan and found her phone in the console. She sent a text to Isabella.

> Have a huge problem. In desperate need of some Izzy advice.

CHAPTER 4
Davis

The smooth texture of the wood beneath his hand breathed life into Davis's soul, and the scent of freshly cut pine sent a blaring memory in his mind.

He and his brother Garrett standing shoulder to shoulder mesmerized by the work their dad did with his table saw. Crackling wood chips beneath the soles of his boots, his vision slightly blurred behind the scratched safety glasses, the sound of the screeching power tool as it tore through the wood, making a perfectly smooth cut.

"Why don't you find a woman to grope instead?" Garrett's voice sliced through Davis's memory as he stepped into the garage.

Davis could come up with a snappy comeback. Or he could ignore his twin. He decided on the latter. He didn't have the energy to put up with Garrett and his comments today.

After the water fiasco at O'Henry's Bar and Grill last night, he'd got to bed late. And to sleep, even later. For what felt like hours, he'd tossed and turned while images of Kelsey popped in his brain. Not only of her dressed in his tank top or in her wet

T-shirt, but the sadness conveyed in her eyes, and the defeated slump in her posture.

He'd been distracted at work all day, unable to stop thinking about their interaction that morning when he found her parked in the lot at the ice-skating rink singing in her minivan. Their conversation had been awkward. And what was worse? He'd agreed to stop by O'Henry's that night. He wasn't prepared to have another uncomfortable conversation.

This issue with her in-laws selling their half of the bar was wearing on her. He wanted to help. But how could he do that without stepping on her toes? Something told him, if he offered to pay off the loans and buy O'Henry's but still have her manage the place, Kelsey wouldn't approve.

Spending time nose-deep in a project and being surrounded by wood, the scent of the pine invading his nose, calmed him. The morning sun had been swallowed up by the early afternoon clouds and brought with it a fall drizzle Davis didn't mind. It gave him the added incentive to be indoors today, as if he needed the permission. But Garrett's presence had the opposite effect on him, and he felt the stiffness in his jaw.

Garrett shuffled next to Davis where he tried to focus on the piece of wood he'd just cut. Garrett remained unusually quiet while he bent and looked on with him, and it made him nervous. Was Garrett judging his cut lines? They'd never butt heads regarding work stuff until the show.

"It looks good," Garrett finally said, easing Davis's apprehension.

Davis glanced over his shoulder, quirking a brow. "Yeah?"

"You know I'd lie to you about many things, but this? Not a chance."

It was true. As opposite as they were, creating and designing had always connected the two of them. That connection was the only hope Davis had in them finishing out their current contract with HGTV.

Renovation Dudes had two more episodes to film before this season was over and Davis could hardly wait. He needed a break. But not from the actual work. The work he didn't mind. It was the cameras. The lights. The crew. The fans.

Fans.

Since when was he—Davis Vance—fangirled over?

"Thanks," Davis said.

"But it doesn't have to be perfect, bro." Garrett slapped Davis on the back.

"Actually, it does. Otherwise, my measurements will be off," Davis grumbled, rolling his eyes at his brother.

"I guess this is why you're in charge of measuring and cutting."

Davis rested a hand on his hip, studying Garrett and noticing the faint sheen of makeup on his clean-shaven face. "Remind me again, what are you in charge of? Looking pretty?"

That comment earned him a punch to the shoulder. "Screw you, Davey."

Davis hated that nickname. Garrett was the only one besides his mom who called him by it. But he hadn't seen her in years.

Garrett strutted around the garage, adjusting the tie at the nape of his neck, ignoring Davis. "I know what you're doing out here."

Tension spread across the top of Davis's shoulders as he picked up the 2x4. "Yeah? What am I doing?"

"You're trying to get out of the shot. You're out here to avoid the cameras."

Busted.

"You know I've always preferred to be out here rather than in there." Davis carried two freshly cut 2x4's through the garage door and into the Larson home which was the current project and episode for Renovation Dudes. "Besides, we both have specific duties. It's in our contract, remember?"

Garrett followed him into the house. "Oh, don't give me that bull. You're always throwing the contract in my face."

They passed two cameramen and a woman fidgeting with a light on a stand.

Davis ground his teeth. Garrett wasn't wrong. That contract was like a ticking time bomb. Each episode, each season they completed he was that much closer to freedom. Though free to do what, he wasn't sure.

"All I'm saying is, you're better at this than me. The camera loves you." Davis leaned the wood against a wall, yanking his hammer from his toolbelt.

Garrett pinched the bridge of his nose, sighing. "Davis, we're twins."

He said it so matter-of-factly as if Davis was unaware of this obvious fact. Because yeah, they were twins. Identical even. But that was on the outside. Inside, the Vance twins were two very different people.

Davis ignored him and went about the task at hand. Framing in a faux fireplace and mantle for the living room they were renovating. The Pineridge home was built in 1985 and was quite honestly in desperate need of more updates. But the show wasn't funded to help with other rooms. This was the part of the gig Davis didn't like. They were only contracted to renovate one room of the homeowners choosing but then the rest of the house remained outdated. Sometimes even lacking some much-needed repairs.

"Look, after this one, we only have one episode left to film this season. We're in the homestretch."

Davis grunted.

But Garrett was right. He could do this. In a few weeks,

he'd be done. At least for six weeks before they began shooting the next season. Their final season. But he wasn't going to think about that. For now, he had his eyes on the prize. The six weeks of solitude after they wrapped up this season. Just him and Cooper, and his canoe, books, and projects. His TBR pile of books was about to topple over. And he had so many projects in his shop waiting to be finished.

Not to mention the tasks at Kelsey's home that needed attention. Ricky, God rest his soul, had been overly consumed by the bar which meant the simple repairs at his home took a backseat. Davis knew she had a lot on her plate, and whenever he was at her place and he noticed a project that needed attention, he itched to be the one to fix it for her. She deserved that much, and whatever he could do to shoulder some of her burden, he'd happily do—if only to see her smile.

A pretty smile he'd been thinking about more and more as of late.

Davis gestured at the other end of the piece of wood. "Hold that for me, will ya?"

Garrett listened, propping up the 2x4 on one side while Davis used his screw gun on the other. After it was secure, he brushed his hand across the wood, his fingers skimming over the screw. The tension released in his shoulders, and he exhaled, the work calming him like it always did. It was so natural to him, like breathing. This was much easier than dealing with people. Less complicated, that was for sure.

"What you need is a night out," Garrett suggested, tugging on the sleeves of his sports jacket.

And there it was. The earlier tension returned tenfold.

Davis's jaw ticked. "I went out last night."

"Hanging out with your platonic best friend isn't my definition of a night out," Garrett retorted, unable to hide the disgust in his voice.

The idea of being friends with a woman and sex being off the table did not interest Garrett in the slightest. In fact, it was so far-fetched, he couldn't even comprehend it. But if he knew what had happened between the two of them the night before, he wouldn't think his evening was so dull after all.

The problem was, Davis couldn't explain what had actually happened between them. Only that the definition of their usual platonic/innocent relationship had become obscure. And if it didn't make sense to himself, then he couldn't explain it to Garrett. Besides his brother would most likely taint it, and ruin whatever this was before it even began.

"I wasn't hanging out with Kelsey the whole night."

He'd talked to Leo for a bit too.

"Oh, that's right," Garrett continued. "You were also working. I saw you coming out of the O'Henry's kitchen soaking wet."

Davis grabbed the second 2x4 and Garrett took one end of it without being asked this time.

"I'm talking about a *real* night out," Garrett continued.

Davis knew what Garrett was going to suggest. That damn Halloween costume party no one could shut up about every fall. But dressing up as someone else for a night, being surrounded by loud, drunken idiots did not sound like his idea of fun.

But he might as well get the conversation over with.

"Let me guess, you want me to go to the Halloween party at O'Henry's? Because that would count as a real night out?" he grunted.

"As long as you don't offer to babysit Kelsey's kids or fix anything for her, then yes, it counts."

Davis sighed, as he used the screw gun to attach the board. "I'll think about it."

"I swear, you have a real boner for her."

Davis jerked his attention at his brother, his heartrate suddenly up. "For who?"

"Kelsey."

"Shut the hell up. You don't know what you're talking about," he retorted, his throat tight. So maybe he felt caught in his recent conflicting feelings for Kelsey, but that didn't mean he was ready to discuss them. Especially not with Garrett.

"Everyone knows it. I don't know who you think you're fooling."

"Just because I'm a good guy doesn't mean I have a . . ." he paused, "a *thing* for Kelsey. We're just friends."

"But I bet you wanna be friends with benefits." Garrett wagged his brows.

His body went rigid, feeling defensive for their relationship, and yet he'd be lying if he said his mind hadn't danced over the idea of that the past twenty-four hours.

The assistant director, Sandy approached them, her attention wavering between them, before landing on Garrett.

"Hey, guys, how we doing? Am I interrupting?" Sandy greeted, tucking her long, curly red hair behind one ear.

"Hey, Sandy," Garrett said, flashing her a wide, white-toothed smile.

Inwardly, Davis groaned, though he couldn't restrain an eyeroll.

"Nope. Just the normal disagreement," Davis admitted.

Garrett waved him off. "He's kidding. We're fine."

"Are we just about ready to pick up on the next shot?" She glanced at Garrett who looked to Davis for instruction.

"You wanted the fireplace completely framed in before we began shooting again and it's almost done."

"Great. I'll let the crew know." Her focus lingered on Garrett.

Davis nodded at her. Not that she noticed, since she was busy checking out his brother.

She stepped closer to Garrett, her eyes blinking rapidly as she lowered her voice ever so softly. "So, Garrett...I was wondering if you had a date to the couples Halloween costume party? The one at O'Henry's."

"A date?" Garrett coughed into his fist.

"Yeah."

Garrett yanked at the tie at his throat. "Um..."

Watching his smooth as silk brother struggle to come up with an excuse filled Davis with more pleasure than it had a right to. He couldn't help but grin and lean back, crossing his arms to catch the show.

Now this was his idea of entertainment.

"I just figured—" Sandy went on, shuffling her feet back and forth— "since I don't know anyone else in town, and it's a couples thing, maybe we could go together."

Davis should be insulted, Sandy knew him, too, but this was too entertaining to care.

"Together?" Garrett's voice cracked.

Davis snickered.

"Yeah, I thought it could be fun to go as Jim and Pam from The Office?"

"Oh, uh...you see, the thing is...Sandy...Davis and I are going together. We have our costumes picked out already."

Davis straightened, uncrossing his arms and his hair flopped in his face. "We what now?"

"Oh." Sandy glanced back and forth between them, a bit of hurt shimmering in her eyes but still a hint of endearment as well. "That's cute."

"Yeah. We thought so."

"Totally," Sandy gushed.

Davis glared at his brother. Just what in the hell was

Garrett trying to pull here? He hadn't agreed to attend the party, never mind dressing in a couple's costume with him.

But he stood there silent because he'd been Garrett's wingman plenty times over the years. Usually, it was to help him get a date, not get out of one. That's how they'd winded up engaged to twin sisters. Suddenly that felt like so long ago.

"But I'll see you there, yeah?" Garrett touched Sandy's shoulder, sliding his hand down her back and her cheeks blushed so hard they nearly matched the shade of her red hair.

"Yeah, okay," she said, smiling.

Of course Garrett would give her that hope. The prospect of a one-night stand with a woman who was only in Pineridge temporarily meant Garrett wouldn't have to commit. And ever since his fiancée Emma died, Garrett couldn't commit to anyone.

As soon as Sandy sauntered off, Davis slugged Garrett in the arm.

Garrett grunted and rubbed at his bicep.

"Couples costumes? I'm not going as your wingman to this thing, and I'm sure as hell not going as your date." Davis ambled away.

Garrett chased after him. "It could be super cool. We could go as Batman and Robin."

"No," Davis grumbled over his shoulder as he went out the door and back into the garage.

"Darth Vader and Luke Skywalker?"

"No."

"Fred and Barney?"

Davis's jaw ticked. "I thought you said, cool?"

"Right. What about Thor and Captain America?"

While that suggestion was moderately appealing, the whole idea was not. Dressing up in a costume, hanging out with people he didn't particularly like, and crowding into a noisy bar sounded like the worst way to spend his Halloween. He would much prefer to stay home with Cooper, watch a movie, and hand out candy to the trick-or-treaters in his neighborhood.

Picking up a 2x4, Davis spun around to look at Garrett. "You know parties aren't really my thing."

Garrett fiddled with the tools on the bench. He released a deep sigh. "And you know I've had a rough few years. Just give me this one thing."

An ache pulsed in Davis's throat. Losing Emma had gutted him. Davis wasn't sure his brother would ever get over her death. But Garrett was quick to forget that when he lost Emma, Davis lost Lissa too. After her sister died, she broke off their engagement, told him she had to be near her parents and couldn't settle down in Pineridge.

While in retrospect, not marrying Lissa had turned out to be a good thing—they had different dreams and plans for their futures. But the last few years for Davis hadn't been all sunshine and rainbows. He'd poured himself into their projects for the show, helped Kelsey around her house and with the kids, taken Cooper and his canoe into the wilderness for days on end.

But as much as Davis wanted to agree with Garrett, it was never just one thing. Never just one favor. He always wanted more. That's how Davis had ended up stuck in a contract with HGTV.

Two years ago, it had been just Davis and Garrett. They had a thriving renovation business. While Davis did most of the manual labor and decorating, Garrett did the behind the scenes. The paperwork, finish work, and designing.

But then word got out somehow that the twin duo was something special. Davis blamed tourism. The mountains and lakes. And that damn love lock bridge in town. It brought tourists from miles. Next thing Davis knew, he and Garrett were being offered a two year, four season contract with HGTV.

As the oldest twin, Davis felt responsible for Garrett. Always had. With parents who weren't around much during their childhood, it had always been Davis and Garrett against the world.

Davis really didn't want to do this—agree to going to the party, agree to dressing in a couple's costume with his brother. But Garrett was right about one thing; he'd had an exceptionally rough year. Rougher than most.

"Fine," Davis grumbled.

"Yes." Garrett pumped a fist in the air.

"But—I'm choosing the costumes," Davis warned.

"Yeah, sure, whatever you want."

The garage door opened, Sandy popped her head in. "Hey, boys. Camera's ready to roll."

Garrett slapped Davis's shoulder and led him into the house. "What are you thinking? Good cop, bad cop?"

Davis said the first thing that came to his mind. Characters from one of his and Kelsey's favorite movie, Dumb and Dumber. Because he already had the costume from a prior Halloween, this would take very little effort on his part.

"Harry and Lloyd."

"Seriously? From Dumb and Dumber?"

"Hey, it's either that or you can take Sandy up on her offer and if that's the case, you'd better start practicing your Jim *look* now."

Garrett chuckled. "Okay, fine. What the hell? Let's do it."

CHAPTER 5
Kelsey

R ain ran down the windows of the Sweet Cakes Bakery while Kelsey got her children situated at a table. Her mama, Rita, loaded them with all their favorites, mini leaf cookies and cake pops in the shape of pumpkins. She looked good today. Most likely running on more hours of sleep than usual and a Bloody Mary to get her going.

Once the kids were distracted, Kelsey joined Isabella at a separate table.

"Okay, spill," Isabella demanded, a coffee cup from The Daily Grind in her hand.

Kelsey glanced over her shoulder, assessing the situation. The last thing she needed was her mama or her children overhearing their conversation. She wasn't sure how to explain these strange feelings to herself, never mind to anyone else.

But with Isabella, she'd have to try. Because it was clear, she needed someone's guidance.

"Spill what? Not sure there's anything to spill," she began. She had to take it slow. This was uncharted territory. She couldn't just rip off the Band-Aid.

"Liar," Izzy teased.

Kelsey finally relented. She'd start with the issue with the business first. "I haven't wanted to say anything because I didn't want you to worry—"

Isabella's brows lifted as she leaned in and interrupted, "Are you kidding? I'm always going to worry about you. That's what friends do."

"And while I appreciate that, this isn't your problem to fix. It's mine."

"I'll be the judge of that. Tell me what the problem is."

Unable to make eye contact with Isabella, Kelsey traced a finger over the paper coffee cup in front of her. "I got behind on the payments for the business loan."

Isabella inhaled a sharp breath. "How behind?"

"Really behind." Her eyes flicked away, the white faux pumpkin garland draped in front of the windows distracting her. "So I took out a second loan, and got behind in those payments too. Izz, I might lose the bar."

"No way, we're not going to let that happen. Tell me how Leo and I can help."

Kelsey's throat thickened and she shook her head. "This isn't your problem."

Izzy placed a hand on Kelsey's. "I think Leo would beg to differ."

Tears pricked at the corner of Kelsey's eyes, and she forced them to stay at bay. She wouldn't let her kids see her cry; God knew she'd done enough of that the past year. Kelsey held up her hand, stopping her friend from speaking any further. "Nu-uh. No way. Leo is trying to open his photography shop. And you guys are still traveling back and forth from here and New York."

"Let's be honest, even if we weren't doing those things, you wouldn't let us help."

Her friend knew her too well.

"First things first—I'm going to talk to the O'Henry's and see if they're interested in either buying back the bar or," she paused, clenching her teeth before saying, "helping me get caught up on the payments."

"What about the house? Can you take out a second mortgage?"

She shook her head. If the bar went under and she lost the house—the only place the kids knew as home with their daddy —she'd never forgive herself. "Losing the house is too big of a risk."

"You should at least try whatever you can. You can't let the bar go without a fight."

"C'mon, you know me better than that," Kelsey said.

"Yes, I do." Izzy smiled before taking a sip of her coffee.

The sound of the rain pounding against the paved sidewalk outside grew louder and Kelsey shivered, pulling her fuzzy cardigan tighter around her. Kelsey could only hope the family business meant as much to Mr. and Mrs. O'Henry as it did to Ricky. As it did to herself.

"You know, I gotta be honest," Izzy began, pressing her hands against the table and leaning across it like she was fixing to tell her a secret. "When you texted me that you had a huge problem and needed my advice, I assumed it had to do with something else."

Kelsey dipped her chin, staring at the apple spice cake with cream cheese frosting in front of her like it was the most interesting thing she'd ever seen. She tucked her hair behind her ears and swallowed, afraid to ask but did anyway.

"Oh, yeah?"

"Yeah. Like why you and a certain Mr. Davis Vance were seen together at the bar soaking wet?" She waggled her dark brows.

Kelsey's body went hot as her mind raced back to that night. The way it felt to have Davis's sturdy body pressed against hers. The vision of him as he peeled off his tank top to give her, leaving him bare chested. She sucked her lower lip in between her teeth as a yearning rattled in her depths, a pulsing of hunger between her thighs.

"Plumbing," Kelsey blurted.

Isabella furrowed her brows, and she tilted her head.

"I had a plumbing problem," Kelsey elaborated. "A leaky shut off. Davis fixed it for me. That's all." She released a shaky breath, halfway through turning it into an awkward laugh. "Why in the world would you think anything else was going on?"

Isabella shrugged. "Maybe I was just hoping." She winced before giving her friend a look of sympathy.

Kelsey hated that look. She didn't want to be pitied.

"Hoping what, exactly? That something was going on between me and Davis?" Her heart raced as she spoke the words. She was grateful her voice remained strong as she said, "That's absurd, you know that, right?"

Charlotte's whines quickly turned into a fit of sobs.

"Not *completely* absurd. You guys have a lot in common. And you get along so well."

"Yeah, well, you know I'm not ready to date. I don't know if I'll ever be ready." Kelsey stood, clearing their table. "Besides, Davis is my best friend. That would be weird."

Even though things felt weird between them already. She would be a liar if she didn't admit that she hadn't been able to stop thinking about Davis stripping off the tank top, how solid his bare chest appeared underneath the florescent lighting, his steady hands as they worked at fixing the pipe. Friends certainly didn't look at one another like that; their eyes devouring every inch of each other.

"I'll try not to be offended by you calling Davis your best friend." Isabella winked, standing alongside Kelsey.

Kelsey waved her off. "You know what I mean, he's my best guy friend and you're my bestie. But if you wanna stay that way, you better not spread gossip around and encourage the Pineridge rumor mill," Kelsey teased as she hurried to the aid of her children.

She hoped her face didn't deceive her by giving away her secrets. Lord knew this town would have a hay day with this one. Before her business became Pineridge's most juicy gossip once again, she needed to make sure it was at least worth it. Until then, she didn't trust speaking about her feelings for Davis in public.

Maybe she should try making sense of them first.

SITTING IN HER MINIVAN PARKED OUTSIDE HER IN-LAW'S house, Kelsey needed a minute to gather her thoughts. June and Zach unbuckled their seatbelts and Zach entertained Charlotte with a game of peekaboo. It wasn't like she was about to ask the O'Henry's for money for herself. It was for the bar, to keep it in the family, and open to Pineridge locals who had come to love it.

During her marriage to Ricky, she'd never been privy to her in-law's finances so she couldn't be certain they could afford to help her. But based on the knowledge she did have, and the part of town they lived in, the only new housing development to exist in Pineridge, she held onto hope. If they couldn't afford to buy back O'Henry's, maybe they would at least be willing to pay off the loans she owed. Because she was quickly running out of time.

Finally climbing out, Kelsey opened the back door and unbuckled Charlotte from her car seat. "C'mon, little one. Time to put on a happy face for your grandparents." She held her to her hip and kissed her on the cheek. Charlotte squealed in delight.

"Grandma said we get to make Halloween cookies today," Zach said as he stomped up the driveway in his rainboots.

"I wanna eat cookies," June said.

"That sounds fun." Kelsey tried to sound upbeat, but her nerves were threatening to make way to a full-blown panic attack.

After knocking, Mr. O'Henry opened the door and smiled wide behind a thick red mustache. "Hey, kids," he greeted as each of them stepped inside. "Hi, Kelsey. How've you been?"

"I'm good. Staying busy, as usual."

He put his hands out to Charlotte and she clung to Kelsey's shirt.

"Aw, maybe you'll have better luck with Grandma," Mr. O'Henry said.

Kelsey felt bad that Charlotte was so particular. But if they didn't want to have a crying baby all night, he might as well not even bother. She hoped he'd be patient and Charlotte would come around soon.

Mrs. O'Henry entered the foyer dressed in a fancy pantsuit and pearls. "Children, we're so glad you're here. Boy, are we going to have fun."

Kelsey's phone rang from the back pocket of her jeans, and it caused her to jump. "Sorry."

"Come to Grandma, Charlotte." Mrs. O'Henry put out her hands and even though the baby hesitated for a moment, she did lean into her grandma.

After handing Charlotte to Mrs. O'Henry, Kelsey slid her phone out, frowning when she saw Julian's name on the screen.

"Please excuse me," she said before accepting the call and stepping away from her in-laws and children. "Hey, Julian, what's up?"

"Sorry to bother you, Kelsey, but the delivery guy from Tapp's just showed up and unloaded the new kegs we ordered and then loaded them right back up again."

"What?" she barked into the phone.

"He said something about our payment not going through."

She pinched her eyes shut and threw her head back as she sighed into the phone. "Is he still there?"

"Yeah, for now. I'm trying to stall him, but I don't think I can for much longer." He paused. "Kelsey, is everything okay?"

No, everything was not okay.

"Please just keep trying to stall him. I'll be right there."

She ended the call and chewed her bottom lip.

Mr. O'Henry looked at her, worry in his eyes. "Everything okay?"

With this new development, now should've been the perfect time to tell them what was going on and ask them to help. But this whole *asking for help thing* was new to her, and now she was distracted and needed to get to the bar in a hurry.

"An issue at the bar. I need to go." She hugged and kissed her children goodbye. "Thank you," she said as she slipped out the front door.

So it was already beginning. If she couldn't afford to pay the vendors, she wouldn't have anything to serve her customers. If she didn't have customers, she would have no reason to keep O'Henry's open.

She needed a solution. And fast. Her brain went to the person it always did when she needed help but was too proud to ask for it.

Can you come by the bar tonight?

DAVIS
It's Thursday.

So?

DAVIS
Ladies night.

And?

DAVIS
Raincheck?

Please.

It felt like forever before a response came.

DAVIS
As you wish.

She would not overthink his response. She would not overthink his response. She would not—*crap*. Too late.

CHAPTER 6
Davis

Not only was Davis exhausted from work, but an extra packed bar that was a favorite by all the locals, was not his scene. Especially on ladies' night. But Kelsey had asked him to come, and she rarely said please. If she needed him, he wouldn't let her down.

Dressed in a pair of dark jeans, a flannel, and a pair of Timberland boots, Davis entered O'Henry's. He wished he would've brought Cooper with him tonight. He preferred his dog's company over most people, and he helped to calm him in large crowds.

Davis ducked his head, tugging his hat down further as he let the door swing closed behind him. The familiar music by Hozier played loud through the speakers in the bar. He exhaled a relieved sigh that so far, the karaoke hadn't begun. He didn't think he could put up with thirty women taking their turn singing a different Taylor Swift song—even if her current music wasn't half bad.

Making a b-line for the bar, he kept his eyes focused on his feet as the twinkling lights draped above him. He didn't want to get stuck talking to a fan, or worse—a tourist. There was only one person he came to see tonight.

"Hey, you came," Kelsey greeted him with a smile.

And darn it if he didn't feel the same attraction hit him like lightning to the chest just like it had the last time he saw her. Tonight, she wore a fitted, bright blue sweater, the material clinging to her in all the right places. The sight of her curves made it difficult to form a coherent thought. And that smile of hers...it had his heart racing, the beating thundering in his ears.

He silently cursed, clenching his fists at his sides. He hoped the past few days had been a fluke, and that the combination of lack of sleep and the length of time since he'd had a girlfriend had affected his common sense. Truth be told, he hadn't gotten laid in a while, but that wasn't what *this* was.

This alluring pull was something he couldn't explain. Never mind handle. He'd never been friends with a woman before dating. His past relationships consisted of Riley in high school that only lasted about three months, Becky, who he dated intermittently while he lived in Denver, and lastly there was Lissa who he'd met through a twin dating app Garrett convinced him to join.

So being friends with a woman first—best friends—before dating was uncharted territory.

Kelsey slid a beer across the bar top and Davis caught the glass. He nodded his thanks, unable to make eye contact with her while his finger wiped at the spilled beer down the side of the glass. Was he acting weird? Because he felt like he was acting weird. Would she notice? Of course she'd notice. This was Kelsey.

As if she too were similarly affected by his presence, Kelsey ran a nervous hand through her straight black hair, her eyes peeking at him from beneath thick, dark lashes. That was unlike her, the shy glances, the awkward silence.

Had something changed between them?

Their friendship was the one thing that remained the same in his life. It was the one constant. Through it all. The breakup with Becky, and the breakup with Lissa.

"I can't stay long," he blurted, too loudly.

She nodded, slowly, wiping a hand over a hip, drawing his attention there. "Yeah, okay. I just need to go over something with you before you go...in the back."

"In the b-back?" he stuttered, his face heating as he fidgeted with the sleeve of his flannel shirt.

The guy standing at the bar next to him signaled Kelsey for a beer before turning to look at him, recognition dawning on his face. "Hey, I know you."

Davis forced a smile.

The guy pointed at him. "Renovation Dudes."

"Yep," Davis grunted, his stomach tightening. He was hoping to slip in and out of the bar tonight without running into anyone who might recognize him.

"My girlfriend is gonna lose her mind when I tell her I saw you."

"I take it you're not from around here?"

"Nah, Wyoming. Just here for work."

While Kelsey filled the man's beer, Davis took this as a sign that maybe he'd made a mistake coming to O'Henry's tonight. The best thing to align the relationship between him and Kelsey would be distance.

He snatched his beer, took a long swig, and then slammed it down before whipping around.

"Hey, where ya going?"

His shoulders tensed. He spun to face Kelsey. Concern smeared across her face, and it instantly riddled him with conflicting guilt.

"Too crowded. I'll come by your house tomorrow. I told Zach I'd let him borrow a flashlight."

"Just stay for a few. Norah and Maddie should be here soon."

Norah and Maddie were fine separately but together, they were too much for him. And why was Kelsey suddenly bringing up Norah? Kelsey had tried to fix him up with plenty of women throughout the years, but he'd never been interested in any of them. For someone who had been his best friend for the last ten years, she really didn't know his type.

Did he even have a type?

"I'm tired. Early day tomorrow." It was a half lie. He was tired, but he didn't have an early day tomorrow. He'd finished his part on the Larson house and had the day off. It was Garrett's turn to work his magic on the designing side of things.

"Liar," she countered, her dark brows raised. "You're not filming tomorrow."

He opened his mouth to speak, then shut it.

Guilty.

"Fine. I'm just tired."

"And you don't want to be here?" she asked it like a question.

He noticed how her bottom lip pushed out, her eyes drifting to the side, unable to meet his stare. He wasn't sure what he wanted, and that was the problem.

"Can you stay for a bit?" she pressed, finally dragging her gaze back to him. A teasing smile replaced the uncertainty, and she gave him a knowing look. "I promise after we talk, you're free to return to hibernation."

"Ha, ha," he said sarcastically.

He should be relieved by the out she was giving him. But what could she need to talk to him about? If it was about this recent, weird energy buzzing between them, he wasn't sure he was ready to discuss it. What he really hoped was that it would go away completely.

Davis checked the time on his phone.

8:00 p.m.

"Yeah, okay, you free now?"

Kelsey grinned and his heart shifted in his chest. "I'll see if Julian can cover me. Give me a sec."

While she bustled around, Davis turned and leaned against the bar, taking a swig of his beer. Scanning the crowd, he tried not to make eye contact with any of the locals. He spotted a couple people from high school, some of the older women from his church, and when he saw Norah and Maddie walk in through the door, he ducked.

"Okay, ready?" Kelsey said, smiling brightly.

His fingers ached and he stroked his throat.

He nodded and followed her through the swinging door with the *Employees Only* sign on it, averting his eyes from focusing on her backside in the black leather leggings. These were new. He'd never seen her wear the pants before. He would've noticed how much they accentuated her shapely ass.

But then, no, he wouldn't have noticed. Because he hadn't checked her out in years.

Passing the kitchen, Davis followed Kelsey into the office, his body hot and feeling the perspiration worsening. He remained quiet as she approached the desk and slid a drawer open. His heart beat harder in his chest with each passing moment. His throat went dry.

As she turned slowly to face him, he caught the uneasiness on her face and the uncertainty in her eyes. On instinct, he wanted to bolt from the office. Somehow, he needed to put their friendship back together, because he wasn't a fan of this uncharted territory.

But then he noticed the iPad gripped in her hand and coming to life.

He frowned, even more confused and rubbed at the back of his neck. "What's going on? You're worrying me."

Kelsey sighed so heavily he could've sworn he felt it rattle in his bones. "Tapp's Brewery came to make their usual weekly delivery until they discovered my payment didn't go through." She hesitated before continuing, her hand trembling as she clung to the iPad. He wanted to be relieved that he was off the hook from having an awkward conversation he wasn't ready to have—about them and their relationship—but she had him worried. "How am I supposed to sell beer if I don't have any?"

He ran a shaky hand through his hair. "Shit. I'm sorry."

"Davis," his name expelled from her lungs with such exhaustion, such desperation it did something in his chest. "I don't know what I'm supposed to do."

"Until you have a plan, let's first figure out how to keep your connections with the vendors. Let me talk to the owner at Tapp's and see if we can make a deal." He was positive she wouldn't agree, and yet, she might've been just desperate enough to take him up on his offer.

"And what about after that? I have less than forty days."

"I mean, I don't know anything about legal stuff. That's not my area of expertise. But we'll figure something out. And then...I don't know..." he hated to say it out loud, but couldn't restrain, "you might have to sell the bar."

She shook her head. "I can't. I won't. Ricky would never forgive me."

The mention of Ricky was like a sucker punch to the gut. They'd talked about Ricky plenty over the last year since his accident. But it felt different now. Suddenly he felt like a jerk for checking her out, for thinking of her sexually.

"Then don't. Then ask the O'Henry's to become a partner or...find someone else."

"Like who? I mean, O'Henry's is the busiest bar and grill in town, but it's not a goldmine." She looked at him expectantly.

Sure, he'd tossed the idea around in his head about helping her out, possibly paying off the debt and maybe even buy the place from her, but he was scared to mention it to her. Besides that, though, he didn't know what to tell her. All he did know was seeing her like this, looking helpless and desperate, made him want to help.

"Besides the O'Henry's, maybe someone else in town would think of it as a good investment. I don't know." He shook his head and pulled her hand into his, he ran his thumb against her smooth skin.

"I just don't know what to do." Her eyes glossed over.

Seeing her weak like this, and vulnerable sent a pang into his heart and on impulse, he dragged her into him for a hug. He wrapped his arms around her, and she rested her cheek against his chest. Her shaky breathing rumbled against him as he held her closer, but he couldn't bear to find out if she was crying.

"I can't lose this place," she whispered.

"I know." He rested his chin on top of her head.

Kelsey gripped his back and his heart raced faster.

"Tell me how I can help."

Help was like a curse word to her. Somehow consumed by negativity.

"Just hug me for a minute longer," she muttered against his chest.

Holding her closer, he longed to take away her pain, her worry. It caused him to feel reckless. He just wanted to help her. Any way he could. She'd not only suffered a great loss over the last year, but she had a tremendous amount on her plate.

Without overthinking it, he rubbed his chin against the top

of her head, caught the hint of lavender from her hair. Kelsey's fingers went to the nape of his neck and intertwined with his hair. An instant craving shot through his veins, zinging south and his eyes fluttered closed. He attempted to shut off his brain, not wanting to think about how this was Kelsey, *touching him*. Rather, he focused on how desperate he was to take away her hurt.

She repositioned her head and suddenly he felt her heated breath radiating on his neck setting a fire to his skin. He moved his hands down her back, gliding even further, until they nearly reached a place they'd never gone before—a place of no return. Once they went there, there would be no turning back.

Was this going to happen?

The office door swung open, a loud bang sounding against the wood. Their attention jerked in the direction, their hands falling away from one another.

Standing in the open doorway was Rita, Kelsey's mom. She had a hand on the door knob while the other clutched a purse. There was amusement plastered on her facial features as she let out a loud cackle, before clamping her mouth shut with her palm.

"Well, isn't this rich," she sneered, her body swaying as she let go of the door.

"Mama? What are you doing here?" Kelsey rushed to her mom's side, throwing an around her to hoist her up.

Davis hurried to Rita's other side.

"What do you think I'm doing, love bug? This is a bar. I came to get a drink."

Kelsey rolled her eyes and Davis's gut pinched. He helped her get Rita to the couch.

"You know you can't drink here, Mama," Kelsey said.

"Why not? That's not fair," she slurred.

"Life's not fair. Remember? You taught me that."

Rita laid back on the sofa, pushing her dark hair out of her face and curling into a ball. "You're a smart aleck, you know that?"

"Yeah, yeah," Kelsey muttered.

"Don't think I didn't see what y'all were doing. I'm watching you Mr. Vance." Rita narrowed her eyes and made the signal that she'd be watching him.

He smiled. "Yes, ma'am."

She put her finger to her lips. "Shh, just don't tell Davis. I think my daughters always had a crush on him."

Davis's lip twitched.

"Mom," Kelsey gasped. "This *is* Davis."

Rita looked confused, her brows knitting together and her lips scrunching.

"Why don't you get some rest, Mama. I'll take you home when I'm off work."

Rita's lips drooped and she clasped Kelsey's hand. "I'm sorry, love bug."

"It's fine."

"No. You have enough to worry about. I shouldn't be adding to your burdens." Tears welled up in her eyes and her lip quivered. "I don't want to be a burden."

Kelsey sighed, but said, "You're not a burden, Mama."

"I'm gonna get help, I swear. For you. And the kids."

Kelsey brushed her mom's hair out of her face. "Why don't you rest. We'll figure out tomorrow, tomorrow."

Rita's eyes drifted closed.

Kelsey's mom might not have been a burden, but she wasn't helping her either by adding more things to her plate. Davis couldn't do much at that moment to help Kelsey with her problem with the bar, but he could help with her mom.

"I can take her home."

"You don't need to do that." Kelsey waved him off. "I'll let her sleep and take her home when I'm off."

"But you're not off for a few more hours. It's not a problem. She's on my way home anyway."

Kelsey chewed on her bottom lip and his gaze went there before he shifted his focus away. "You sure?"

He cleared his throat. "It's fine. Happy to."

"You're a liar. But I'll owe you big. Like usual." She smoothed her hands down her sweater, and his eyes immediately followed her movements. He jerked his attention back to her face, her cheeks beginning to fill with a rosy glow.

A glow *he'd* caused.

"What are friends for," he choked out, forcing an attempt at a nonchalant shrug. He hauled Rita off the couch, bracing an arm around her.

"Thank you."

"No problem. I'll text you once she's home safe and sound."

"You're the best," she whispered, her throat bobbing. He knew she didn't like asking for help, but she should know better by now; he'd always be there for her, no matter if she asked or not.

Because they were friends. Just friends.

Only, he had to remind himself of what that meant.

In all honesty, he owed Rita Sanders. She may have just saved him from making the biggest mistake of his life.

CHAPTER 7

Kelsey

Asking for help was one thing. Begging was something entirely different. Going to her in-laws to ask for money so she could save the bar felt a lot like begging. But with only thirty-five days remaining, she was running out of time.

Checking the weather app on her phone had been a mistake. It verified the usual—it would be a cool fall day in Pineridge. But at least there would be blue skies and full sun, giving way to a beautiful mountainous landscape. The cooler temps and rain the week before resulted in early snowfall in the Colorado mountains. While it was sure pretty to look at, the sight of snow was a horrific reminder of Ricky and the accident.

Acid burned Kelsey's throat as she pulled a cream knitted sweater over her head and yanked on a pair of freshly laundered jeans straight from the dryer. She buttoned and zipped them as she hopped around in her bedroom before rushing downstairs and into the kitchen. The same pair of jeans used to fit snug around her hips and thighs. But there was something about grief that messed with your appetite.

It messed with a lot of things.

Kelsey scooped the pancake mix from a box into a bowl, pouring in the measured water and whisked it. At least pancakes were something even Charlotte could eat and the other two loved which hopefully meant they'd all get out of the house with zero crying. She could hope.

With her mind busy and distracted on what she'd say to the O'Henry's when she dropped the kids off, she couldn't muster the appetite for pancakes herself. Instead, she drank a cup of coffee and popped a handful of chocolate covered raisins into her mouth and called it good.

"C'mon you two, get your shoes on," she called to June and Zach as soon as they were finished eating breakfast.

"I don't wanna go to Grandma and Grandpa's. I want to stay with you," June whined.

"It's only for a few hours. Besides, it should be fun. They're taking you to the fun center."

"I want you to take us to the fun center."

Well darn it if the mom-guilt didn't punch her straight in the gut.

"Mommy has to go to work today."

"We can go with you," June said.

"If you go with me, Mommy won't get any work done."

June frowned but put her shoes on.

Kelsey had a love/hate relationship with O'Henry's Bar and Grill. After Ricky died, the last thing she wanted was to be at the bar. It reminded her of Ricky, and it hurt too much. But once she finally returned and opened it back up, it was the place she felt closest to him. Now, pulling her away from the bar for more than even a day was difficult.

Lately, Davis had been trying to convince her into going out on the canoe with him and Cooper. The river that stretched through town was just calm enough to put in at. She always had a good excuse to give him. The kids, the bar, too tired. While he often settled for a Disney movie night at her place that resulted in helping her carry sleeping kids to their beds, he never complained.

Not sure what she did to deserve a friend like Davis. She had a moment of panic while she picked Charlotte up and plopped her on the kitchen counter. Things between them the night before had escalated. At first, she assumed it had only been a moment of weakness when she checked him out while he stood before her bare chested, offering his mostly dry tank top to her.

But last night—*last night*. The memory of what it felt like to have his hands on her back, the warmth radiating through her sweater, sent her heart racing even now. The connection between them was so intense, it frightened her.

Charlotte babbled causing Kelsey to blink back the memory. She threaded the baby's pudgy arms into her jacket. The little girl normally fussed when she had to be restrained with things like coats and shoes. But she was distracted by a stuffed dog.

Kelsey swallowed, forcing herself to be present with her kids. "Alright, I'm counting to ten. Everyone better be out of this house and in the car by the time I finish, or we aren't getting pizza on the way home tonight. One, two, three…"

The two oldest were out of the house before Kelsey could get to four. Pizza worked like a charm. In a few years, she'd have teenagers and she'd have to up her game to things like video games or iPhones. Things she hoped she'd be able to afford. If she got her finances figured out now.

The O'Henry's were reasonable folks. They'd always liked Kelsey. Before she and Ricky had even gotten married, they'd welcomed her into the family and treated her like a daughter.

Since Ricky passed, they often offered to babysit the kids,

and they brought over groceries and dinners. If they didn't want to or couldn't afford to help her with her loan issues, she was sure they had lawyer friends who might be willing to help and would at the very least, buy her some time. With just over a month remaining, she didn't have much longer to come up with a solution. And as each day ticked by, it felt as if her grasp on the bar slipped more and more.

Kelsey drove to her in-laws across town where the upper class of Pineridge residents lived and unloaded her kids from the car. As she walked up the driveway and front steps with jittery nerves, her boots crunched against the fallen maple leaves. She rang the doorbell like she always did, now at least.

Before, she followed Ricky inside after he'd turn the knob and walk right in like he owned the place. The O'Henry's never batted an eye to his behavior, but something didn't feel right about her doing that now that he was gone.

The door opened and Mr. O'Henry stood there, a wide smile and crinkling eyes, reminding her of Ricky. If he were older. If he'd had the chance to grow older. Her throat thickened. But she managed a weak smile.

"Good morning, Kelsey. Hey, kids. C'mon in." He put his hands out for Charlotte, but the poor girl refused, clinging to Kelsey's jacket in her small fists.

"Hi, Jack," Kelsey greeted her father-in-law as she entered the home with her youngest still in tow against her hip and slipped her shoes off. She abandoned them in the front entryway where the kids had already tossed theirs and followed Jack through the house.

"Who's ready to go to the fun center?" he asked with much enthusiasm.

"Me, me, me!" June shouted.

Mrs. O'Henry stood in the kitchen, placing colorful donuts

on a serving tray. "Me, too," she said. "But who's ready for a donut first?"

"I want a donut," Zach said.

"Hi, Kelsey, how are you?"

"I'm fine, thanks." She wasn't. She hadn't been fine all year. But did Mrs. O'Henry want the full truth on how she was?

Because the full truth was, she was terrible. She was worried and stressed. And mostly, she was lonely and felt abandoned.

"You mentioned on the phone you had something to discuss so I thought donuts for the kids would be a good distraction."

"Good idea." Kelsey tried not to think about how she'd already served the kids a sugary breakfast, and now they'd be eating an even sweeter snack. At least she wouldn't have to deal with the sugar rush followed by the crash.

"What about Charlotte? Does miss Charlotte want a donut too?"

The baby fussed, squeezing her hands, and reaching for Mrs. O'Henry who took Charlotte into her arms and picked up a pink donut with sprinkles. Charlotte's eyes widened and she licked her lips.

"I think she approves." Mrs. O'Henry giggled, setting Charlotte into an old wooden highchair. She buckled her in and put the sprinkled donut onto the tray. The highchair had been used by all the O'Henry children, including Ricky when he was a baby.

Kelsey's heart squeezed.

"There. They look settled. For a few minutes at least. Why don't we go into the living room." Mrs. O'Henry led the way.

"Would you like some coffee?" Mr. O'Henry offered.

"No thank you."

She was also already jittery enough. Not only because of

the caffeine. She was dreading the conversation she was about to have with her in laws. What if they'd only been nice to her because of Ricky? And now that he was gone, they didn't have to pretend anymore?

Mr. and Mrs. O'Henry sat on high-back chairs in the formal living room where a giant grandfather clock took up an entire corner and expensive art hung on the walls. Kelsey sat across from them, knees buckling together while she wiped her sweaty palms down her legs. She didn't have time for beating around the bush. And she wasn't the kind of person to walk on eggshells either. While she did attempt to have the best manners around her in-laws, she was still Kelsey.

"I've fallen behind in my loan payments," she blurted.

"On the house?" Mr. O'Henry asked.

She shook her head. "On the bar."

They looked at one another and Kelsey's heart skidded. *What did that shared look mean?* But there wasn't time for reading people or for assumptions.

"I couldn't keep up with paying the vendors, then the bills, so I took out a second loan against the business, then I couldn't keep up with those payments. Now, not only are they passed due, but in just over a month, the bank is going to close the business. And possibly put a lien against the house," she rambled.

Mrs. O'Henry tucked her hair behind her ear, and she pushed her lips out before speaking. "Oh, Kelsey, I wish you would've come to us sooner."

Her heartbeat picked up speed. The air in the room felt thin and she struggled for breath. While her in-law's expressions appeared worrisome, their reactions were passive, making them difficult to read.

"We'd like to help, in any way that we possibly can," Mr. O'Henry said.

Kelsey's eyes flicked to him. His red hair was lighter now than it had been ten years ago, but his green eyes were the same. Like the ones she'd gazed into a million times. The ones she looked into when she confessed her never ending love to, made promises to, committed her life to.

"But we sold the business to you and Ricky for a reason," he continued.

"Business is good. We're always busy," Kelsey insisted.

"It's not about business. We just have a lot of funds tied up elsewhere," Mr. O'Henry explained.

"We'll see what we can do," Mrs. O'Henry said, leaning forward and placing a hand on top of Kelsey's. "But don't worry, we won't let you lose the house."

Kelsey flinched and eyed them desperately. "And the bar? What about the bar?"

"The house is most important, don't you think?" Mrs. O'Henry asked.

"If I have to, I'll sell the house and use the money to pay the loans off for the bar," Kelsey replied.

"My grandchildren are not going to live in a bar," Mrs. O'Henry said, straightening.

She was right, of course. Kelsey was sounding crazy. But she was desperate. She could feel the bar slipping through her fingers and she couldn't let that happen. She wouldn't.

"That's not what I meant. We could rent something."

Mr. O'Henry held up his palms. "Let's not get ahead of ourselves, all right? Let me talk to a friend of mine, he's an attorney in Denver. There's gotta be a death loophole of sorts. Let's find out if this is even legal."

The unpaid loan bills piling up, the past-due notices, the bank phone calls—it felt legal to her. She'd borrowed money that she was unable to pay back. Seemed straightforward to her.

And yet maybe Mr. O'Henry was onto something. With Ricky dying, maybe she could get an extension of some sorts.

"Thank you, I'd really appreciate that," she said, though she'd be lying to herself if she didn't admit she'd been hoping for a quicker fix. The last thing she wanted to do was ask them to help her financially, but at the same time, now she was stuck waiting.

"I can't make any promises, but I'll put in a call and let you know."

Crossing her legs, Mrs. O'Henry leaned forward. "Sweetie, maybe letting the bar go isn't such a terrible idea."

That she was even suggesting that, caused Kelsey's skin to tingle in anger. After all the work the two of them and Ricky had put into the bar, Kelsey was shocked. All she could do was stare at Mrs. O'Henry blankly while she continued.

"You've already cut back on employees, which suddenly makes sense now, but it's causing you to work yourself to death. You can't afford to take any more short-cuts."

With her heart hammering, Kelsey scooted to the edge of the chair, tucking her hair behind her ears. "But I don't mind the work. To me, it's worth it. Saving the bar, I mean."

Mrs. O'Henry sighed as if she were exhausted and looked at Mr. O'Henry.

"Don't get us wrong, we love the bar as much as you do. It's been in our family for decades. But sometimes you have to know when to cut your losses," Mr. O'Henry said.

Charlotte cried from the other room.

"We can discuss this more later," Mrs. O'Henry said, standing.

Kelsey jumped to her feet. "Please, just call your friend. And in the meantime, I'll weigh my options."

Mr. O'Henry nodded. "Promise. First thing in the morning."

"I think that's a good idea." Mrs. O'Henry gave Kelsey a weak smile before she embraced her.

The desperation to say something more clawed at her throat while her fingers trembled at her sides.

After Mrs. O'Henry pulled away, her eyes solemn, she said, "Just remember, those kids already lost their father, don't put this need to keep the bar above being there for them." She spun around and crossed the room to tend to a fussy Charlotte.

"While I appreciate that, I can't stand by and watch their legacy snatched away from them." Kelsey turned and raced out of the room.

She left the house in a hurry, rushing down the steps, through the leaves, without even saying goodbye to the kids. Otherwise she may have said something she'd regret. She loved her in-laws, but sometimes, she didn't understand them. Mr. O'Henry's parents started the bar decades before. O'Henry's had been in the same building, the same location, in the heart of Pineridge since the beginning.

There had to be someone in the town that loved the bar enough and who also had the money, to help her save it. But who?

CHAPTER 8
Davis

Overthinking was Davis's forte.

He could overthink something to smithereens. Which was why he was having to remeasure everything on the Larson job. He couldn't get his brain to concentrate. It was preoccupied; over analyzing the intense moment between him and Kelsey.

Cooper lay, curled in a ball on the floor, his brown eyes gazing up at Davis.

"Don't give me that look." He pointed the measuring tape at the dog. "I know what you're thinking. And no, just because I love her as a friend doesn't mean I love her more than that."

Never, in all the years he and Kelsey had been friends had his hands traveled her body. Never had her fingers gone to the nape of his neck. Never had his mind wandered to the places it had—a longing to explore her further.

It was almost as if for ten years, he had blinders on, unable to see Kelsey as the woman she'd grown up to be. She'd been nothing more than his best friend. A person he confided everything to. His anguish when Garrett grieved the loss of Emma. His sadness when Lissa broke his heart and moved away. He shared with her his regret of signing the contract.

Now, the blinders had been removed. He was seeing Kelsey for the first time as not only a loving, intelligent, and determined woman, but an attractive woman at that. She had a rocking body with a backside he suddenly craved to touch.

No, not blinders. It had been months since he'd got laid. That was the explanation. Nothing more.

Except it *felt* like more.

There had been the comment made by Kelsey's mom, *I think my daughter has always had a crush on Davis*. Had she said that because there was truth to it, or had she said it because she'd been completely wasted?

Either way, the comment caught him off guard, and caused him to over analyze his friendship with Kelsey. It had made him wonder, what could be.

It downright irritated him.

He had no business questioning their relationship. He'd never done it in the past. So why now? All it was doing was screwing everything up. Not only their friendship, but now his job.

This house was in the middle of filming. It was scheduled to be the last episode aired this year. Meaning, not only did the remodel need to be completed, but the house also had to be fully decked out for the upcoming holidays. He'd leave that task for Garrett to handle. Christmas hadn't been a favorite holiday of his since he was a child and his dad had left.

The front door of the Larson house flew open, bringing with it a gust of autumn wind and withered maple leaves as Kelsey burst inside. Cooper lunged from his spot on the floor and he let out a string of barks until he recognized the intruder and they turned into an excited howl instead.

Davis dropped the measuring tape from his hand, the metal winding up with a snap. "Kelsey? What the hell?"

"Hey, sorry to bug you, I just need to talk for a sec." She closed the door behind her, tightening her jacket around her while she wiped her boots off on the front rug. Cooper met her in the middle of the room, and she petted him before plopping herself down on the step of the sunken in living room.

His stomach muscles tensed. Instantly his mind was at attention, replaying the vivid moment from the night in the bar's office. The overwhelming scent of her hair, the powerful heat transferring from their bodies as they inched closer. He mentally tried to prepare himself for what was to come. The mention of that exact awkward moment and how it shouldn't have happened, how it *couldn't* happen again, and that it meant nothing.

Davis let out a low, shaky breath before bending over and snatching up his measuring tape. "Yeah? What about?"

He busied himself with the measuring of the kitchen cabinets. Maybe if he kept himself preoccupied his reaction to her words wouldn't be as noticeable. He'd be prepared for the blow.

But when she didn't speak, he took a risk and glanced at her over his shoulder. She looked small sitting on the step, knees tucked to her chest, and her lower lip hidden between her teeth. Her dark hair was messy and wind-blown but swept away from her face.

With her eyes downcast, a pang hit him in the center of his chest and a sudden over protectiveness washed over him. He hung his head and set the measuring tape down before shuffling to the step and sitting next to her. Cooper joined them, propping his head on Davis's knee and he couldn't resist petting the dog's head.

He half expected Kelsey to rest her head on his shoulder

and burst into tears. But he was grateful she didn't. He didn't fully trust himself to console her in a friendly way.

And they were just friends.

Wrapping her arms around her knees, she stared in the space in front of her. "So, I finally went and spoke with the O'Henry's. They can't afford to help with the loans."

Davis filled his cheeks with air before releasing it in a puff of unbelief. Partly his relief was the result of Kelsey's topic of conversation. The last thing he wanted to do was discuss what went down between them.

Forcing himself to focus on her and the issue with the bar, he didn't look at her out of fear of distraction. He knew far too well Kelsey wouldn't want his pity. She came here for a solution. But did he have it to give?

"So what now?"

She turned sideways on the step to face him, leaning her back against the open doorframe, and he allowed a peek at her from the corner of his eye. The sight of her worriment was enough to zone in.

"I made an appointment to meet with my accountant tomorrow afternoon," she said, tucking her hair behind her ears.

"That's good."

Cooper finally relaxed, laying down on the floor and closed his eyes for another nap.

"Mr. O'Henry also said he'd call a lawyer friend of his and see if there's any kind of loophole, you know...since the owner of the business died."

He nodded along with her as she continued to speak, not able to look at her once again.

"It's not an answer, but it's a start."

"Can you afford a lawyer?" he asked, already knowing the answer.

"No. But hopefully this guy will do it as a favor to Mr. O'Henry? I'm not really sure. He's in Denver and since this is a local bar, I can't see him being passionate enough to help."

He nudged his knee into hers. "C'mon, you don't know that."

"Besides doing it as a favor to Jack, why would he want to help a mother of three small children save a bar?" She laughed sarcastically, the sound dying in her throat.

"It's not just a bar. It's a restaurant. It's a business. Your family business and your livelihood. He'll get that."

"Maybe..."

Davis would offer to help. In any way he could. Including financially. But it was pointless. Kelsey was too proud to ask for help, never mind accept it. Most importantly from him. Yet, he couldn't keep himself from at least trying.

"Let me help."

She sat up straight, her face going stony. "You are helping. By being my friend and letting me vent."

"That's not what I was referring to."

Her eyes went wide, and her brows rose. "I know what you were referring to and the answer is no."

"C'mon, Kels. Quit being so proud—"

"It's a big fat NO," she cut him off. "And it has nothing to do with pride. With a dead-beat father who skipped town when I was little and an alcoholic mama, I'd say that ship sailed a long time ago."

She stood and he did too, rubbing his suddenly sweaty palms down the fronts of his Carhartt's. Cooper sat up, noticing the shift in the air, and studying Kelsey as she paced the living room hardwood floor.

Davis crossed his arms, watching her as well. "Okay, stubborn ass. If it isn't pride, what is it then?"

She stopped walking and spun to face him. "It's principle."

He called her bluff. "Principle is just a fancy word for pride."

She narrowed her eyes at him. "I think we both know I'm far from fancy."

This comment got a stirring inside him, and he chuckled. It was a thrill quite different than what their usual banter caused. And he had to admit, he didn't hate it.

A devious smile slid onto her lips and his chest expanded enough for him to sigh. Things for her might've been crap right now, but the two of them—their friendship—was fine. They were still Davis and Kelsey.

The earlier tension in his shoulders released. "As always, let's agree to disagree."

"Fine." She gazed around the room while she stepped toward the mantle he'd built. She ran her hand along the old barnwood he'd installed to stick out past the rest of the fireplace.

He couldn't help but track her eyes, to try and read them, to wonder what she saw and felt as she ran her fingers over the wood. Her opinion had always mattered to him. Even more so since he and Garrett had signed the contract with HGTV. Kelsey would give it to him straight. If he'd done shit work, she'd let him know.

"This is beautiful," she said, her fingertips still grazing the wood.

He rubbed the back of his neck, the compliment feeling different than usual, and his cheeks warmed. "Thanks."

"Where'd the wood come from?"

"The Patterson's old barn."

She gazed at him over her outstretched arm, her fingers stilling their movement. "And Garrett was okay with that?"

"It was his idea."

"So sad. All that property just sold back to the bank. The barns torn down. The animals sold...Lissa moving away."

He nodded, his throat thickening. She didn't have to go into detail. Mentioning Lissa was enough. They rarely talked about his ex. In all honesty, there wasn't much to say.

When the only woman Garrett had ever loved enough to commit to, died along with her parents in a helicopter crash in Hawaii nearly two years ago, it was more than sad. It was infuriating. It was cruel. And it had completely wrecked Garrett.

And in turn, he supposed he'd been wrecked too. Emma's twin sister, Lissa had been too distraught to stay. Or to keep her parent's farm. She sold everything as fast as possible. In what felt like a blink of an eye, he'd too lost the only woman he'd ever loved. Or at least loved enough, Davis thought they had a future together.

Losing Emma Patterson turned Garrett into a bigger player than he'd been before. Now, he was out of control. He'd dated and slept with so many women, Davis had lost count. That had been the main reason Davis had agreed to the contract for the show with HGTV.

Garrett had been the strong one when their dad ended up being a complete flake.

This was Davis's chance to return the favor.

The front door opened again, both of their attention swinging in the direction just as Garrett stepped inside the house, shifting a box in his arms to a hip. Cooper only glanced at him momentarily, too familiar with Garrett and his spontaneity. An instant chill entered with him, and Davis felt the distance between him and Kelsey immediately.

Garrett took one look at Kelsey and a big, goofy grin spread on his lips.

If she didn't have three kids, or *baggage* as Garrett would call them, he'd probably pursue her.

"Kelsey," Garrett said, tipping an imaginary hat.

"Hey, slacker. Nice of you to finally show up," she muttered.

"Hey," he replied, incredulous. "Somebody's gotta do the shopping. You and I both know, this guy isn't gonna do it." He nudged his chin in Davis's direction.

"True," she agreed.

Davis could fake being insulted but what would be the point? It was true. He hated shopping and he hated interior designing. That was Garrett's expertise.

"I come bearing gifts." Garrett held out the box.

"Everything's done. I just put up the mantle."

Garrett set the box on the floor and strolled over to the fireplace. He inspected the barnwood mantle Davis had just installed. Part of Davis wished he knew what was going through Garrett's mind. If he was thinking about the Patterson's farm. The barn. Emma.

"It looks great. As always, little bro." Garrett smacked Davis on the back and spun back around, returning to his box.

The brave face Garrett put on was beginning to grate on Davis. It was as if he wouldn't allow himself to feel anything at all. Not for Emma. Not for her death. Not even for the demise of their relationship. Instead, he dove into work and women. And not in that order.

Davis wished in that order.

"Wanna stick around and help me decorate this place?" Garrett held out two candles toward Kelsey, brows raised and a bright smile on his face.

"No way, not a chance you're roping me into doing your work." She crossed the room heading toward the front door, zipping up her jacket before braving the wind. "I gotta get back to the bar. I've been gone long enough. Julian could have set the place on fire by now."

Davis chuckled. Even though she was most likely wrong. Julian knew his way around that bar backward and forward. If Kelsey handed over the reins long enough to trust him to be in charge, she'd know that.

"Hey, will you be at the Halloween costume party?" Garrett asked just as Kelsey gripped the doorknob.

"You mean the one at my bar?" she teased, narrowing her eyes. "Of course I'll be there."

"Who're you going with?"

Davis's chest tightened. "Garrett," he hissed.

She dropped her attention to the floor. "I'm not going with anybody. I'm working that night."

"What about your costume? It's couples' costumes."

"Garrett," Davis snapped, louder this time.

"What? She knows I don't mean anything by it, right, Kels?"

Her jaw ticked and Davis wanted to punch Garrett for being so insensitive.

"The party is at my bar, I don't have to follow any dumb rules. I don't have to dress up at all." She opened the door and stepped outside.

"Oh, come on. Where's your Halloween spirit? I bet you'd make one sexy witch." Garret waggled his brows.

Davis shot his brother a glare as heat crept up his neck. He was sure that Kelsey having tiny humans who called her *Mom* was a turn off for Garrett. Maybe he'd been wrong, and if so... well if so, they would have a problem.

Davis met her in the open doorway. "Don't listen to him. You don't have to dress up."

She cocked a brow. "What, you don't think I'd make a sexy witch?"

"Foot in mouth, bro," Garrett said from behind him. "Foot. In. Mouth."

More heat rose from beneath his collar. His face had to be ten shades of red by now. He rested a shoulder against the doorframe and folded his arms across his chest. "I didn't say that. All I'm saying is...do what you want."

"I always do." Kelsey winked at him but leaned to the side, her gaze finding Garrett. "Guess you're both gonna have to wait and see. Bye, boys." She fluttered her fingers and sauntered down the walkway.

After she'd climbed inside her minivan and closed the door behind her, Davis whirled around.

"Just because you're heartless doesn't mean you can treat people like that," he snapped.

"Like what? And I'm not heartless. Kelsey gets me. It's fine. We're cool." Garrett placed the two candles on top of the mantle, stepping back with hands rested on his hips to admire them.

"Reminding her the party's a couples' thing doesn't help. You're only reminding her she's alone."

"Kelsey is tough. I doubt she's still pining after Ricky. He's gone. Just like Emma. She needs to do herself a favor and learn from the pro."

Davis's brows rose. "Who? *You?*"

His brother nodded confidently, pulling two vases from the box. "That's right. She needs to get laid."

Davis nearly choked on his own saliva.

Garrett shrugged. "Just saying. It worked for me."

"Yeah well, thankfully she's nothing like you."

"I don't think it's a bad idea for her to at least get a date for the Halloween party. You're her best friend, do you want her to be single forever?"

"Of course not."

And yet, the thought of Kelsey having a date didn't sit well with him. Thinking of some random guy—or worse—a guy like

Garrett, making her laugh, running his hands through her hair, kissing her, it made his chest tighten. It wasn't that he wanted to be that guy necessarily. He just didn't want anyone else to be with her.

Crap. What did that mean?

If he didn't want anyone else with her, did he mean anyone else besides him?

"Just leave her alone," Davis muttered.

"Fine. Just saying."

"Yeah, well, just get to work."

"Don't act like you're the only one working here," Garrett fired back.

"I got here early. I'm hungry. I'm gonna go get something to eat."

"Fine. Bring me back a sandwich, will you?" Garrett called as Davis went out the front door just as the film crew pulled into the driveway.

Davis groaned.

He'd thought Garrett was the last person he wanted to talk to right now, but no. It was most definitely the film crew. Or the producer. Or anyone related to the show.

"Davis, buddy, how goes it?" Franklin, their producer greeted as he hopped out of the vehicle before it had a chance to even come to a complete stop.

Davis grunted, his only reply.

Franklin walked alongside Davis as he hurried to his truck.

"So, listen, the crew and I have been talking and we think it would be a stellar idea if you undid another button on your flannel's, maybe even skipped the t-shirt underneath."

Davis came to a screeching stop and turned to Franklin, his chest already heating. "You serious?"

Franklin shrugged his shoulders. "Let's be honest. Sex sells."

"This is a family show," Davis said between gritted teeth, growing more annoyed with Franklin by the millisecond.

"It is, it is," Franklin said, his salt and pepper hair flopping as he nodded, pretending he was thinking about that. But they both knew better. Franklin wasn't considering Davis's words at all.

Davis tried again. "Our viewers range from children to my great grandmother's friends. I don't think me showing a little more skin is necessary."

"It's not so much skin as it is your muscled physique. The hair on your chest. C'mon, Dave, you're a strapping young man. Let's show the viewers that."

Dave?

Davis yanked open the door of truck. "I think Garrett shows the viewers enough for the both of us."

"You're not wrong, big guy."

Big guy?

"But if it's all the same to you, Mr. President and I think it will boost the ratings in the next episode."

Davis hopped into his truck and proceeded to button up the top two buttons on his flannel very, very slowly. "It's not all the same to me," he said before slamming the door shut.

As he started the engine and pulled his truck away from the curb, he didn't look back at Franklin. He didn't have to. He was pretty sure the guy was still standing there, mouth agape, hands on his hips. Probably his mind was spinning out of control on how he was going to tell Mr. President and be sure his job wasn't in jeopardy.

When Davis had agreed to the show, it was already obvious that one of the angles was that he and Garrett were not only brothers but twins. It would make it appealing to viewers— identical twin brothers who were carpenters and who were in business together. The advertising team had used their looks and their skills to promote the show. Both tall, dark blonde hair, lanky but toned, talented, with friendly and trustworthy smiles. Garrett brought the sex appeal; Davis brought the family appeal. That had been the show's angle.

After two seasons, why change it now?

Whatever the reason—Davis didn't care to find out.

CHAPTER 9

Kelsey

If anyone could ever convey such intense pity with just one look, it would be Maria Velez. In high school she'd been the epitome of a younger J. Lo. Even still, she portrayed the beauty of the famously talented singer/actress. At the moment, she was about nine months pregnant but still managed to have flawless hair and makeup.

When Kelsey was pregnant with Charlotte, toting around Zach and June, she looked like a sloth who'd swallowed a watermelon. If anything, Kelsey hoped Maria would give her some grace and possibly use that pity to work some magic with her finances. Though based on the solemn look in Maria's brown eyes, it wasn't promising. Kelsey's shoulders tensed.

With a slight shake of her head, Maria spoke softly when she said, "I'm so sorry, Kelsey. But with the second mortgage on your home, and the current housing market along with high interest rates, you wouldn't make enough if you sold. Not even enough to break even."

The dread hit her low in the belly with a dull thud. This wasn't the news she'd been hoping for. First, her in-laws couldn't help her, and now she'd just been informed that not only would she not be making enough money to pay off the business loans if she sold the house, but she would also be upside down. She'd been dealt one bad hand after another the past year. It felt like all the cards were stacked against her.

"What about another loan? A third loan?" Kelsey's heart raced, her fingers trembling.

Maria folded her lips in between her teeth as she gave long, slow blinks. "I've ran all the numbers. Both the business and your personal, and again, I'm sorry, but it's just not feasible." She leaned across the desk as far as her rounding belly would allow, glancing around before saying, "Kelsey, they're about to put a lien on your house."

Her head spun and her chest hurt, acid burned in her throat.

This wasn't her last resort, she knew. But convincing her mind to focus on that instead of on the defeat that thudded in her chest was useless. The feeling of losing control, of dropping all the balls she'd been juggling, came to the surface.

She stood on wobbly legs. She needed to leave the bank before she released the pent-up anguish and tears. "Thank you for your time. And good luck with the delivery. I'll be sure to send a gift."

Back to square one.

Kelsey pushed out the doors of the bank, gulping in the crisp air and forcing back the impending tears. She had too much to do to wallow in her circumstances. Instead, she headed straight for The Daily Grind, then she'd hit up Sweet Cakes Bakery. A Pumpkin spice latte and a piece of her mama's cinnamon apple cake would have to do the trick. At least for now.

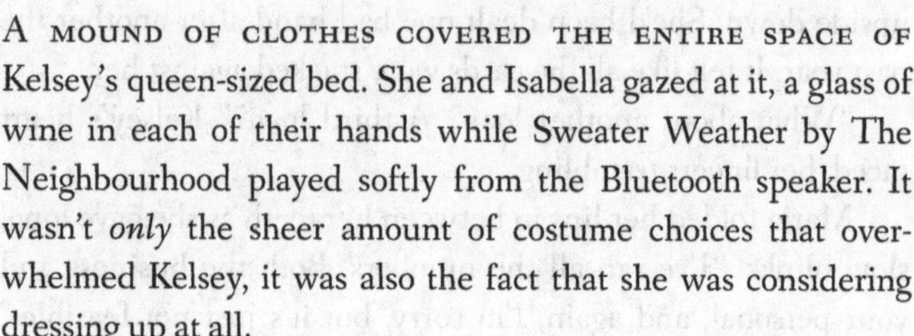

A MOUND OF CLOTHES COVERED THE ENTIRE SPACE OF Kelsey's queen-sized bed. She and Isabella gazed at it, a glass of wine in each of their hands while Sweater Weather by The Neighbourhood played softly from the Bluetooth speaker. It wasn't *only* the sheer amount of costume choices that overwhelmed Kelsey, it was also the fact that she was considering dressing up at all.

While all her friends and people attending the party dressed in couple costumes, she would be reminded, once again, that she was alone.

She gulped the remaining inch of her wine before setting her glass down and dropping onto the bed dramatically, instantly drowning in the clothing. Isabella distractedly rummaged through Kelsey's closet and mumbled, "No, no, no."

Isabella and Leo had their costumes picked out over a month ago. Baby and Johnny from Dirty Dancing. Even Norah, who hadn't been out much since she and Landon split, was going to the party. She was dressing up as a female/sexy version of Danny Zuko and Maddie was going as Sandy Olsson from Grease.

"What about this? You could go as Lilo and take June's Stitch stuffed animal?" Isabella asked, holding up a red Hawaiian print dress Kelsey hadn't seen in years.

The dress had been shoved in the back of her closet since a Luau themed party they'd hosted at the bar. It was Ricky's idea. A way to bring morale after a summer forest fire burned nearly 800 square miles up the mountain. Ricky was always thinking of things like that.

"Well?" Isabella blinked at her.

"That's just sad. Going as a couple costume with myself. I'd be better off choosing a solo costume, or not dressing up at all."

Isabella tilted her head to the side. "I think it would be creative."

Kelsey groaned, throwing her arm across her eyes. If she could get Julian to cover her at the bar, she wouldn't have to be there at all. That was the only reason she was in this predicament. Because she'd be at the bar working. But she didn't want to be the only one not in costume. Maybe Garrett had been right in encouraging her, maybe a sexy witch wasn't such a bad idea.

"Fine. We'll keep looking." Isabella shuffled through more clothing in the closet.

"How about I just pick something and make up a costume?"

Isabella ignored her.

"Ah-ha. I got it," Izzy said.

Kelsey sat up and leaned back on her elbows.

Isabella held out a pastel blue suit.

Kelsey had worn the suit only once. Davis had a matching one in orange. The two had competed in a costume competition years ago. Dressed in Harry and Lloyd costumes from their favorite movie Dumb and Dumber, they'd won first place.

It was so long ago it felt like a lifetime. Or like someone else's life.

Before kids. Before Ricky. Before life had become so complicated.

Kelsey pursed her lips, surprised she was seriously considering it.

"Dumb and Dumber, right?" Izzy asked.

"Yep."

"It's perfect. It's part of a couple costume, but you don't

have to necessarily have the other guy to complete the costume."

"Lloyd," Kelsey amended.

"It's so iconic, everyone knows him."

"I suppose." Kelsey stood and searched in the back of the closet for a step stool. Locating it, she set it up and climbed it to rummage around on the top shelf of her closet. Finally, she found what she was looking for. A pastel blue top hat.

Isabella's eyes widened and she snatched it from Kelsey. "Ahh, this is too perfect." She set the hat on her head, admiring herself in the full-length mirror and then snorted a laugh at her reflection.

"Give it here." Kelsey held out her hand. "You could never pull off this look. It's too nerdy."

Izzy gasped. "I can be nerdy."

"Oh, honey, you couldn't even if you tried." Kelsey smiled, setting the hat on her own head, and presenting herself to Isabella, a smile stretching across her face.

"And somehow, you're right. You can totally pull off the look. And still be completely adorable."

"Ha," Kelsey scoffed, slipping the hat off and pushing her fingers through her hair. She reached for a bin in the back of her closet. "I think I might even have a blonde wig in here somewhere."

"Here's a thought—why don't you ask Davis if he still has his Lloyd costume and would want to do a couple costume with you?"

Kelsey whipped her head up. "Wh-what? What for? Why would we go as a couple?"

Isabella blinked at her.

Kelsey's cheeks burned. "I just mean, I'm sure he doesn't still have it."

"Okay, weirdo, what's with you?"

Was she being weird?

"What? Nothing. It's just that, I'm sure he's already going with someone. Everyone's had their costumes planned for weeks. You know how Davis is."

Isabella pushed her lips into a thought. "Yeah, that guy is definitely a planner."

"A lot like someone else I know." Kelsey elbowed Isabella, smirking and praying she'd changed the subject enough.

"Ha, ha," Isabella replied, sarcastically.

The thought had crossed Kelsey's mind. Asking Davis to buddy up with her for the couples' costume party. But with how off things had been between them lately, she didn't want to ask. She needed things to go back to normal. She missed her best friend.

And yet...

The past week she'd been unable to stop thinking about Davis without a shirt on, completely bare chested and sculpted. Don't even get her started on the way it felt to have his fingers travel down her back, to have his mouth so warm and near. It had been completely wild and irresponsible. But even worse and most shocking? As his hand had traveled down her back, hovering dangerously close to her backside, she hadn't wanted him to stop.

It had been a long time since she'd felt pleasure. A long time since she'd been touched by a man. A long ass time since she'd teetered on the edge of ecstasy and had her mind blown.

A tingling sensation headed south, and she swallowed.

"Did Davis help you out with your problem?" Isabella asked, interrupting Kelsey's tactless fantasy.

"Mmm? What?" Her brain stumbled, unable to fully make words.

She had a problem all right. And unfortunately, it was something Davis couldn't help her with.

Or *shouldn't* help her with.

"You said you were gonna talk to him about helping you possibly find someone in town who might want to invest in the business Did you talk to him?"

"Oh, that. Yeah, I did."

"And?" Isabella stretched out the word.

"And of course all he did was offer to help financially."

"Naturally." Isabella found a cowboy hat in Kelsey's closet and stuffed it on her head, posing in front of the mirror.

"So of course, I said no."

"Of course." Spinning around to face Kelsey, Isabella took the cowboy hat off her head and adjusted it on Kelsey's. "When is that man ever gonna realize his money's no good to you?"

Kelsey gave a lopsided smile into the mirror at her reflection. "Probably never."

"You might be the only person in town who could care less about Reno Dudes."

"It's true. And yet, why does it feel like he's gotta remind me of it?"

"I don't know, but if it makes you feel any better, I don't think he actually likes the attention. Or the money."

Isabella was right, he didn't. But lately it felt like it was becoming an issue. More women in town were beginning to notice him. More tourists in the bar were asking about him than ever before. Most of the time the tourists hung on Garrett. But as the show progressed, more were seeing straight through that charming facade of his and realizing Davis was the genuine one. He was charming without even trying.

"Part of me thinks Davis regrets signing that contract at all," Isabella said. She was still talking but Kelsey was only half listening.

Over the past week, she'd been allowing herself to wonder about the "what ifs", or the "what could've beens". Even though she and Davis had always been strictly friends, what would've happened if he hadn't left for Denver? Between the time after high school graduation when Isabella had gone to New York and she and Ricky had gotten together, she and Davis had been inseparable.

From musicals to concerts to movies, they'd seen them all together. There had been a time, a moment, a flicker, when she thought maybe, just maybe there could be something more between them. But then Ricky asked her out and Davis encouraged her to say yes. Davis left for Denver a few years later.

When he returned to Pineridge two years ago, Kelsey was married with two kids and another baby on the way. They picked up where they'd left off—*almost*. They still saw every Jim Carrey and Adam Sandler movie together, but they were strictly friends.

"What do you think?" Isabella asked, refilling Kelsey's wine glass.

"About the contract?"

Isabella nodded, taking a sip of the pinot grigio.

Of course, Davis had disclosed his thoughts on this topic to her, but Kelsey was put in a tough spot when it came to her best friends. She made it a priority not to tell one another their secrets.

"I think you might be right. At least a little. Davis loves what he does. But as far as the cameras and all that nonsense, you know he hates attention. Even if it is positive."

Kelsey found the short blonde wig she'd been looking for and she positioned it on her head, as she checked in the mirror. Isabella left the cowboy hat on her head and plopped onto Kelsey's bed, sitting crisscross applesauce.

"Makes you wonder why he agreed."

Kelsey chewed her lower lip, picking up her full wine glass and joining Izzy on the bed. "Love." She shrugged.

Isabella's eyebrows squished together. "Love?"

"Yeah. For Garrett. I'm sure it's a good distraction. All those old feelings about Emma and her death must be coming up after using the wood from the Patterson barn on their last house project," Kelsey said.

"It's so sad. And I bet you're right." Isabella leaned against the headboard. "I can see why you're so close with Davis."

"He's the best." Her thoughts spiraled, turning nostalgic as images of the ways Davis had been there for her in just the past year played in her mind.

"Now you see why I was jealous when he moved back to town."

"Jealous? Why?"

"Because, he was your best friend after I left for college. He was your Izzy," she teased.

Kelsey smiled, studying the wine in the glass while she swirled it around. "No one could ever replace you. But he was a fine runner-up."

"Fine is right," Isabella teased, pushing a toe into Kelsey's leg.

But Kelsey couldn't look at her. She was afraid if she did, Izzy would see straight through her. She'd definitely notice the affection in her eyes. Because as each day passed, Kelsey didn't know if she'd be able to hide it much longer.

The truth was, the feelings she held in her heart for Davis far outweighed the definition of a friend. Would a friend look at her in the way he had while her T-shirt had been soaked through? Would a friend lean in so close as if daring a kiss? Would a friend offer to go with her to Denver for a night to meet with a lawyer who'd agreed to discuss her situation?

Okay, so a friend would most likely offer to do the latter. Isabella definitely would. Except Kelsey hadn't asked Izzy. For one, Izzy was busy, and for another—a reason she was afraid to admit to herself—she wanted it to be Davis who went with her.

An entire night away.

Not only would it be the first break she'd had since Ricky passed and she'd been soloing this parenting gig, but it would also be a chance for the two of them to be alone. A chance to maybe figure out what was going on between them. And either do something about it, or not. Kelsey wasn't a patient woman. And she didn't like this beating around the bush. She didn't have time for that nonsense.

Only, she just hadn't told Izzy yet.

"So..." she began, feeling the pulse in her throat. "Speaking of Davis, he offered to go with me when I meet with that attorney in Denver."

Isabella's attention snapped from her phone and landed on Kelsey; brows raised. "Really?"

"Don't say it like that." Kelsey bumped her shoulder into Izzy's playfully. "He just didn't want me to go alone," she said it nonchalantly, even though her skin buzzed with anticipation of the upcoming trip.

"Don't say it like what? Like I'm a teensy-weensy bit excited that you're getting out of town for a night...with Davis?"

"Yes, exactly. With Davis," she attempted to make her voice sound even.

"Fiiiiine," Izzy whined, rolling her eyes and sighing. "You're right, it's just Davis. But I am excited you're getting away. Even if it is for just one night. You've been so busy with the bar and the kids. I think it will be really good for you."

"Izz, I'm going to meet with an attorney, about saving my business...I'm not going on a vacation."

"I know," Isabella replied, incredulous. "But if you don't at least make Davis take you out for a drink that night, I will."

"I will let him know." Kelsey smiled.

And with that, her brain whirled. She was unable to shut off her mind from thinking about the upcoming trip to Denver. Two uninterrupted hours in the truck with Davis, there, and back. One night in a shared hotel room.

She wasn't sure how she'd be able to handle it once the time came, because now, only thinking about it, caused a searing heat to travel through her body, creating a throbbing ache between her thighs.

CHAPTER 10

Davis

Despite the several times he and Kelsey had made the trip to Denver for concerts, this was different. They'd shared an almost-kiss, and he'd touched her in ways that friends don't touch. If Kelsey's mom hadn't interrupted them, Davis was certain he would've delved in and found out all the things he'd been wondering when it came to Kels, and activities that involved zero clothes.

It made zero sense. And all he was really sure of—he needed to stop thinking about it.

He needed to stop thinking about *her*.

Davis stepped out of the shower, wrapping a towel around his waist, and tucking in the edge at his hip. He looked at his reflection in the mirror as he raked his fingers through his damp hair.

Unfortunately, the cold shower hadn't helped in the way he'd hoped. He was still worked up. Maybe it had something to do with the fact that he and Kelsey were about to spend a full twenty-four hours together.

Alone.

In a hotel room.

While them going and doing this together wasn't unusual, it had been several years since they'd made this trip. And this would be the first one since Ricky passed, the first one since she was single again. Thinking about it like that made him feel gross. He was a jackass.

As he dressed in a pair of dark jeans, his nicest flannel and a North Face vest, his phone vibrated against the counter. Kelsey's name displayed on the screen.

KELSEY

Change of plans.

Davis's heart felt as if it stopped beating in his chest. Was she bailing on him?

What's up?

KELSEY

Pick me up at the Whitley's instead of my place.

He exhaled a breath.

Will do.

Why the change in location he didn't really care, she'd fill him in later. All he was relieved about was that she was still able to go. With running the bar, taking care of her kids, and helping her mom, any number of things could interrupt their trip away this weekend.

Davis needed this getaway maybe as much as Kelsey did. Things with Garrett and Renovation Dudes had him feeling as if he were suffocating. Between the tension with his brother and then the show's producer, Franklin suggesting he bring more sex appeal as they neared the last episode, he felt on edge.

Garrett was stretched out on the sofa, attention on his phone when Davis emerged from the bathroom. Cooper laid on his dog bed but perked up when he saw him. He probably sensed that Davis was fixing to leave him. He considered taking him along, leaving him with Garrett was a bit nerve racking.

Garrett cocked a brow at him. "You're going to see an attorney dressed like that? You wanna borrow one of my suits?"

"I have my own suits," he mumbled as he wrestled on his boots. "And I'm not seeing the attorney, Kelsey is meeting with him alone."

"Then what's the point of you going? I'm pretty sure Kelsey can drive herself, she's a capable woman, that one." He sat up and swung his legs over the edge of the sofa.

"Call it moral support."

"Just seems like an unnecessary trip to the city when there's plenty we could be doing here."

Davis's gaze snapped to his brother. "*We?*"

"Please tell me you're at least getting some action out of this?"

Picking up a piece of paper off the kitchen island, Davis waved it in the air, signaling Garrett's attention and ignoring his comment. "Here's the instructions for Cooper. They're simple—basically, don't forget to feed him."

Hearing his name, Cooper bounded over to him and sat, wagging his tail. Davis petted the dog's head and mumbled several, *good boys*.

Garrett followed, walking him to the door. "Yeah, yeah, Coop and I will be fine. We get along great, don't we boy?"

Cooper barked in response as if in agreement.

"Thanks for staying here."

"No problem."

"And one more thing—no women."

Garrett waggled his brows and Davis's gut tightened.

"I mean it, Garrett. I don't want out of town fans who are obsessed with you knowing where I live. If you don't mind, take them back to your house."

"Fine, fine," he replied, waving him off. "But can you do something to return the favor?"

Grinding his teeth, Davis ambled toward the front door where he picked up his bag waiting there. Cooper followed on his heels. As if Davis owed Garrett anything. He'd already given him the next two years of his life. What more could he possibly want from him?

"Yeah? And what's that?" he asked over his shoulder.

"I'm being serious here. I need you to relax. Forget about the show, and the cameras, and the fans. And just have a good time. Have fun. If you remember how, that is." Garrett smirked.

Davis's shoulders relaxed. "Thanks. He crouched and scratched Cooper's ears. The dog licked his face. "See ya, Coop. Be a good boy. Take care of Garrett," he whispered.

DAVIS PULLED HIS PICKUP INTO THE WHITLEY'S DRIVEWAY and put it in park. He ran his hands down his pant legs and debated getting out of the truck. What was the etiquette here? This wasn't a date. They were simply two friends heading out of town together.

Except they weren't. This was more. They were driving to the city. They were staying in a hotel.

Davis groaned and ran his palms over his freshly shaven face. What had past Davis been thinking? Booking only one hotel room for the two of them. Pre-plumbing mishap, the one room wouldn't have been a problem. They'd shared a hotel room numerous of times. Hell, before Ricky entered the equation, they'd even shared a bed and neither of them had blinked an eye.

But post-plumbing mishap, post-near kiss, sharing a room felt wrong. He couldn't stop seeing the wet t-shirt, the vision of it clinging to her skin.

Yep. This was definitely going to be a problem.

Climbing out of the truck, he exhaled a long sigh. He shut the door and took his time shuffling down the pathway to the front steps.

"Get a grip, Vance," he mumbled under his breath.

The front door swung open before he could even knock.

"Hey," Kelsey greeted, a wobbly smile on her lips.

She was dressed in gray slacks and a matching suit jacket with a blue silky blouse underneath. He'd never seen her look so professional, and it was off-putting. It wasn't her. But the brightly colored shirt brought out the blue in her eyes. That along with the low v of the blouse giving him a decent view of her tempting cleavage was doing a fine job of distracting him from the depressing suit.

"Hey?" Davis tugged at the collar of his flannel where he'd left the top few buttons undone, mostly he did it out of spite to his producer, Franklin. He'd leave as many buttons undone or done up as he damn well pleased.

She dipped her chin to the side, exposing skin he was suddenly fantasizing pressing his lips against.

"Davis," June exclaimed, shoving past Kelsey, and launching herself in Davis's arms.

He caught her midair and swung her around. She reared back to get a better look at him, furrowing her brows.

"You look funny."

Davis chuckled.

She patted both of his cheeks in her hands. "Where'd all your hair go?"

He shaved his face earlier that day. He wished he could've said it had been on impulse. But no, he'd thought about it, and he knew how much it bothered Kelsey when he kept a constant unshaved look.

Davis's gaze flickered to Kelsey. "I wanted to make your mama smile."

Kelsey's cheeks blushed a soft red and she tucked her hair behind her ears.

"I think it worked," June said happily.

Kelsey waved him off. "Alright, don't act like that's the only reason. I know your deepest secrets, remember?"

His throat thickened. "Secrets?"

"Yeah, Franklin asked you to shave. Thought it would hike up the ratings." She winked.

"Oh, right. Totally."

Kelsey flashed him a smile, it was probably the same smile he'd seen about a trillion times before. But now, it looked different. It caused her blue eyes to sparkle and at the same time sent an ache of satisfaction in his chest. If all it took on his part to manufacture that smile, was for him to shave, he'd do it every damn day.

Kelsey cleared her throat. "Okay, we should go."

He set June down and she hugged his waist. "Bye, Davis."

"Bye, kiddo."

A baby screamed from inside the house. Charlotte's cry could be easily deciphered. His gut tightened, worried this trip wasn't going to happen. She was running out of time and needed a solution. He hadn't given up the idea of offering to help her out completely. The only thing holding him back was her. He was almost positive she'd never accept.

"Oh hell, we didn't get outta here soon enough," Kelsey grumbled.

Mr. Whitley rushed into the front entryway. "Go you two. Get out while you can."

"It's okay, Mr. W. I can calm her down," Kelsey insisted.

He took her by the shoulders and shoved her toward the door. "Don't be silly. We can handle things from here. Believe me. Now go." Mr. Whitley snatched up a bag from the floor and pressed it into Davis's chest.

Kelsey hugged Mr. W. before taking the steps behind Davis. She yanked her bag away from him.

"You don't have to carry my bag."

"I don't mind."

"Yeah, well, I'm more than capable."

"Oh, I know." He thought a comeback was warranted. But at the same time, she'd been trying extra hard to prove her independence. He'd let her have this win, even if it was small. He kept his mouth shut.

They climbed into his truck in silence. After tossing her bag into the cab and buckling in, she began syncing her phone to the truck's stereo.

Davis chuckled, shaking his head. "I haven't even backed out of the driveway yet."

"Your point?"

Hozier's voice poured through the speakers, growing louder as Kelsey turned up the volume. Because that's what Hozier's voice did. It poured like liquid running over, seeping into nooks and crannies of your soul. And it was in that moment, the silent conversation and music transcendence stretching between the neighborhood and the open road, when Davis relaxed.

They'd been rewarded with a sunny fall day, and the further they drove, they were welcomed with views of the snow-capped mountains and hillsides of red maples and golden aspens. But with the temperature expected to dip below forty degrees in Denver that night, he was glad he decided to wear the vest.

Glancing Kelsey's way, he found her focused on her phone, her lower lip pulled between her teeth.

"Everything okay?"

"Yeah, I was just checking in on my mama."

"She good?"

"She seems more herself this week. Her old self," Kelsey corrected.

"That's great."

"It is." She smiled at him, and his chest expanded.

He quickly returned his attention to the road stretching in front of him. "So what happened today, why the change in location for pick-up?"

"Oh, right. When I was dropping off the kids at the Whitley's, Mr. Hoffman heard me pull into their driveway and said my van was making a weird noise. He told me to park it at his place and offered to take a look at it while I'm gone."

"I could've checked it out for you, if you would've let me know." He tightened his grip on the steering wheel.

"Davis, you don't have to be there every time I need something. You don't have to catch me when I fall," she said.

But what if he wanted to?

What if he wanted to be the one to catch her each time she fell? Each time she couldn't do something on her own? Or each time she needed a hand to hold?

With his throat thickening, he said, "I know."

"Besides, you're already helping, by driving me to Denver."

When he dared a look at her, and found that enchanting smile on those tempting lips, he nearly lost control of the vehicle.

As the song came to an end, Kelsey turned the volume

down a bit as she said, "If you can sing the next song that comes on word for word, I'll let you choose where we have dinner tonight."

"What?" he asked, taking his eyes off the road for a second to look at her once again.

"But if you can't, I choose."

He shook his head. "Oh hell no, there's no way I'm letting you pick."

"What? Why not?"

"If you pick, we'll be stopping at some hole in the wall diner, and I'll be the one up all night with my head hanging over the toilet from food poisoning."

"I can't help it if you have a weak stomach," she teased.

"It's not weak, it's just not used to eating the crap yours is."

"That just means you haven't conditioned it."

"Well I'm not going to start now. Sorry," he muttered.

Kelsey leaned forward, turning up the volume on the stereo. "Guess you better try hard then."

He caught her smirk from the corner of his eye and relented, unable to help the grin that tugged on his lips. This back and forth between them, this banter, it was exactly what Davis needed. It was a reminder of their friendship and why they got along so well even when they didn't have much in common. He'd been so desperate to get things back to normal when he shouldn't have worried at all.

He eased into his seat and tapped his thumb against the steering wheel to the beat while he began singing the song.

Per usual, Kelsey couldn't hold back, she joined in with him at the chorus, belting out the familiar lyrics.

When his voice cracked on a high note, they both busted up laughing. At that moment, the world righted itself once again, giving him his best friend back. Even if they'd be stuck eating at the worst dive in town and he'd most likely end up with a belly ache, those few minutes, laughing with her would make it all worth it.

DAVIS PULLED HIS TRUCK INTO A PARKING SPACE IN FRONT of a low-rise building in downtown Denver. It was close to dark even though it was only almost five o'clock. This attorney friend of Mr. O'Henry's had squeezed Kelsey into the end of his schedule for that day, meaning she had the very last appointment.

Kelsey unbuckled her seatbelt with shaky hands. She flipped the visor down to check herself out in the mirror. She looked great, though she probably wouldn't take his word for it. He could tell she was anxious.

"You got everything?"

She picked up a large purse from the floorboard, pushed the visor back in place and flashed him a brave smile. "I think so. Okay, wish me luck." She straightened her shoulders before opening the door of the truck and climbed out.

"Good luck," he hollered before she shut the door.

He watched her until after she'd gone inside the building, his heart hammering in his chest. This meeting was a big deal, and she was nervous. *He* was nervous. If this didn't go well, and the attorney didn't offer a solution, he'd have to seriously consider his own.

But would offering to help her out be worth the risk? Not only would she deny him, but it could also alter their friendship. She hated when he, not only offered to help, but offered to help financially.

And paying the loans back, offering to help save the bar, was a big one.

When his phone chimed, he half-expected it to be Kelsey, asking him to come inside and attend the meeting with her. Or maybe, he was hoping.

FRANKLIN

Hey big guy!

Davis groaned and continued reading.

FRANKLIN

Heard you were away this weekend but wanted to fill you in on the newest memo taking effect on Monday. I'm attaching it. Thanks!

When he opened the memo and scanned it, his stomach dropped, filling with a heavy dread. Mr. President had enlisted not only a wardrobe change for both Davis and Garrett, but a new angle for the show. It seemed Franklin's friendly chat had an ulterior motive, soften him up before the official memo went out.

Davis chucked his phone onto the passenger seat and his pulse picked up speed. He clenched his hands into fists before slamming one down onto the dash. Where did they get off telling him what to wear? Or how to wear it? And what about changing the angle of the show? Now they wanted both he and Garrett to bring the sex appeal. Mr. President stated it would be better all-around for their viewers.

Davis's phone chimed again, this time he was relieved when it was Garrett's name flashing on the screen.

GARRETT

Just ignore Franklin's text for now. Don't look at the memo until you get back.

Too late.

> **GARRETT**
> Don't let your panties get in a bunch. I'll talk to him.

> You better or I will.

> **GARRETT**
> Don't worry, bro. I got this.

Davis set his phone into the console. Garrett was right about one thing, there was nothing he could do until he was back home. Even though he was tempted to head into the building and show the memo to this attorney. Based on their previously signed contract, there was no way this was legal.

Exhaling a deep shaky breath, he pushed his seat back. He propped his crossed ankles on the dash and pulled the brim of his hat over his eyes. For once in his adult life, he'd let Garrett handle things for him. He had enough going on, what with helping Kelsey and the complicated feelings growing for her.

CHAPTER 11

Kelsey

The appointment with the attorney was useless. Not only did he shrug off her impending tears, but he hardly looked at her. During their less than fifteen minute meeting, he commented at least four times that he was happy to be able to do a favor for Mr. O'Henry. He'd handed her a printed sheet of paper summing up the legalities after the death of someone when they own a business as a shared entity, meaning her.

By the time she left the office, she felt mistreated and belittled. And even worse, completely lost. The loans were her responsibility. There were no grace periods. She might as well wave the white flag, because the meeting with the attorney was her last resort. Losing the bar felt more real than ever.

Fighting back the tears, Kelsey rushed out of the office building and hurried down the stone steps just as nightfall hit. Darkness enveloped Davis's truck, making it difficult for her to decipher if he was still inside. When she yanked on the door handle, he startled in the driver's seat.

Davis lifted his outstretched legs and adjusted the hat on his head. "What happened? How'd it go?"

It was a natural question, expected even, but it still hit her square in the chest. "Based on my luck, it went exactly how I thought it would." Her fingers trembled as she buckled the seatbelt.

"Uh oh."

"There's nothing he can do."

"Are you sure? He knew your situation?"

"Yes," she snapped.

He glanced away.

The regret slid through her almost instantly. Davis had been nothing but kind to her, going out of his way to help her at the bar, brainstorming with her, and now driving her all the way here for this useless meeting. "I'm sorry, I'm just...upset."

He shrugged a shoulder. "You don't have to apologize. I get it." He rubbed at the back of his neck, resituating in his seat.

She released a long, slow breath. "Guess I'm back to square one."

Davis seemed to consider this, his lips twisted to the side and his eyes were unable to focus on hers. She knew he was already trying to come up with a solution on how to help her. It touched her, the way he cared for her so tenderly. Regardless of how their friendship had been developing into something more as of late, he was still the same attentive Davis. And maybe her feelings for him grew stronger in that moment because of that fact.

"Kels, I'm sorry. But we're not going to give up. Between you and I, we'll think of something."

"Thanks." She forced a smile.

Despite the bad outcome at the attorney office, they still had the rest of the night ahead of them. She'd promised Izzy she'd make Davis take her out for a drink. And she needed it more than ever now. Besides that, he'd lost her wager, meaning she got to pick where they were going to eat dinner.

Pulling out her phone from her purse, she Googled the best bar and grill outside of Denver, coming up with an extensive list. The one she picked would not only need high reviews, but it would have to be near a hotel. Because tonight, Davis wasn't only taking her out for a single drink, they'd be consuming enough that she wouldn't remember her life was in complete disarray.

Maybe they'd drink enough that all their inhibitions would be lost, and they'd be open to act on impulse alone. And just maybe, they'd finally come clean about their feelings for one another.

WITH HER HANDS PRESSED TO HER HIPS, KELSEY BEAMED as she gazed up at a neon sign with two of the letters completely out and one flickering.

"You can't be serious," Davis grumbled at her side. "You made me cancel our perfectly nice hotel reservation for this?"

Warmth expanded in her chest. "It's perfect."

"You won by a technicality. You made me laugh."

"But I still won," she boasted, pressing her palms on Davis's back, and shoving him forward. "C'mon, I'm sure it won't be that bad."

"How many times have I heard you say that before?"

She snorted a laugh. "I'll buy you a beer and you'll be fine."

Call it nostalgia, but Kelsey loved checking out other bar and grills. It was fun to see how they decorated, what food they had on their menus, what types of beer they had on tap. Besides, the comments on Yelp had said they brewed their own beer and there was a perfectly fine hotel within walking distance. She'd always been curious if O'Henry's could brew their own beer, it would save them from having to pay vendors.

"Fine, let's just hurry inside. It looks like it may rain."

A patron exiting the bar held the door open for them. Kelsey nodded her thanks before taking in the condition of the inside.

Live band?

Check.

Crowded?

Check.

The scent of grease?

Check.

Kelsey had a good feeling about this place. She led the way to a small booth near the back of the bar. Across from the booth was a row of pool tables and just beyond that, a few dart boards hung on the wall. She slid into the booth and Davis hesitated before joining her on the other side.

While O'Henry's had a clean and friendly reputation that this particular bar may have been lacking, it carried a familiar cozy vibe Kelsey could appreciate. Glancing across the table at Davis it was clear by the expression on his face, he wasn't feeling the same vibes.

He furrowed his brows as he studied the menu. It was cute how his lips scrunched to the side. Always the overthinker and cautious.

"See anything interesting?"

"Interesting is not how I'd like my food described."

She snorted a laugh.

"But do I see something that's remotely safe? I hope so." He set the menu down before rubbing his hands across his thighs.

"Well?"

"Cheeseburger and fries."

"I think that's a solid choice."

A server dressed in a simple t-shirt and jeans came by and they placed their order. Kelsey went with the same as Davis. You couldn't go wrong with a burger and fries. She ordered a chocolate stout, while Davis chose a brown lager. Both perfect options for fall.

Davis sat across from her, his back straight, glancing over his shoulders. He needed to loosen up. Despite her feeling down, she was trying to make the best of her night. This was her first time away from the kids in almost a year. To say she'd been busy the past several months would've been an understatement. Between juggling the bar and the kids, and her mama, she'd barely had a moment to herself, never mind a chance to even breathe.

Being away from all her responsibilities had her skin buzzing. She had this overwhelming sense of being carefree. She wouldn't allow Davis's over cautious mood dampen her good time. She had every intention of making the most of this trip. First thing on the agenda; getting Davis to loosen up.

The server set two pints of beer onto their table with a smile. "Can I get you anything else while you wait for your food?"

"Two more beers, please?"

"What?" Davis asked, his glass almost at his mouth.

"Yep, that's right. Just keep 'em coming." Kelsey grinned at the server who winked before sauntering away.

She chugged half her beer before coming up for air. It wasn't the best beer she'd tasted, but for a stout it went down smoothly.

"Whoa, go easy there?" Davis said.

"You can't be serious? We're not driving. My kids are being taken care of. I've got no responsibilities tonight."

"Fine." He nodded, taking a sip of his beer.

She leaned across the table, the beer already working its magic and granting her a boldness she had no right possessing. "Unless you can think of another reason I shouldn't be drinking?" She was so obviously challenging him.

If he was worried they'd drink too much, make bad decisions, push the limits of their friendship, he'd dance around the caution but he'd tell her if he wasn't worried. If he was confident in their friendship, he'd let this go.

With a straight face he said, "Nope. Can't think of any other reason."

She leaned back against the booth, satisfaction blooming in her chest. "Good. Then you better keep up."

He gazed at her for too long, clearly challenging her right back, his eyes darkening and a flicker of mischief she recognized. He lifted his glass and held it out to hers.

"You're on."

She couldn't help it. Heat furled inside her chest and her lips curved as she clinked her glass against his.

They both drank, watching one another over the brim of their glasses and there was a dip low in her belly. This night was about to get interesting.

Kelsey was already two beers in before their food arrived. That much beer on an empty stomach was not a good idea. But watching Davis line his empty glasses across the table gave her the nudge to carry on.

Davis slammed yet another empty glass onto the table. "We can stop this friendly challenge at any time."

Friendly? Was it still? Because it felt like something more. Like maybe they were trying to prove something. Maybe that they were still just friends despite the plumbing fiasco and their embrace in her office. Like maybe they needed to convince themselves they could remain friends and forget those things ever happened.

Or maybe...they'd had nearly enough alcohol to throw their inhibitions to the wind and get wild. To act on this overactive hunger inside her. To satisfy this growing desire burning between her thighs.

She gazed up at him from behind the glass to her lips. "Oh, we're not stopping. I mean unless you want to stop," she teased. "You're the one with the weak stomach."

"It's not weak. It's...sensitive."

She flicked her wrist. "Potato, patahto."

He signaled the server and when she stopped by their table, he ordered two more beers without taking his eyes off Kelsey.

Her cheeks burned and her toes curled inside her shoes.

He leaned across the table, eyes darker than normal, his thumbs tracing the condensation on the glass. It had her on the edge of her seat. Something as simple as wiping a thumb on a glass had her turned on. The action was hot and stimulating and had her craving to have those thumbs on her, tracing against her skin, dragging down the curves of her body.

She swallowed the lump in her throat, pressing her thighs together.

It was clear—he was not going to back down. She nearly caved, giving in and calling him the winner right then. Only, she felt an urge to keep going. Maybe it was because she felt the need to prove something to Davis. That she didn't need him or anyone else worrying about her or taking care of her. Or maybe she just needed to prove something to herself.

And if it was only that last one—it was enough for her.

CHAPTER 12
Davis

Davis had seen Kelsey tipsy more than once in his lifetime. He'd seen her drunk a handful of times too. And tonight, she was definitely tipsy. They'd gone past their usual banter and moved right into flirting.

And a flirtatious Kelsey was something entirely new.

It was hot and exciting, and if she didn't stop, he would surely offer to push this relationship to the next level. With an emphasis on hoping the next level was them finally sharing that most anticipated kiss. If it went beyond that, he wouldn't complain.

Pushing the door to their hotel room open, he held it for her to enter first. She stumbled inside, laughing. He entered behind her, closing the door.

She'd barely been in the room for more than two seconds and she was already kicking off her shoes. She tossed her purse onto the floor, then flopped onto the bed.

The bed.

What the?

Davis spun around, just to make sure. But nope. His eyes hadn't deceived him. There was only one bed.

In the past, before Kelsey and Ricky had gotten together, a shared hotel room, even a shared bed wasn't a problem. But that felt like a lifetime ago. And sharing a bed with Kelsey, right now, after the flirtatious actions on both their ends, felt like a very bad idea.

He didn't trust himself to not step over the imaginary friendship line they'd drawn in permanent marker years ago.

She pushed off the bed and wriggled out of her jacket, tossing it onto a chair before she began unbuttoning her blouse.

Davis's throat went dry, and he scratched the back of his head, glancing away even though he was tempted to look. "Um. What're you doing?"

"I gotta get out of this outfit. It's so scratchy and restrictive."

"Okay, but, Kels, there's a bathroom."

She snorted a laugh. "Oops. Sorry. You're so modest, Davis."

"Not modest, just," he paused, not even sure what to say. He searched through his fuzzy brain, sifting through words, but unable to grasp any. The alcohol was clearly messing with his ability to form the right words from his database.

Davis dropped both of their bags onto the floor and when he glanced up, Kelsey had already stepped out of the gray slacks and stood there in a bra and panties.

Very lacey panties.

"Whoa." He shielded his eyes.

"Sorry." She giggled again. "Hold on, almost done."

He swung his attention back to her slowly, watching as she tugged a sweatshirt from her bag and then flung it across the room at him. It smacked him in the face and his teeth bit down against his lower lip.

Hard.

"You may have everyone else fooled into thinking Garrett is the player, but you forget," she paused, placing her hands on her hips, and drawing his attention there, before traveling up her torso, zoning in on the cotton bra hugging her full breasts too tightly. "I've been your best friend for years. I know your deepest, darkest, secrets."

He tossed her back the shirt and she pulled it over her head before plopping onto the bed again and leaning back on her hands.

While she was right about one thing, they had been best friends for years, she was wrong about the secrets part. Because if she knew his biggest secret of all, she would never have agreed to allow him to drive her this weekend.

Unaware himself, he'd been harboring feelings for her. But for how long? Who knew.

Davis's eyes dragged over her slowly. Too slow. Deliciously slow. The smooth skin on her legs, leading to black, lacey panties, and a perfect bellybutton he'd seen a hundred times in less than innocuous situations—trips to the pool and beach, changing into costumes.

But now? Now everything about her, especially that dark, sultry look in her blue eyes, and her soft lips, somehow poutier than normal, lured him in.

Looking at her in this way was wrong. He ran his hand over the back of his neck and mustered the strength to put an end to this. He crossed the room and reached his hands out to her.

"C'mon, you can finish getting changed in the bathroom." He yanked her up and nudged her in the direction of the bathroom, doing his damnedest not to look at her backside in the barely-there underwear.

She didn't argue, which was saying something. A whole lot of somethings. Either she'd realized this was a mistake, or she didn't feel like arguing.

He flipped the bathroom light on for her and she stood inside, her dark hair looking wild. It took all his strength to shut the door with him on the other side of it.

"Wait. Bag?" she called.

Right.

"On it." He grabbed the duffel, and she opened the door just as he was about to knock.

"Thanks." She smiled and reached for her bag.

Their fingers grazed before he released it, and tiny jolts of electricity buzzed through him. It took everything in him to not pull her straight into his arms. Instead, he took a tentative step backward and she shut the door.

He dragged his fingers through his hair and spun around, eyes landing on the queen size bed that was a no-go. He needed to get that issue figured out quick, because if a single touch of her fingers made him ache to grab her and pull her close, there was no possible way he could lay next to her half-naked b body all night.

"Hey, I'm gonna go to the front desk and see if they can get us a new room."

The bathroom door opened. Kelsey stood there dressed in an oversized sweatshirt and a pair of cotton shorts. Okay, so maybe not half-naked, which was a slight disappointment. What was worse was that even fully clothed, so simple and relaxed, she tempted him like a kid in a candy store.

Damn, his head was a disaster when it came to her.

"What's the problem? Why would we need a new room?"

He placed his hands on his hips. "Uh, did you not notice? There's only one bed."

She glanced at the bed she'd just been sprawled out on only a few minutes before. She shrugged. "What's the big deal? We've shared a bed before."

"Yeah, but that was a long time ago. It hasn't been since, since...before..." his words died in his throat.

"Um...maybe we sleep head to toe or something," she suggested, hunching a shoulder, and biting her lower lip.

"You do know that's what everyone suggests when faced with this dilemma? Like in every movie. What are we now? A cliché?"

She gasped mockingly. "Never."

He pushed a fist into her shoulder softly. "Shut up."

"You know I'd never let that happen. As much as I love movies because they're so predictable, I do hate clichés."

"I know you do."

"Uh...we sleep traditionally, head to head," she said next.

"That's not any better," he mumbled, his imagination of the two of them in bed side by side running wild.

"Well, I don't know." She threw her hands up. "All I know is, it's late and we should just try to get some sleep."

Sleep. Now that was a great idea. He inhaled a deep breath.

It had been a long day. And they had to get up early and leave by check-out time and make the drive back to Pineridge. Kelsey had to get home to her kids and the bar. Davis had filming. Even if part of him was dreading and praying for car trouble that left them stranded in Denver for days.

But breaking his contract wasn't an option. Neither was messing things up for Garrett.

"Sleep is a great idea," he said finally.

He rummaged around in his bag for his toothbrush and toothpaste and slipped into the bathroom. Maybe if he took his time, she'd be sleeping by the time he went back into the room. It would sure make it a hell of a lot easier for him to actually get sleep.

But no such luck. He'd taken his time, dressing in joggers

and a white t-shirt, and brushing his teeth. He'd even let his electric toothbrush run through twice. Yet when he stepped out of the bathroom, Kelsey was sitting on the side of the bed, a knee propped up, talking softly into the phone.

He cleared his throat and she glanced at him over her shoulder.

"I should go. Give the kids a kiss for me. Thanks again." She slid her phone onto the nightstand. "Mrs. Whitley."

"Uh, everything okay?"

"Yeah, I was just hoping to talk to the kids before they went to bed."

"No such luck?"

"Apparently Mr. Whitley took them ice skating and they were exhausted."

He chuckled. "Sounds about right."

"It's probably best this way. My head is still spinning a little." She smiled all lopsided and goofy, pushing her fingers through her hair.

He decided in that moment, he liked how her hair looked since she'd grown it out some, making it long enough to drape over one shoulder.

And that was it. He wasn't going to notice how that left her other shoulder exposed, revealing the soft skin there. Nope. Nothing.

Remembering how Kelsey usually liked to chug water after drinking a few beers, he returned to the bathroom to fill a glass with water and brought it back to her. "Here, thought you might want some water."

She narrowed her eyes at him as she took the glass. "You know you don't have to take care of me."

If I don't, who will? Is what he wanted to say. But knew he couldn't. That remark would send her ranting. Apparently just giving her the water was bad enough.

"It's just a glass of water. Don't over think it." He rested his hands on his hips.

"Ha!" she said mockingly. "Says the king of over thinkers."

His jaw ticked as he clenched his teeth together.

Flipping back the covers, he chose to ignore her. But that didn't mean he didn't feel the press of her stare on him. It was obvious she wanted him to argue with her, but what wasn't obvious, was why?

"All I'm saying is, I don't need your help," her voice was softer. She yanked back the covers.

"Just get in the bed."

He was losing his patience. Losing his restraint from yelling at her that she *had* asked for his help. Or worse, lose his restraint and confess he had feelings for her. But he couldn't be sure if they were real, true feelings. And he couldn't risk it if they weren't.

They both crawled into bed at the same time, from the corner of his eye he caught sight of the creamy skin on her thighs. The shorts were so short they revealed a hint of her butt cheeks. But it was enough. More than enough.

He exhaled a throaty groan and yanked the covers over himself quickly, an attempt to hide his impending erection. After switching off the lamp on the nightstand, he laid on his back, propping an arm behind his head. He stared at the glowing ceiling as the pool in the courtyard reflected against it.

Kelsey was quiet. Something of an anomaly for her. But he felt her eyes pressing into him like a drill press squeezing against a piece of wood. Almost as if she was waiting for him to say something.

Risking a glance at her, he regretted it instantly, the way she looked at him sent him into a trance that had his head reeling. This was Kelsey. His best friend. He had no right wanting her in this way.

"I'm sorry," she whispered.

He turned to face her then, laying on his side and propping his arm underneath his head. Her face revealed a kind of exhaustion that shouldn't exist. It was unfair, her situation. Everyone counting on her like they did. The last thing he wanted was to be another thing begging for her attention.

"I don't need an apology," he said, his voice came out sounding gravelly.

"Unfortunately, you signing up as my best friend also means you get the brunt of my sassiness."

"Lucky for you, it doesn't happen that often."

"You mean, lucky for you," she teased.

His lips tugged at the corners.

They stared at one another, neither brave enough to say another word. He honestly didn't know how he would survive this night without doing something completely idiotic, like confessing his feelings for her. Or worse, pulling her into his arms and exploring every single inch of her body with his hands and mouth.

CHAPTER 13
Kelsey

Every nerve ending burned with a yearning Kelsey couldn't explain. Laying there, sharing a bed with her best friend while the reflection on the glowing ceiling illuminated his face, set her body on fire.

Maybe the room was too hot. The temperature set too high on the heat. That made much more sense. More sense than resisting acting on a growing fascination with the familiar body lying next to her.

This craving, this desire building between her thighs was insane, and she demanded an explanation for her body betraying her. She and Davis were friends. That's all they'd ever been. Even before Ricky.

Maybe if she didn't look at him, she'd be fine. Yeah, that would work. The world would then align itself once again. She turned her face to stare at the ceiling again. Definitely not as enjoyable.

"I don't mind, ya know?" he said, his voice scratchy against the quiet hum of the swooshing fan.

"What's that?"

"Being your punching bag."

She gasped. "You're not. I've never treated you that way. Have I?"

"No, I'm just saying, I can handle it. Use me...for whatever."

She swallowed hard. *Whatever?* He had no idea what he was saying.

The yearning she felt for him made her want to act on these feelings she'd had for him for the past couple weeks. But what if it was the alcohol giving her liquid courage? What if he turned her down?

She needed to chill and just go to sleep.

But when she rolled to face him once again and her eyes flicked up to meet his, she found him staring at her. His own eyes darkened, and his long, black slashes swept over her. A shudder racked her body.

"Davis, I—"

"That's what I'm here for." He reached a hand out and pushed a strand of hair away from her face.

Without overly thinking it, she reached a tentative hand toward him, dancing a finger down his chest, her fingertip sliding against the smooth skin of his pec. The intake of his breath at her touch sent a hum in her depths.

She should've put a stop to it right then. It was dangerous. They were hovering over a land mine. One wrong move, wrong touch, wrong word spoken could cause an explosion. In a single moment their entire friendship could shatter into oblivion.

Could their friendship afford to take that chance?

Being drawn in as if under a spell, she leaned closer to him. When he rubbed her shoulder and slid his hand down the length of her arm, she regretted wearing the sweatshirt to bed.

As her hand traveled lower, his stopped on her hip, where he gave it a squeeze. She pulled her lip in between her teeth, and he reached his hand around to her back, sliding it inside her sweatshirt and she shivered. The roughness of his calloused hand against her skin electrified her need for him and she released a suppressed moan. His fingertips dug into her back.

"I want to be here for you," he said, his voice low and gruff.

"For this?" she couldn't help but ask and then snorted a laugh that she tried to cover with her hand. "Wow, am I sexy or what?" She didn't expect an answer.

"More than you know."

In what felt like one swift motion, Davis took her into his arms, pulling her on top of him. She didn't want to think, only act, but she couldn't help it. She was impressed by his maneuvering. By his skills in this department. This was a side to him she'd never experienced before. And it ignited something fierce inside of her. A passion. She frantically pulled his shirt up his torso, and he helped by ripping it all the way off.

He was beautiful, as he laid on display beneath her. Unable to resist, she rested her palms on his chest and ran them against the firm muscle, gliding them over his rippled abs. He fisted the hem of her sweatshirt and yanked it over her head.

Without speaking, and as he watched her with hooded eyes, she unhooked her bra, releasing her breasts. She tossed the bra over the edge of the bed, dropping it to the floor.

Davis stared at her as she straddled him, fully exposed, yet he didn't touch her. He simply gazed at her with an appreciation only someone who genuinely loved her could. She could see the way he saw her. Imperfectly perfect. Wanted. Desired.

It was a beautiful moment she wanted to cling to, capture the look in his eyes and cherish it. Take a mental photo of it. So she never forgot.

Davis ran his fingers up the curve of her hip, featherlight and cautious, even as his gaze smoldered. She could tell he was holding back, savoring this fragile moment trapped in time.

Her pulse raced when he lifted his hand higher, his rough fingertips leaving goosebumps in their wake. He let out a soft groan, his large palm cupping her ribs, and slowly, torturously so, he inched toward her breast—

And then the magnificent and delicate moment imploded.

Kelsey's phone rang, the sound intrusive. But what was even worse, the ringing competed with the rumble of Davis's stomach.

She clasped a hand over her mouth, hiding a laugh.

"Don't laugh. This is your fault. It's that damn food." His stomach gurgled again.

Kelsey suddenly felt vulnerable straddling him half naked. She clambered off him, searching the floor for her shirt and covering her bare chest with it once she found it. Her phone continued to ring, and she read the contact just before she answered.

Mama.

"Hey, Mama, what's up?"

"Hi, love bug."

From Kelsey's peripheral, she caught Davis hopping out of the bed and racing to the bathroom. She winced, covering the mouthpiece of the phone while she hollered, "Sorry!"

"I w-was wondering...if you could pick m-me up? J-just real quick like," her mom said.

Kelsey threw her head back and groaned, dropping onto the edge of the bed. Her mom had been doing so much better lately. "Mama, I can't. Remember, I'm out of town for the night."

"I swear, love bug, it'll take jus-just two seconds."

"Mama," she half shouted, frustration building in her chest. "Do you hear me? I'm not home. I'm in Denver."

"Denver? What the heck you doin' in Denver?" her words slurred.

Kelsey was distracted by the closed bathroom door. Torn by the conversation with her mom and Davis who might need her. This feeling was something she'd hoped she could've avoided by going away for the weekend.

"Davis and I came for that appointment with the attorney Mr. O'Henry set up."

"Oh, that was this weekend? Why didn't you r-remind me? I tol' you I'd watch the kids."

"It's fine. They're with the Whitley's."

Her mom grunted into the phone, but Kelsey ignored it. She wasn't one for picking fights. It was easier to let her mom vent and for Kelsey to stay quiet.

"Where are you?" she asked.

"Downtown. Cosmos bar."

"Let me see if I can get someone to come get you. Don't leave Cosmos." Kelsey ended the call with her mom and her thumb slid through her list of contacts on her phone.

Julian was running the bar and Izzy lived near the mountains. The Whitley's were close to downtown, but she'd already asked enough of them. Her thumb landed on Howard Hoffman. He was the closest, but he too had just helped her. Wasn't there a limit to how many favors someone did for one person? Because Kelsey was pretty certain she'd reached it with every person in her life. And she hated to think that.

Crossing her fingers, she hoped the long-term friendship between Howard and her mom was still strong. She checked the time first. Howard went to bed early and it was almost ten. She sucked in a breath and prayed.

Howard picked up on the second ring.

"Hello?"

"Hey, Mr. Hoffman, it's Kelsey. Kelsey O'Henry," she specified when he didn't respond.

"Kelsey? Everything okay with your van?"

"Oh yes, it's fine. Um..." she hesitated. "I was wondering if you could do me a favor?"

"What's wrong?"

She dropped her chin to her chest. "It's my mama."

There was a sigh followed by a long silent pause on the other end of the line. She didn't need to elaborate further. He knew her mama well enough to know.

"Where is she?"

"Cosmos."

"Tell her to sit tight. I'm on my way."

Relief flooded her chest, and she pinched her eyes shut. "Thank you. Please, come by anytime next week for a beer on the house."

"It's not a problem." Mr. Hoffman hung up the phone.

She hated that nagging feeling of owing someone. And if it wasn't for her alcoholic mother or dead husband, she wouldn't.

The sound of the toilet flushing interrupted her pity party. She'd almost forgotten about Davis. Which in turn meant she'd almost forgotten about the intimate moment shared between them in the bed only minutes before.

Picking up a pillow, she buried her face in it. She needed advice from a friend. And not the friend who was currently holed up in the bathroom of their shared hotel room. Over ten years of friendship and not once had they ever shared a romantic moment.

Now they'd shared three in the last couple of weeks. Was mercury in retrograde and she needed somewhere to invest this new chaotic energy? Was her dry spell finally catching up with her? She and Ricky did always have a healthy sex life.

Whatever it was, she needed to make sense of it. And fast. Before something happened again.

She never thought she'd be thankful for her mama's addiction. But she may have very well saved her from making a huge mistake, causing the ruin of their friendship. She decided against texting Isabella. Confessing her feelings to Izzy would mean they wouldn't be private anymore, and she had to admit, keeping this thing between her and Davis hidden felt more exciting.

Instead, she went to the bathroom door and knocked gently. "Hey, you alright?"

"Yeah, I'm good."

But if he was good, he wouldn't still be locked in the bathroom. Maybe he was just embarrassed. Which he didn't need to be with her. Later, she'd tease him relentlessly, sure, but right now, she wanted to help. She wanted to be there for him like he was always there for her.

"Do you need anything? Some ginger ale or something?"

There was a pause before he said, "No, I'm fine. Thanks. You should get some sleep."

"You do remember who you're talking to, right?"

"Yes and you should remember I'm the last person you need to worry about."

"Pft," she grunted and whipped around. She snatched the room card off the desk. "I'll be back," she hollered before slipping out the door and not bothering to wait for a response.

With no luck in the vending machine, Kelsey took the elevator to the lobby in search of ginger ale.

Still no luck.

Giving up, she bought one can of 7-Up, two bottles of water, and a set of playing cards from the girl working in the lobby. By the time she returned to the room, Davis was in the bed, his back toward the door. Her chest tightened as disappointment slid through her. It was silly. She was fully aware. But she hoped he was feeling better and maybe they could play cards.

She tiptoed around to face him, and found his eyes closed.

He looked peaceful. The stomachache must've worn him out. She smiled at him, setting down the 7-Up and water on the nightstand next to him. She rounded the foot of the bed and flipped off the bedside lamp before slipping into the bed.

Lying next to him, facing his back in the darkened room, she felt a dull ache, a need to be closer to him. Her fingers tingled with the urge to touch him. Even though only inches separated them, he felt so far away in that moment. The fear that their friendship would be different in the morning made it feel as if it was hard to catch her breath.

Losing the bar was one thing but losing Davis would be unbearable.

CHAPTER 14
Davis

The two-hour drive back to Pineridge was torturous. Davis couldn't decide which incident made it more awkward—their intimate moment in the hotel bed, or his stomach issues that sent him fleeing for the bathroom.

Definitely the stomach issues.

The goodbye on Kelsey's front porch had been almost as painful as the small talk they'd forced in the car. Usually, he went inside and saw the kids. They seemed to enjoy his company as much as he loved theirs. But today, he couldn't drive away fast enough.

Maybe the thing that made it worse, Kelsey hadn't teased him about his stomach issues. She hadn't gloated about the diner being her choice. She hadn't offered to go to his place to take care of him. All things best friend Kelsey had done in the past. This told him one thing: The friendship he'd grown accustomed to and appreciated no longer existed.

And it was his fault.

As Davis made his way home, his phone chimed. He checked it at the stop light.

GARRETT
Got my costume. We're all set.

The Halloween costume party at O'Henry's sounded even less appealing than it had before this past weekend. And after it? It sounded downright awful. He'd rather smack his thumb with a hammer.

As Davis pulled into his driveway, his phone chimed again, and he groaned. For a guy who had an endless supply of friends and women, Garrett sure bothered Davis a lot.

Kelsey's name appeared on his screen and his chest tightened.

KELSEY
We forgot to make a plan for the pumpkin patch. You still up for it?

It had become a tradition of theirs. He and Kelsey going to the pumpkin patch together every October. Some years it looked different. It had been just the two of them for a few years, then he tagged along with her and Ricky, and a few years it was Ricky and Kelsey and a kid or two. Then there was a few when Lissa came too. This year it was almost as if they'd come full circle and it would be just the two of them once again.

The fact that Kelsey was asking him if they were still going had him feeling all kinds of messed up.

Of course.

KELSEY
Good.

Tomorrow still work?

No follow up response had him even more on edge. She always had to get in the last word.

Davis climbed out of the truck and snatched his bag from the backseat before heading to the front door of his house. His home was small in comparison to Garrett's new, modern bachelor pad he'd bought, and the two brothers designed together. But Davis wanted a home that felt like a home. Something that looked like someone lived there. Cozy, warm colors, soft leather couches. Kelsey had helped him pick out blankets and candles and even live plants.

After greeting Cooper, Davis unzipped his bag and turned it over, dumping its contents onto his bed. His phone chimed again.

KELSEY

She followed the text with a winking emoji.

He closed his eyes and the tension previously taking residence in his shoulders released. The tease. The reminder they were okay. It was all he needed.

AFTER THE MEETING WITH HIS FINANCIAL ADVISOR WENT in his favor, Davis knew that before he had an official offer drawn up, he needed to discuss his plan with was Garrett first. He owed him that much at least. Getting him out of the house, away from the attractive film crew helpers, and the lights and cameras, would be the safest environment.

Are you home?

GARRETT

Yep

Can you meet me at Sweet Cakes in 20?

GARRETT

Better make it an hour

But your house is only 10 min away

GARRETT

I'm entertaining a lady friend

Unless things have changed in that
department, I'll see you in 30.

And I'm being generous

GARRETT

It's been so long since you've gotten laid, I
bet you could meet me in 10.

What a funny guy.

Davis grumbled but couldn't restrain a smile.

PARKING IN FRONT OF SWEET CAKES, DAVIS CLIMBED OUT
of his truck and tugged his Tapp's Brewery hat down further. It
was nearing five o'clock, and the outdoor string lights down the
sidewalks of Main Street had already flickered on, illuminating
the shops. The fallen leaves under his boots crunched as he
strode across the sidewalk and went inside the bakery. Instantly
his senses were on overload after being hit by pumpkin and
apple scents.

Rita Sanders stood behind the counter, talking to a few young children. She looked good, happy even. When she glanced up and smiled at him, he approached the counter.

"It's so good to see you, hon," she greeted, wiping her hands down the front of a white apron.

He nodded once. "Good evening, Miss Sanders."

She waved him off. "Oh you, stop with that Miss Sanders nonsense. It's Rita. Always has been, especially for you." She winked.

The last time he saw Rita was after he drove her home from O'Henry's. "How's business been?" he asked, making awkward small talk.

She put up her hands. "Can't complain. There's something about autumn...the crisp air...the spiced treats...the trees changing color...that's just magical, don't you think?"

Autumn was pretty great. But autumn in Pineridge was breathtaking. He wasn't sure he'd go as far as calling it magical, though. "It is the best season."

"I'll bet this is the most magical season for you yet." She gave him a wide, knowing smile.

His face went hot, and he yanked at the collar of his crew-neck sweatshirt. Had Kelsey told Rita about the almost-kiss? Or the intimate moment in the hotel bed? "I...uh...what?" he stammered.

"Hey, Davey," Garrett called from behind him.

Spinning around, he didn't think he'd ever been so grateful to see his brother. "Hey."

"Did you order yet?" Garrett asked, perusing the baked goods behind the case.

"I was just about to."

"I'm starved. Worked up quite an appetite...if you know what I mean." Garrett threw an arm around him, squeezing his shoulder as he waggled his brows.

"I think everyone knows what you mean," Davis said through gritted teeth.

It felt as if all the eyes in the bakery were zoned in on him and his brother.

"Hey, Miss Rita, give us two pieces of your famous apple spiced cake and two slices of your pumpkin loaf," Garrett said, smiling brightly.

Garrett was always doing that, ordering for him whenever the two of them were together. He wasn't the one who'd spent the afternoon in bed with a woman, burning calories the best way possible, so he wasn't that hungry. Maybe he wanted a slice of apple pie. Or nothing because his stomach had been twisted with nerves most of the day as he'd prepared to talk to Garrett. But arguing about it would do no good. He'd give Garrett what he couldn't finish.

"Here you go, boys," Rita said as she set two plates on the counter.

Garrett slapped a twenty-dollar bill in front of her. "Thanks."

They took their plates and found an empty table near the window.

"Whew," Garrett exclaimed as he sat down and stabbed a fork into the apple spice cake. "I am exhausted." He blew out an exaggerated breath. "This woman I met at Cosmos the other day has hardly let me sleep. It makes sense, she's leaving tomorrow, but still. It's been wild, bro."

A bit of protectiveness coiled itself into Davis's chest. "Garrett, maybe you should slow down."

Shoveling a big bite of cake into his mouth, Garrett said, "What are you talking about? Slow down. I'll slow down when I'm dead. The dead don't hurt like the rest of us."

"Garr..." Davis leaned across the table.

"Davey, I'm fine. You worry about you. Like when you're

ever gonna get a date again, never mind have sex again. I think I should be the one worrying about you."

He had this urge to tell him about Kelsey, but he couldn't. He wouldn't. Not yet.

"Fine. All I'm saying is, you don't gotta prove anything to anyone by trying to be this player. You don't gotta live up to the reputation Franklin or Mr. President is trying to present you as on the show."

"That's not what I'm doing. Get a grip. I'm just having fun."

"Fine. Whatever."

"What did you wanna talk about anyway?"

He'd nearly forgotten the reason why he wanted to meet Garrett. O'Henry's. "Right...so I have a business opportunity... and I wanted to discuss it with you before I jumped into it."

Garrett frowned, and he stopped chewing the extra-large bite of pumpkin loaf in his mouth. "What kind of business opportunity?"

"So...Kelsey has been struggling with paying the loans at O'Henry's and..."

"Davey, no," Garrett cut him off. "You are not bailing her out just 'cause you have a boner for her."

His body tensed as his pulse sped up. He couldn't deny the accusation, but that wasn't why he wanted to do this. "That's not what this is about."

"No? Because ever since you met that chick ten years ago, she's been stringing you along and you haven't had a real relationship."

His nostrils burned. "She has not. She was married. And I've been in plenty of relationships. Lissa? Or have you forgotten about her? And her twin sister, Emma?"

Garrett swatted his plate away from him. "You don't want to go there, bro."

"Maybe I do." Davis challenged his brother with his eyes focused and narrowing at him.

Leaning across the table, Garrett lowered his voice, "Look, I don't know what this is about, whether you're unhappy with the memo that went out and the new angle of the show, or something else, but whatever it is, I can assure you, buying out O'Henry's is not the answer."

"That's not what I want to do, if you'd just listen. I want to be partners."

"With Kelsey?" He looked hurt, the way his eyes were downcast and his shoulders slumped.

"I'm not planning on quitting the show. I just want something to fall back on when the show has run its course. Because I hate to break it to you, but one day, it will."

In the middle of their heated discussion, Davis felt the unexpected presence of someone standing near their table. He jerked his attention up to find a woman he recognized.

"Hey, Sophia."

She dipped her chin, fluttered her eyelashes, and smiled. "Hi, Davis, right?"

His brows pinched together. Not only had Sophia asked for him, but she'd also deciphered which twin he was. "Yeah."

"I was wondering if you had a date already to the Halloween couples costume party?"

Was she really asking him out? And in front of Garrett?

Garrett cleared his throat. "Sorry, darlin', but he's already got a date. Me."

Her cheeks blushed. "Oh."

"But that doesn't mean we can't save a dance with your name on it." He winked and she giggled.

"Sounds good, I'll see you then." She fluttered her fingers at them both as she backed away from their table.

"What the hell was that?" Davis asked.

"What?" Garrett shrugged. "It's not like you would've done something about that."

He wasn't wrong, Davis didn't want to go with Sophia, but it was that a woman seemed to finally be into him, not Garrett and he'd gone and cock-blocked him. "That's not the point."

"You're too busy pining after someone you don't have a chance with because you'll never measure up to the expectation of her dead husband."

"I know you're pissed, but leave her out of this."

"Leave who out of what?" Kelsey asked, suddenly standing at their table.

"Oh...hey, Kels," Davis said, rubbing the back of his neck.

Her brows furrowed. "What's going on?"

Garrett pushed his chair out and stood. "Why don't you ask Davis, I'll let him fill you in." He stomped off, pushing forcefully through the door.

Heat filled Davis's cheeks and his heart raced.

"Whoa, what's got his panties in a wad?"

"It's nothing. Just brother stuff."

She pursed her lips as she stared after the door before returning her attention on him. "Show stuff?"

"Not this time." He wasn't entirely lying. Though this time it had more to do with Kelsey and O'Henry's.

"Sorry, I didn't mean to interrupt," she said as she took Garrett's seat across from him and proceeded to break off a piece of his remaining pumpkin loaf and shove it into her mouth.

He quirked a quizzical brow at her and a smile pulled at the corner of his lips.

"What?" her voice went up. "I'm hungry. And it didn't look like he was coming back."

A chuckle escaped him.

"How about you? How's your appetite?" She waggled her dark brows at him, and he shook his head in amusement.

"It's fine. As you can see." He gestured at his plate with the mostly uneaten baked goods. Poking the fork into the moist apple spice cake and taking a huge bite. Still chewing, he said, "Perfect, even."

An enticing smile grew on her lips. "Oh good. Because I was gonna say, if it wasn't, I'd be happy to take those off your hands. You know my mama's apple spice cake is my favorite."

"I know." He smiled.

The way she gazed at him, studying him while he pushed the fork through the moist cake again, caused his skin to tingle with heat. He could feel her hunger for his cake, or was it hunger for him, he couldn't be sure. Oh hell, he hoped it was for him.

All he knew for sure was, this moment stretching between them was so incredibly intimate and hot. It was a damn good thing there was a table in between them. As the seconds ticked by, it became increasingly more difficult to keep his hands to himself.

With her intense gaze unwavering from him, he held the fork out for her. She took her time leaning in, giving him a peek at the glorious dip of her cleavage. The cake dangled only mere inches away and a coy smile played on her beautiful mouth.

At last, she finally closed her lips around the fork, and desire shot through him in an instant, heading south. As her eyes fluttered closed in pleasure, he craved for the chance to satisfy her in the way this cake clearly was. Davis never thought food, or eating could be sexual, but as he fed her the bite of cake, it was hotter than the most delectable foreplay he'd ever experienced.

As she pulled away agonizingly slow, he sucked in a breath. When she eventually opened her eyes, she caught him staring at her, but he didn't look away. Instead, he allowed the lust to burn between them in their held gaze.

"What did I tell you," Rita said, drawing them out of their private moment and they both whipped their heads in her direction. "This is gonna be the most magical season yet." She winked at him again and hugged her daughter's shoulders before shuffling away as fast as she'd arrived.

They looked at one another, Kelsey's cheeks a bright pink and his face as hot as an August sunburn, and they shared a knowing smile.

A smile that said, *this thing is going to happen*. And it better be sooner than later.

CHAPTER 15

Kelsey

Even if the tourists were obnoxious, Kelsey didn't mind. Because it meant business. And the extra business would make O'Henry's sound more appealing to a potential partner. Not that she wanted a partner. But it would sure make it easier to not only help financially but to also shoulder some of the responsibilities.

Getting an attorney would be pointless. That's what she'd been told anyway by the attorney she'd met with in Denver. She had no grounds for anything legal as far as Ricky's death was concerned. She hadn't stayed current on the payments, the bank had every right to shut her down, sell, and take back the money that was rightfully theirs.

"Excuse me, miss?"

Kelsey glanced over her shoulder as she filled a glass of Tapp's Brewery pumpkin beer. An attractive man dressed in a navy-blue long-sleeved Henley stood near the bar, a crooked smile directed at her. She'd never seen him in O'Henry's before.

Another tourist. She resisted an eyeroll.

"What can I get ya?"

"How's the pumpkin beer?"

"Depends." She set the beer down in front of a woman.

"On?"

"How much you like pumpkin."

"Hmm..." he considered this but didn't check the chalkboard over her head for further choices. Instead, he continued to watch her curiously with a smile.

Her cheeks burned from his examination. She filled a taster with the local pumpkin brew and set it in front of him.

"Taste it and let me know if it's worth a full glass."

"A pint *is* a big commitment."

"A man who takes his beer seriously, I approve." She smiled.

He sipped it before letting out a satisfied sigh. "Sold."

"You got it...coming right up."

She felt his eyes trained on her again while she filled the glass and set it before him.

"Thanks...you got a name?"

"Kelsey."

"Thanks, Miss Kelsey."

"Not a problem." She tucked her hair behind her ear.

"Kels?" a familiar voice called as she spun around.

She glanced over and found one of her closest friends in Pineridge approaching the bar. Dressed in black leather pants and an off the shoulder burgundy sweater, Maddie was sure to hold the attention of all the O'Henry's patrons tonight.

"Hey, Maddie."

"Need a couple shots of tequila before I get the nerve to get on the stage for karaoke."

"Okay, girl, I got you." Kelsey filled two shot glasses and handed them to Maddie before sliding a bowl of lime wedges in her direction.

"Thanks, lady."

"No, thank *you*. I can't wait to hear you sing."

"Well that will make one of us."

"You'll be great."

Maddie threw back a shot, wiped her mouth with the back of her hand and then slung back the other before stuffing a lime wedge into her mouth.

The guy in the Henley leaned in closer as Maddie sauntered away.

"A friend of yours?"

She gave a non-committal shrug. "Pretty much everyone who walks through those doors is a friend of mine."

"Does that make me a friend?"

"I don't even know you."

"How rude of me. I'm Christian." He shook her hand.

From her peripheral she caught sight of her favorite dog; Cooper, Davis's golden retriever, as he weaved through the crowded bar and bounded toward her. As happy as she was to see Cooper, that meant his owner wasn't far behind.

Typically, she loved seeing Davis at O'Henry's. It meant he wasn't holed up at home or working on projects alone. But after the erotic cake feeding earlier that day, she'd done nothing but fantasize about sharing a whole lot more than food.

She bent and embraced the dog. "Hey, buddy."

"Is he another friend of yours?" Christian asked, an amused smirk on his face.

"He is." She scratched under his ears and when she straightened to stand, her eyes locked with Davis's. Heat pooled in her chest.

As he advanced toward her, she could feel her blood pumping through her veins with each beat of her heart. Davis stopped in front of her, neither saying a word, until Cooper nudged his wet nose into her hand, and she shuddered.

Christian leaned closer. "Another friend of yours I presume?"

"Um...yep. This is Davis. Davis...Christian."

Being the gentleman he always was, Davis shook the stranger's hand, but he eyed him skeptically.

"And you are?" Davis asked, surprising Kelsey at his boldness.

"Just a tourist. An interested tourist," he emphasized *interested* as he flashed her a suggestive smile.

Kelsey choked and cleared her throat, as she moved back behind the bar.

"You look familiar," Christian said, his brow furrowed at Davis.

Davis shrugged. "I get that a lot. I guess I have one of those faces."

Kelsey knew how much Davis hated the attention because of the show and tried to change the subject. "Davis, can I get you something?"

"Uh..." Davis cracked his knuckles, a nervous tell of his. "I was actually hoping we could talk."

Her breath hitched. He wanted to talk? As much as she knew it was necessary, the bar was slammed. And this conversation couldn't be hurried. It was big. Bigger than big.

"We're busier than expected and I'm shorthanded. Sophia called out tonight."

"Okay, no worries." He patted his thigh, a command for Cooper to come. "Then I'll just catch up with you tomorrow at the pumpkin patch."

"I'm really sorry." Was she though? Because it felt more like relief in her chest rather than remorse.

"Actually, I guess I'll take a beer, since I'm here."

She tilted her head to the side. "Oh, yeah, of course."

Davis never stuck around O'Henry's for the heck of it. She filled a glass and handed it to him with as she pursed her lips.

"Thanks." He nodded once at her, took a sip of his beer then turned his back to her, leaning against the bar.

Just what was he up to?

A song began playing loudly and next, Maddie's voice reverberated through the bar's old tinny speakers. Attention went to Maddie, and it gave Kelsey a moment to breathe. The awkwardness between Davis and her, and the tourist who appeared to be flirting with her, though as much as she hated to admit it, she might've been a bit naïve. Maybe he was just being friendly. Maybe he was lonely.

She was all too familiar with lonely.

As Kelsey served a few other customers, she kept Davis in her peripheral. He finally took a seat on a barstool with his back to her. Cooper laid on the floor, his chin resting on one outstretched paw.

"So..." Christian said to her, his eyes expectant. "What time are you off tonight?"

She wanted to laugh. As the owner, was she ever off?

"We close at two. Then there's the cash drawers and receipts and locking up. I'll be lucky if I'm out of here by three."

"You're working the closing shift?"

"When you're the owner, you're always working the closing shift."

"Ohh, so you're the owner."

She nodded.

Technically, she still was. For about three more weeks at least. The reminder of the timeline hit her like a jab below the ribs.

"This is great, I was actually hoping to talk to you when you have a moment."

"Me?" was all she could say. Her ears burned.

"You're busy tonight. What about tomorrow?"

The air in the bar felt thin and she fought to catch a breath. As loud as Maddie's voice reverberated through the mic, Kelsey was very aware of Davis's presence and there was no way he wasn't hearing this entire conversation.

"Sorry, I already have plans. I'll be at the pumpkin patch all day."

"That's unfortunate. I leave Monday. Maybe we could meet for coffee before I head out of town?"

"Um, yeah...maybe."

"Let me give you my number. There's something I'd like to discuss with you. If you're up for it, let me know."

"Um...sure."

Davis stood and faced her. Leaning over the bar. "Mind if I get the check?"

"You're leaving already?"

"Yeah, I should get Cooper home. Not everyone appreciates a dog in here."

"Well, I'm the owner, and I don't mind."

Davis's attention went to Christian as he said, "It's getting too crowded in here."

She wasn't sure she liked this quality of Davis's. Was this jealousy? "Fine. And don't worry about it. You know your money is no good to me." She forced a smile.

He grunted and yanked his wallet out of his back pocket, tossing a ten-dollar bill onto the bar top.

"I'll see you tomorrow." He spun around and whistled. "Coop, let's go."

Cooper sprang to his feet, obeying.

"I'm going to take off too, here's my card. Call me." Christian winked as he handed her a business card and then he was gone.

She wanted to call after Davis and ask him to stay and let him know that she did want to talk to him, but a loud screech sounded through the bar. The old sound equipment complaining. It had to be babied, everyone knew that.

Yet, when she glanced at the sound booth, horror vibrated in her chest. Her mama was making her way to the stage, a mic in her hand.

Oh hell.

The song began and her mama swayed on the stage, one hand holding the mic near her mouth and the other in the air. Kelsey had no doubt in her mind her mama was about to cause a scene.

With Davis on his way out, that would leave her, and Maddie and Julian left to handle her. Depending how wasted she was, Kelsey worried the three of them wouldn't be enough.

But she spotted Davis near the door and he turned around, making eye contact with her. She shrugged and willed a wobbly smile. He dropped his head, rubbing a hand over his neck and headed back to her.

Wordlessly, she and Davis stood next to one another watching as her mama sashayed her hips across the stage, flirted with the crowd, and tore off her sweater.

When the song finished, her mama stepped off the stage, nearly falling and Davis rushed to help. Kelsey pinched her eyes shut for a moment, keeping her head down as she hurried to her mama.

When she reached her, she had a bloody shin and was laughing. But Kelsey couldn't muster sympathy for her. She was doing all she could to keep the business afloat while trying to save it, and her mama wasn't helping matters.

"Mama, we had a deal. You're not supposed to be here," she snapped, hooking an arm under her elbow to help her up.

"Kelsey," Davis warned.

"What?"

"Not now," he said, taking her mama's other side.

"No, no, Kelsey is right. We did have a deal. I'm not supposed to be here. Because being at a bar might tempt me to drink." She leaned in close to Davis, pushing a finger to her lips. "But...shh. I have a secret. I'm already drunk."

"Shocking," Kelsey muttered, rolling her eyes.

"Oh, love bug, I was really trying," her mama said.

"I know you were, Mama."

"Hey, y'all need some help?" Maddie asked.

"It's okay, I think we got it," Kelsey said.

"Do you want me to call her an Uber?"

"I can take her," Davis offered.

But Davis had already done enough. Despite Kelsey hating feeling needy, he was always helping her. He didn't deserve this. He was supposed to be celebrity in their town. But some glamorous life he lived—best friends with a widower and taking care of her alcoholic mama.

"No, it's okay. She can sleep it off in the office."

"You sure?"

If her mama slept here, it usually meant Kelsey was stuck sleeping there too. That would mean she wouldn't be getting to her in-laws to pick up the kids and take them home that night.

"It's fine."

But as they each took a side of her mama, Howard Hoffman appeared, like a knight in shining armor, offering his arm, and giving relief to Kelsey.

"Here, let me help," Howard said.

"Thank you." She released her mama's arm, handing her off to Mr. Hoffman.

This was the second time he'd rescued her. It was humiliating. But she was grateful all the same.

"If you're still working, I'd be happy to take her home," Howard offered.

"Don't be silly, I couldn't ask you to do that."

"It's not a problem. And you're not asking, I'm offering."

She bit her lip, considering.

"Howard," her mama slurred, "My hero."

"Not too shabby being called a hero. I've been called much worse." He chuckled.

Having her mama away from the bar was a much better idea than the both of them sleeping there that night. Then she'd still be able to pick up her kids and let them sleep in their own beds.

"Are you sure it's not a problem?"

"Positive."

"Okay," she relinquished. "Thank you."

"Goodnight, Mama. I'll check in with you tomorrow."

"Night, love bug," she sang as Mr. Hoffman escorted her to the door.

Davis stood next to her while they both watched her mama go.

"Sorry," Davis said softly.

"What are you sorry for?"

"Because, you have a lot going on. You can't seem to catch a break."

She shrugged. "Everyone has a lot going on. And my break comes tomorrow. When Julian is running the bar and we go to the pumpkin patch. That's my break." She smiled. She was relieved it came naturally. It gave her hope their friendship hadn't been rocked entirely off its foundation. Besides that now, she had the urge to rip his clothes off when a few weeks ago she wouldn't have thought twice about his rippled abs.

"Alright, I'm gonna head out. You sure you're gonna be okay?"

"Yep. Go on. I'll be fine. See you at noon." She patted Cooper's head and gave Davis a quick hug.

After he and Cooper went out the door, she released a breath and spun around. Yet it wasn't the crowd surrounding the bar waiting for drinks that caused her gut to pinch. It was that Christian was still there, seated at the end of the bar, staring at her.

He'd witnessed the entire disaster.

CHAPTER 16

Davis

Being only miles away from the mountain meant it was cold enough in Pineridge, Colorado to freeze your nuts off in October. People were lying if they said you'd acclimate to the weather if you lived there long enough. Davis dressed in layers in preparation to meet Kelsey and the kids at the pumpkin patch. A long-sleeved Henley, a flannel, followed by a jacket.

Besides the two years Davis lived in Denver and the year before he'd been in Hawaii, he'd lived in Pineridge his entire life. And if anything, he was getting less used to the cold. The reminder of Hawaii with its warm, sandy beaches was a kind of cruelty all on its own.

Davis parked his truck and climbed out, inhaling a much-needed breath of fall air. Cooper bounded out of the truck behind him before he slammed the door shut. His phone vibrated in his front pocket. Kelsey, telling him where she and the kids were.

As he trudged through the makeshift parking lot of farm terrain, panic throbbed in his chest. He'd been to see his lawyer and had the legal offer drawn-up to pay off all back payments needed to be co-owner of O'Henry's, and all that was left was to present it to Kelsey. The rolled-up papers awaiting her signature stuffed in the back pocket of his jeans felt like a ticking time bomb. He knew her well enough to understand she wouldn't be thrilled at first.

But what he was counting on, was the part that came after. The understanding and realization that he wasn't only doing this to help her. This was his ticket out of renewing his contract.

This could be the answer both were looking for.

He just needed the perfect moment to present it to her.

Davis passed the kettle corn and candy apple stand and found Kelsey where she said she'd be. Waiting in line to buy tickets for the corn maze.

"Davis!" June shouted, jumping into his arms.

"Hey, kiddo."

"We've been waiting for you," Zach said, sounding annoyed but was quickly distracted by the sight of Cooper.

"You're late," Kelsey said, worry streaked in her expression. "Everything alright?"

"Yeah, fine," he half lied. The pumpkin patch with her kids wasn't the right place to discuss his offer, or their relationship status, he realized in that moment.

"Can you give me a piggy-back ride?" June asked.

"Sure, hop on." He knelt and June climbed on his back, tethering her arms around his neck.

At the front of the line, Kelsey bought their tickets and she handed Zach the map to lead the way. Charlotte was snug in a pack against Kelsey's front. Davis and Kelsey followed behind Zach closely, an awkward silence between them.

Cooper ran ahead, heading up the lead with Zach.

"So, everything go okay with your mom yesterday?"

"Yeah, Mr. Hoffman got her home safe and sound. I saw her this morning at Sweet Cakes. She looked..." her voice trailed.

Because he was pretty certain he knew what she looked like. She looked exactly like herself. Which meant she most likely started the day with a drink.

"She's been doing so well lately. She told me this morning, before last night, she hadn't had a drink in six days."

The slump in her shoulders made his chest ache. "That's good though. Sounds like she's trying."

"Yeah, I guess," she mumbled, her fingers reaching out and grazing a corn stalk as they turned a corner in the maze. "Ya know, I think Howard might have a thing for Mama," Kelsey said, changing the subject.

Davis quirked a brow. "A *thing*?"

"This is the second time he's come to her rescue. And once for me."

Davis shrugged. "That doesn't mean anything. Mr. Hoffman is a nice guy."

"He is but I'm telling you, I think it's more than that. Did you know the two of them dated in high school? Before Mrs. Hoffman, before my daddy."

He turned his head to look at her. "No, I didn't know that." It was surprising, considering Pineridge was a small town, and everyone knew everyone else's business.

Zach must've taken a wrong turn because he stopped and spun around, and next thing Davis knew they were headed back in the direction they'd just come. June wiggled to get down and he lowered himself until her feet touched the ground and she rushed up with her brother.

"Mrs. Hoffman has been gone for over ten years and I've never heard of him dating since. I'll be honest, I'm not super excited about the idea. You know I love my mama, but she's a hot mess. She needs rehab not a boyfriend."

She wasn't wrong. He agreed with her one hundred percent. But the woman had been a mess as long as he'd known her. Maybe rehab wasn't enough. Maybe a cheerleader, a support person, a partner was exactly what she needed.

"I don't know, maybe a guy isn't a bad idea."

She turned and stared at him, lips pursing. "You serious? Because if you say maybe she just needs to get laid, I'll slug you."

He nearly choked, raising a palm in surrender. "Damn, I'm not saying that."

Though maybe that's exactly what *Kelsey* needed. He knew she'd been faithful throughout her marriage and even after. Close to a year was a long time. He could somewhat relate. It had been over six months for him, and he felt like all it would take was another steamy cake feeding and he'd explode.

A part of him, the part he wasn't ready to admit out loud, wanted to be the man she chose to spend a night with, and ultimately, all the other nights afterward.

"No, I wasn't going to say that."

"Good. Because I'm fairly certain she hasn't been lacking in that department."

That was too much information. "I meant, maybe a guy to be her partner, her support system, wouldn't be a terrible thing. You've been that for her since your dad left. Might be nice for you to get a break."

She pressed her lips together, forming a smile. "It's a nice thought. But I still think she needs rehab."

"Oh, she definitely needs that too," he agreed.

The urge to bring up their relationship and how it had clearly shifted over the past two weeks sat at the brink of his mind. As much as they needed to discuss it, he couldn't help but worry the kids would interrupt them.

They walked a bit further, taking a right at a scarecrow and then a left at a wheelbarrow full of pumpkins, followed by another left, and next thing he knew they were back at the scarecrow. The straw, shifty-eyed bastard grinned at Davis maliciously.

Zach studied the map, irritation seeming to build in his posture.

"Hey, little man, mind if I have a go at it?"

Zach pouted and handed over the map a bit reluctantly.

Davis gazed at the map for a moment while Cooper chased the kids through their corner of the corn maze that he was beginning to worry they'd never find their way out of. But then he saw it; their exit.

"How about we try this way?" He traced a route on the map with his finger.

"Okay, but I'm the leader," Zach said, tearing the map from Davis's grasp.

"Me too," June yelled.

Both kids ran up ahead with Cooper on their heels.

"Thank you," Kelsey mouthed, relief shining in her blue eyes.

He was relieved too. The pressing issue of his offer was beginning to wear on him, it wasn't typical for him to keep secrets from Kelsey. And this one felt huge. Though maybe even bigger was the intense feelings he'd been having for her.

After surviving the corn maze, taking a group selfie at the exit to prove their victory, and enduring a rather lengthy line for kettle corn, they sat at a picnic bench. The kids ate their kettle corn and sipped on hot chocolate while Charlotte sat on a blanket on the ground. She ate applesauce from a pouch, but the two older kids snuck her a piece of popcorn or two that Davis was unsure she was supposed to eat.

But Kelsey wasn't the overbearing mom. She didn't keep the kids on a short leash. She let them explore and try things. It was something he'd always admired about her. She'd been the carefree one out of the two of them. Davis was the one who was rigid, afraid to take chances, needed a push before making any big decisions.

Which was why this decision he'd made so easily had him worried. He hadn't gotten the approval from Garrett, but he was sure his brother would come around eventually. And normally he'd go to Kelsey. But this decision he had to make all on his own.

Kelsey nudged her shoulder into his. "Hey, everything okay with you?"

"What do ya mean?"

She scrunched her lips together. "I don't know, you seem distracted."

"I do?" He cracked his knuckles.

She furrowed her brows and danced her fingertips down the front of her neck. "Yeah...you're making me nervous?"

He was making *her* nervous? Because just being in her presence was making him so nervous his palms were sweaty despite it being less than fifty degrees outside.

Davis wanted to have not only the conversation about their relationship, but about the offer while they were alone. But maybe, presenting the offer to her out in public and with the kids around would mean she couldn't freak out at him. If his offer offended her, she wouldn't yell in front of all these people.

On second thought, maybe she would. Kelsey didn't care what people thought. But the sooner he got this off his chest, the better.

He rubbed at the back of his neck. "You caught me."

"I knew it. Okay, spill it."

"I've been meaning to talk to you about this for the past week."

Her expectant expression shifted to worriment, and she fidgeted with the sleeves of her jacket.

There had been a lot going on between them lately. They hadn't had a chance to even discuss what went down in the hotel room, never mind in her office. And if he even mentioned cake, he'd get aroused in an instant. At the pumpkin patch didn't feel like the right place for that.

"Things between us have been...different, so I don't want you to think this has anything to do with that. Kelsey, I—"

"Hey, you two," Maddie's greeting interrupted his already jumbled words.

Davis jerked his head up and found Norah and Maddie standing near the picnic table.

"Hey, ladies, what are y'all up to?" Kelsey asked.

"Ugh, day date," Norah grumbled.

"At the pumpkin patch? That's cute," Kelsey replied. "I'm so glad you're out there dating again, Norah."

Davis frowned at their intrusion.

"I talked her into it," Maddie admitted.

Kelsey grinned. "Of course you did. Who's the lucky guy?"

"No one you know," Norah said, squeezing onto the picnic bench next to Davis.

His chest tightened as he scooted closer to Kelsey and fidgeted with the popcorn bag in front of him.

"Davis, can you pretend to be my on again off again boyfriend so I can shake this guy?" Norah asked.

Suddenly attentive, he whipped his head up to look at her. "What?"

"Norah, no," Maddie whined.

"We both know this guy isn't for me and this date is gonna go nowhere."

"But you gotta at least try," Maddie said.

"Believe me, I tried." Norah turned to Davis, giving him a pleading look. "Please, Davis. Just for a few minutes."

He bounced a knee while his heart raced.

"You sure?" Maddie asked, looking at Norah.

"I'm sure. I'm not ready for all of this."

"Oh, I don't know...I don't think it's not a good idea," he stumbled through his words.

"C'mon, Davis, help a friend out," Kelsey said.

Davis looked at her, surprised she'd encourage this. But of course, why wouldn't she? She was not only a good friend to him, but she was also a good friend to Norah. If Kelsey didn't think there was anything going on between the two of them and they were just friends, this would make sense. But things didn't add up and he was more confused than ever.

"You sure?" He looked pointedly at Kelsey.

"Why would I care?" Her eyes challenged him right back.

A stiffness twinged in his neck, and he gave an exaggerated shrug. "Okay, well I mean, if you don't mind?"

"The kids and I will be fine." She smiled.

But he knew her. And he knew that smile was fake.

"What about our conversation?" he asked.

"Let's talk tomorrow night. At the costume party."

"Fine," he agreed, climbing off the picnic bench.

"Yay, thank you." Norah jumped up, joining him.

"Now what am I supposed to do?" Maddie asked.

"I guess you get to take your pick between the two guys," Kelsey replied, brows raised.

"Are you sure you aren't ready to get back on that horse?" Maddie asked Kelsey.

Davis couldn't resist, his eyes shifted to Kelsey just as hers flicked to him. Heat expanded in his chest. He wanted to say something. Instead, the sensual eye contact between them was enough to remind him, this thing between them wasn't even close to being over.

"I'm sure. Maybe someday, but not yet."

His shoulders relaxed.

"C'mon, Norah, let's get some pumpkins and then I'll take you home." He held a hand out to her.

Norah smiled at him, setting her hand in his.

The two men from their double date headed toward them with candy apples.

"Thank you," she whispered to him.

"Bye, kids. Be good for you mama," Davis hollered. "See you tomorrow, Kelsey."

"Oh, yeah, sure. Just go leave me to explain. No problem," Maddie complained as he and Norah began to walk away. "You be sure to tell that twin brother of yours I'm doing just fine without him."

He nodded.

And Davis felt the eyes of everyone on he and Norah as they strolled away hand in hand.

Kelsey

Monday was for new beginnings.

Or something like that. After she left the pumpkin patch and went home the day before, she'd held the business card Christian had given her and contemplated calling him. He was an investor who worked in Denver. She hated the idea of going into business with someone from the city.

But since word had leaked around town that she was at risk of losing O'Henry's, no one else had come forward and made her an offer. So, Kelsey had called Christian, and he agreed to meet her that morning before he headed out of town.

She searched the Daily Grind, bleary eyed from the lack of sleep the night before. There was something about the risk of losing your family business and having feelings for your best friend that made it impossible to sleep.

Christian stood up at a table near the back and gave her a wave. She smiled and stepped in line to order herself a coffee. Today, she'd get an extra-large Americano. She needed *all* the shots of espresso. If she could, she'd shoot them straight into her veins.

After making small talk with the barista while her drink was being prepared, Kelsey joined Christian at the table for two.

"I'm so glad you changed your mind and agreed to meet me," Christian said, smiling brightly as he shook her hand. He presented the empty seat across from him and she gingerly sat down.

"I'll be honest, I'm still a little confused as to why you wanted to meet with me." Kelsey took a sip of her coffee, thankful for the inch of cream she'd requested as to not burn her tongue.

"Confused? I'm an idiot, I should've come into the bar earlier in the week. Then hopefully we could've done this sooner."

Was that a line? Was this guy hitting on her? Or was this only business? She wasn't very good at this stuff.

"What were you doing in Pineridge this week?" she asked over the brim of her coffee cup.

"Work." He peered at her, and she felt a light flutter in her chest. Even though this wasn't a date, the way he looked at her made her think that maybe, someday dating would be possible. "And let me just cut to the chase, I don't normally mix business with pleasure. I didn't solely want to meet with you because I think you're beautiful, but it was also because I have a proposition for you."

Her heart raced and her mind swished with confusion. She'd known this meeting was strictly business, and yet the flattery was a surprised bonus.

"As I'm sure you saw on my business card, I work for an investment company in Denver and I'm very interested in buying O'Henry's—"

"Wait. What?" she interrupted.

"I assumed you knew that?" He raised his brows.

She set her cup down and flexed her fingers, her heart racing. "I knew you worked for an investment company, yes, but I didn't know you were interested in buying O'Henry's. Like completely."

"I've already met with the O'Henry's, and they voiced their reservations over you losing the place. So, we'd like to offer you the manger position. Of course you'd get the whole package, retirement, paid vacations, health insurance," he rambled, but it was difficult to hear with the thundering in her ears.

She jumped to her feet, her chair scraping against the floor. "Are you freaking kidding me?"

"Whoa, whoa," he said, raising his palms as his eyes scanned the cafe. "There's no need to get worked up. Let's keep this professional, shall we?"

She glanced over both shoulders and sat shakily once again. "Professional? You're the one who was flirting, and you want to keep this professional?"

"Oh, um..." he paused, rubbing at the back of his neck. "You thought I was flirting?"

"It doesn't matter," she bit out, heat fanning across her cheeks.

"Look, the way I see it, it's a win win for you. The bar stays open, and you can still call the shots. All without the headache."

"No," she ground out.

"I think, if you have a chance to look over our official offer—"

"No," she cut him off and pushed against the table to stand again. Blood pounded in her ears. Her fingers trembled and when she spoke again, the words vibrated in her chest. "Thank you for the offer, but I'm not selling."

Because of course she would still be cordial. She was Kelsey O'Henry. She pushed out the door, her name being called behind her, but she didn't turn around. She'd been so stupid to think an investor from the city would make her a serious offer, and to think they might allow her to remain as a partner. In doing so, they wouldn't make as much money. But to her it wasn't about the money.

Tears built in the corners of Kelsey's eyes before breaking free. She shuffled into the bakery next door. Her mama stood behind the counter, filling the display case with her delicious pumpkin spice macaroons. One would never guess the night before she'd been drunk as a skunk, serenading O'Henry's with one of the worst renditions of *She Will Be Loved* by Maroon 5 she'd ever heard.

"Hey, love bug," her mama greeted her in singsong and a happy smile until she took in her face. "Uh oh. Come give your mama a hug and tell her all about it."

Kelsey collapsed into a heap of blubbering sobs, clinging to her mama. It was times like this she was grateful her mama was at least an experienced alcoholic. She had her routine down, knew how to sober up, which meant she already smelled like booze. She probably needed that Bloody Mary to get her going this morning after last night.

But she was still her mama and she loved her fiercely, she only hated the disease. At times, she had some strong feelings about her dad too for his hand in her mama's choices.

"You got any salted caramel macarons to spare?"

"For my only daughter? Absolutely."

The time had finally come for Kelsey to tell her mama about the business stuff. She needed to come clean about being unable to pay the loan payments. But she would keep everything about Davis to herself. Her mama had made it obvious she adored Davis. Kelsey planned on spilling all the tea to

Isabella during their next coffee session and ask for advice. Because at this point, she felt lost. She didn't know what to do with her love life.

The business had to take precedence.

Even if her heart hammered in her chest when she thought of Davis, even if a shiver of pleasure went through her when he touched her, even if she lost all inhibitions when she was with him.

Sex had to be off the table.

So much for dusting out the cobwebs from her lady parts. Mothballs might as well take up residency down there too. Because this dry spell was apparently here to stay. Her lady parts were about to have a long winter.

Orgasm-apocalypse here we come.

CHAPTER 18
Davis

Garrett, the typical prick, texted Davis letting him know he'd be late to the Halloween party and would meet him there. It's not as if this were a date or something but this had been Garrett's idea. Davis hadn't even wanted to go to the party.

Originally, he'd planned on staying in and handing out candy to the trick or treaters. He loved having a quiet evening in on Halloween, seeing all the creative costumes.

But nope. Here he was, dressed in an old costume, going to O'Henry's. Not only was he not looking forward to the overcrowded bar, but he also still had the papers rolled up and stuffed in the inside pocket of the orange suit jacket. Getting Kelsey alone tonight to discuss it would be impossible. But the longer he didn't tell her, the harder it got.

Parking in the O'Henry's lot, he gazed at the bar, anticipation buzzing through his veins. As much as he wanted to see Kelsey, he despised crowds. Even worse, drunk crowds. And even worse yet, drunk crowds dressed in costumes.

Everyone trying too hard. People hooking up. Tourists in

town, only there to see the famous love lock bridge. One's that learned Renovation Dudes was filmed there—people noticing him. Then right away asking if he was Garrett or Davis. The disappointment when they learned he wasn't Garrett.

It was all too much.

But he'd promised Garrett he'd be there. He wouldn't break his promise. Even if the prick didn't even have the decency to show up on time.

Grumbling under his breath, Davis climbed out of his truck and stuffed the hat on his head. With a sigh, he headed to the door. When he stepped inside O'Henry's, loud Halloween music boomed through the speakers. His eyes scanned the crowd. Lots of costumes he expected. Batman and sexy Robin, Mr. and Mrs. Smith, Jim and Pam from The Office, some he had no clue who they were supposed to be.

He felt out of place being there. Especially being there alone. Everyone else had the other half of their couple costume but his other half might've stood him up.

His eyes scanned the crowd, trying to find Kelsey behind the bar, but she wasn't there. He frowned and spun around. He debated leaving. Garrett didn't need him there. If he knew his brother well enough, and let's face it, they were twins so of course he knew him, he'd find a hot tourist within the first five minutes and ditch him. What was the point of him being there?

But then he saw her.

Kelsey.

She straightened from leaning against the bar, pushing a baby blue hat down over a short blonde wig. She'd dressed in her Harry costume. With him wearing the Lloyd costume, it was as if they'd planned to come to this party as a couple. His gut pinched and he felt the urge to talk to her now. About the offer and about his feelings for her. As much as he'd tried to stuff them down, they weren't going away. There was something there. Something more than friendship. And he wanted to act on those feelings. He wanted to see where this thing between them could go.

He crossed the room, weaving through the crowd, his eyes set on her. But then he saw Garrett—his twin brother—seated at the bar in front of Kelsey. Her smile had been for Garrett. Davis knew that smile. She looked smitten.

It felt as if a balloon popped in his chest and then deflated.

"Garrett!" a woman screamed, taking him off guard as she wound her arms around his neck.

Maddie.

She swung him around and he had to crane his neck to see Kelsey and Garrett.

"Hey, Maddie. It's Davis." He unhooked her arms gently, giving her a friendly pat on her back.

She winced. "Oh, sorry. But did you know you and your brother are dressed in the same costume? Did you plan that or was it some twin telepathy thing?"

Maddie was clearly already buzzed based on her actions and slurring of her words and not being able to tell him and Garrett apart.

"Definitely not planned. I thought he was gonna dress as Harry."

"And which one are you?"

"Doesn't matter. Excuse me."

"Okay, but save a dance for me."

"Sure," he muttered.

He had no intention of doing that. Maddie was a nice girl, but it was obvious to just about everyone that she had a thing for Garrett. And Garrett would probably have a serious thing for Maddie if he could ever be serious about anyone ever again.

That last thought only made him worry more as he headed toward the bar where his brother sat, flirting with Kelsey. He arrived just in time to see Garrett and Kelsey both sling back a shot.

"Hey," he hollered, louder than he probably needed to. "What's going on?"

Kelsey's eyes flickered back and forth between the twins, her face falling.

"Wait. Garrett, you didn't tell me you two dressed in the same costume."

Garrett turned and scrutinized Davis and Davis stared right back at him.

"That's because I didn't know. Bro, what's up? Why did you come dressed as Lloyd? You know Jim Carrey is my man. Plus, I could never be a Harry. Lloyd is the lady's man."

Davis refrained from releasing a snappy comeback. "You knew this was the costume I had."

"How would I know that?" But Garrett didn't wait for Davis to respond before continuing. "Just go home quick and change. I would, but I've already been drinking. Kelsey and I are already two shots in."

"Really? You never drink while you're working."

Kelsey hunched a shoulder. "Why should everyone else get to have fun at my bar? Besides it's not going to be my bar for much longer so what do I care?"

"You don't know that. Aren't you still trying to find a partner?"

Kelsey glanced away, as if she was unable to look at him. "I met with a prospective investor from Denver who offered to buy O'Henry's, without the option as a partner. It's no use, Davis. I've run out of time. It's over." Her words came out sounding broken, the defeat in her posture was felt in his chest.

He had a way to help her, even if she probably didn't want it. Maybe she'd feel as if she didn't have a choice. He needed to get her alone and discuss it, tonight. No more delaying it.

"It's not over. Not yet."

"Who are we kidding?"

"Can we talk for a minute?" he asked, pleading with his eyes.

She peered up at him, biting her lower lip.

"Bro," Garrett said, back handing Davis in the chest. "You're bringing her down. She wants to have fun."

"It's fine," she said, waving Garrett off.

But he was right. This was a party. And she deserved a night of fun.

"I'm fun," Davis remarked.

Garrett busted up laughing. "No, no, sorry. You're right. You're fun. We know that. But right now, you're sorta killing the vibe."

Kelsey snorted, picking up the tequila bottle and filling two shot glasses. "He's not wrong."

Garrett was a bad influence on her, and he didn't want him rubbing off on her. The way Garrett had been handling Emma's death was unhealthy and he didn't want that kind of coping for her. Davis's best bet to keep an eye on her, would be to join in.

"Fill one for me too."

She tilted her head, mischief in her eyes. With raised brows, she said, "You sure?"

He kept his gaze trained on her as he nodded.

"Things just got interesting," Garrett said.

"Okay, now it's a party," Kelsey sang out.

As the three of them lifted their shot glasses, the heated tension buzzed between him, and Kelsey gaze a slight smirk right before they all slung back the alcohol.

"Woohoo," she cheered, pumping a fist into the air.

"Drinking on the job is just something I've never seen you

do before." He sucked a lime into his mouth, the citrus biting at his tongue.

"Then I guess this is a new side you haven't seen before." She leaned in closer to him.

Garrett bobbed his head to the music, distracted by the usually attractive women in their town now even more so in his eyes with their costumes of sexy nurses and witches, Vivian's from Pretty Woman, and J.Lo's.

"Oh, I think I've seen all the sides of you," he replied, unaware of the huskiness in his voice until after the words were out.

She tilted the hat on her head to get a better look at him. "Is that so?"

"Well, you are my best friend."

"Friend?" She laughed sarcastically. "Is that what we are?"

"More or less." He grinned.

"Which is it? More or less?"

"What do you think?" he growled.

"Tell me more." She leaned across the bar, her cleavage on display in the white button-down shirt turning him on.

"The Kelsey I know takes a lot of pride in this place. That's the Kelsey I know." And oh, hell, he was going to say it because it needed to be said and this conversation was way past due. "That's the Kelsey I love."

Her eyes widened, turning glassy.

He'd told her he loved her plenty of times before. They were best friends after all, and that's what best friends did. But this time felt different. And they both knew it. This time it was like a confession hanging out on an explosive line between them.

She sniffed but smiled. "Shit, Davis, if you had given me a chance, I could've told you that Julian is taking over for me at ten. So I can have the rest of the night off to enjoy the party.

The kids are with my in-laws tonight. They're taking them trick or treating. I was hoping," she paused, dipping her chin to her chest. When she glanced back up at him, her blue eyes dark, he sucked in a breath, and she continued, "you and I could have a drink together and maybe finish that conversation from yesterday. That overdue conversation we've been meaning to have."

He didn't know what to say, so he simply nodded.

"I'm upset about the bar, yeah. And I'm planning on drinking too much tonight. But that's what my friends are for. You, Isabella, Maddie, Norah, and yeah, even Garrett. You'll all keep an eye on me."

Davis inhaled, his shoulders releasing their tension. Garrett usually had ulterior motives when it came to women, even Kelsey. He'd said it to him a few weeks ago. He'd go for Kelsey if she didn't have kids. But maybe, tonight he'd seen a new side to Kelsey. One where she wasn't looking for forever so her being a mom wasn't an issue. But Garrett also had to know how Davis felt about Kelsey so he was positive he wouldn't pursue her.

"Whatever you're gossiping about, save it, we're here to party and have fun," Garrett said.

"C'mon, join us for the next shot, will you?" She tilted her head and made her way back behind the bar.

Davis watched her from a distance as she filled three shots of tequila once again and then their eyes locked on one another's. The sultry look she gave him told him he was in trouble.

Trouble in the best way possible.

He exhaled, long and slow, before joining them.

Isabella hurried up to the bar, cutting off his path.

"Wait for me, I want in on this next one. It's not very often I get to drink with my bestie."

Kelsey grinned and filled a fourth shot glass. But before they could drink, Maddie and Norah showed up.

"Count us in too," Maddie said.

Before long, it felt like half the bar crowded together and they all took a shot at once.

Maddie shouted, "Woo-hoo! Let's all make some bad decisions tonight!"

And the crowd erupted in a cheer so loud, it vibrated in Davis's chest. It was difficult to *not* have fun. As much as Davis hated to admit it. But it had been a long time since he felt included in something and not out of default because he was Garrett's twin.

He glanced over at Kelsey and found her staring at him as she wiped the back of her hand against her lips. His heartbeat pounded in his ears, and he swallowed.

One way or another, tonight he was going to reveal his true feelings for her and act on them too.

CHAPTER 19
Kelsey

Kelsey sucked on a lime wedge, the citrus awakening her taste buds. She was four shots in, and her eyes burned as she stared at the men opposite her. Two men who were twins and dressed in the same costume.

At first, when Davis had walked into the bar, she'd thought her vision had gone blurry from the alcohol, making her see double. But she'd only had two shots at that point. Now that she was four shots in, she was grateful the men had finally separated. Not that she'd ever confused the two. One was her best friend, and the other was the biggest man whore in Pineridge.

Julian shuffled toward her. "Alright, Kels, you're free."

"Thanks. I owe you."

"No, I owe you. Because of you, I just got out of puke duty. My youngest stuffed herself full of Halloween candy."

"Eww, yeah, you're right. You're welcome." She rounded the bar and met Izzy on the other side.

"I'm glad you get to have some fun tonight."

"Well at this point, the kids are already in bed, so I might as well," Kelsey said.

"So are we dancing or doing Karaoke?" Izzy asked.

Kelsey thought about it, her eyes zoning in on Davis where he sat at a table nursing a beer. When he confessed that he loved her earlier, the declaration sounded different than any other time before.

It felt different too.

Things between them for the last few weeks had been building and now, maybe they were ready to find out what this was. Or better yet—act on it.

Tonight could be the night.

If I Can't Have You by Shawn Mendes played and the music vibrated through her veins and buzzed across her skin.

"Dance," she finally answered Izzy as she and ambled toward Davis. When she reached him, she said, "Hey, you wanna dance?" His eyes drifted lazily up to meet hers. When they locked, there was a low dip in her belly.

He glanced over his shoulder before looking back at her, fire in his gaze. "Kels," he groaned, and the rumble rattled something loose inside her. "You know I don't dance."

"Humor me," she said, smiling seductively and presenting a hand to him. "C'mon, you don't even have to do anything."

He quirked an intrigued brow at her, and her cheeks burned. He set his hand in hers and she instantly yanked him toward the bar.

"Uh, the dance floor is that way," he protested.

A laugh bubbled out of her. She was a bit more than buzzed than she'd first thought. But it was okay because this was a safe space and she felt light and free. When they reached the bar, she dropped his hand and hoisted herself up on top of it

Davis cupped his hands around his mouth, "What are you doing?" he yelled.

She hooked a finger at him.

"You really must be drunk if you think I'm getting up there with you."

"Not drunk. Not yet," she said, her hips beginning to shake to the music.

"Are you sure you've got the right twin?"

"Davis, get your tiny tush up here right now," she demanded, tugging on his arm.

"Fiiine," he grumbled.

Suddenly, him up there with her, she was stricken with stage fright. A self-consciousness she'd never felt around him. This was Davis. She didn't get nervous around him. But tonight, she was. Because he was looking at her with hunger in his eyes.

Hunger for...*her*.

His desire for her ignited her skin and caused her hips to rock again. When he flashed her a devilish grin, her own lips spread into a smile.

Kelsey placed her palm on his chest, running it down his abs where he felt solid and hard beneath the thin button-down shirt. She had the craving to undo those buttons, very slowly. She bit her lower lip and then spun around in his arms, backing up into him. His grunt was loud enough for her to hear, and it encouraged her to continue dancing. She pushed her butt into him, her hands pumping into the air in time with the music. She bent at the waist, her hat falling off and she kept her backside in the air as a few cheers sounded in the bar.

When she straightened and spun around so she was facing Davis once again, she gripped his hips and forced him to two-step with her briefly, guiding him along as he stayed pressed against her. The feel of his craving for her, so firm and hard sent a thrill of pleasure racking her body. He smiled relentlessly at her, giving her an adorable shake of his head. With both hands flattened against his chest, she slid them down as she lowered her body in front of him. The song came to an end, and she stood once again, tilting her head, and gazing up at him and finding his eyes dark.

When the cheering quieted, she said in singsong, "He dances."

Davis grinned and warmth blossomed in her chest. Oh boy. Yep, he was no longer in the friend zone. Not after his smile alone did that to her. Turning her on was one thing, but causing her heart to explode, that was something entirely different.

"Guilty." He hopped down and held her waist, helping her off the bar.

"That was fun, right?"

He shrugged. "I guess."

"C'mon, why can't you just admit it?"

"Okay, it was fun."

"Kelsey, you were a goddess up there! I had no idea you had those moves," Izzy said, wrapping Kelsey up in a hug.

"Oh yeah, I've got moves." She winked at Davis as she took a sip of a beer.

The combination of the alcohol, the dance, and losing O'Henry's had her feeling daring. Risky even.

Davis gently pulled the bottle from her, "Okay, how about we cool it with that and let's get you some water."

Heat coiled through her, and she snatched the bottle back. "No, Davis. Stop. I don't need water."

"Fine." He put his hands up in surrender. "I was only trying to help."

Davis was only worried she'd end up like her mama, that's what it was. And she wouldn't. He knew the burden her mama had caused, and she'd never let herself get out of control like that. It hurt that he didn't trust her.

"Ugh," she groaned. "You're always just trying to help. Maybe I don't need your help. Have you ever thought of that?"

"You're right. You don't need me." Davis stepped back a few feet, staring at her. "I'm sorry." He spun around and stalked off.

"What was that about?" Isabella asked after he was gone.

Kelsey watched him go, her eyes burning. "It was nothing."

"Nu-uh, that definitely wasn't nothing. And that whole dance up there, that wasn't nothing either." Her finger twirled in the air.

"I don't know." Her cheeks warmed. "Lately, things between us have been...complicated."

Isabella's eyes widened.

"Don't," Kelsey warned.

"Okay, okay, I won't say anything. Except," she said, clasping her hands in front of her and her eyes going all dreamy, "aww...how cute would you guys be together?"

"I don't do cute. Or men...not anymore."

Isabella bumped her hip into Kelsey's. "Listen, I know you're not ready to date so I'm not going to push you—"

"Good, then please don't."

"But sometimes, people come into our lives unexpectedly. Some opportunities present themselves to us when we're least expecting it."

"Davis always needs a project. He just wants to fix me."

"Sweetie, I don't think that's it."

"Really? Because can you actually see the two of us together? We have different priorities and responsibilities. I have three kids and an alcoholic mama, so let's face it, it's more like having four kids. He has a TV show."

Isabella lifted her arms at her sides. "He loves you, Kels."

"Yeah, well, not like that. And I'm done with this conversation. I plan to have fun the rest of the night, while I can."

"Okay, you're right. I'm done. How about karaoke?"

"Yes, please!" Kelsey dragged Izzy toward the stage.

After three songs, one solo and two duets, Kelsey chugged a glass of water. She'd done pretty good putting Davis in the back of her mind while she'd been distracted by karaoke. But now, sitting alone her curious eyes couldn't resist a trip around the room.

One Vance twin dressed in a Lloyd costume sat at a table with two women she didn't recognize. The other Vance twin also dressed in a Lloyd costume approached her, at first, she assumed it was Davis until she got a closer look.

"Hey," Garrett said, propping on a stool across from her.

"I thought you were Davis at first," she admitted.

"Do you want me to go?"

"No, no, don't be silly. I just saw the Lloyd over there with those women and assumed." She gave a flick of her wrist.

"I guess my brother is better in the lady department than I thought. Who knew?"

She shrugged, trying not to glance in Davis's direction again.

"You knew," Garrett said, quirking a brow when she glanced up at him.

"What?"

"You two with your, *we're just friends*, you guys don't fool me. I may not know you that well, but I know my brother. And it's obvious he has real feelings for you."

"No, he doesn't...he couldn't...we don't." Her head felt fuzzy.

Music played through the speakers for a few beats before a voice sounded out.

"Do you want to dance?" Garrett asked.

She widened her eyes and bit her lower lip, considering before finally relenting. "Um...sure."

Garrett took her hand and led her to the dance floor. He rested their joined hands against his chest and pressed his free one to her lower back. She sunk into him, resting her cheek onto his chest. His heart thumped slow and rhythmic. She exhaled a long breath and allowed her eyes to close.

Even if Garrett was a player, constantly toying with Maddie's feelings, Kelsey knew he had a big heart. One that had been broken when his fiancée died. The two of them had this in common, a bond that connected them.

They weren't that different she realized in that moment. Neither of them had been dealing with their grief in a healthy way. While he'd been distracting himself with work and the TV show, and endless women, Kelsey had been distracting herself with juggling the kids, the bar, and her mama.

When Garrett's hand slid further down her back, she jerked her head up. She yanked her hand free from his grip and smacked him in the chest.

"Can't blame a guy for trying." He chuckled.

"Garrett, you're a sweet guy...when you want to be." She smiled and gestured between them as she said, "But this, you and me, it's never gonna happen. Do everyone a favor, including yourself, and give a relationship with Maddie a real shot. At the very least, ask her to dance." She went to her tiptoes and pressed a kiss to his cheek before she spun around to search for Davis.

Only she didn't have to search for very long. When she turned around, he stood there, fists clenching at his sides and a tightness in his eyes. Heat flushed through her body, and she gulped in a breath.

The hurt expression he portrayed as she advanced toward him caused a dullness in her chest. After being friends for so long, the one thing that had always kept their relationship strong was that she never had a thing for Garrett. So whatever Davis thought he just witnessed, could've threatened whatever had been tethering their friendship along. Even if it had been nothing, to someone witnessing their interactions moments before, it could very well have been misconstrued.

Never during the ten years of their friendship had she been the cause of that look of pain and betrayal.

CHAPTER 20

Davis

The hope of confessing his feelings to Kelsey not only slipped away but imploded the moment his eyes took in the horrific sight of Garrett and Kelsey dancing together. *Slow* dancing. Garrett's hand suspended alarmingly close to Kelsey's backside and her cheek pressed against his chest.

Of all the women in the bar tonight that Garrett could've hooked up with, why did he want Kelsey? And what was worse; he thought he knew Kelsey. He thought she was smart enough not to be sucked in by his brother's charm. He wasn't sure if he should be disgusted or just disappointed. Instead, he couldn't push away the impending feelings of jealousy that racked his body.

After Davis had excused himself from the two women he'd met who had come to Pineridge to see the infamous love lock bridge, he had hoped to ask Kelsey if she wanted to dance. A slow dance this time, out on the real dancefloor. But after that display, he shook his head at Kelsey and pushed outside, sucking a gulp of air. He tore off the orange hat and fisted it in his hand.

As he leaned against the building, he debated leaving. But he worried about Kelsey and how she'd get home. Even if his brain did go to places he didn't want it to. Like maybe Garrett had already offered to take Kelsey home.

He groaned and pushed the heels of his hands into both eyes and groaned.

"Hey, bro, what are you doing out here?" Garrett asked.

Davis brought his hands down and tried to hide his whiplash of feelings from seeing Garrett not only standing next to Maddie but holding hands with her. He cleared his throat. "Just needed some air."

"We're heading out," Garrett said.

"Oh, already?"

"Yeah." Garrett widened his eyes and lifted his brows as he gesticulated at Maddie. "It's getting late. Party is slowing down."

Davis nodded, his brain still trying to play catch up. Did he have it wrong?

Garrett walked backward, tugging on Maddie's hand as he spoke, "But hey, don't get air for too long. You should really get back in there. I think someone's waiting for you."

"'Night," Maddie said.

"Yeah, goodnight." Davis watched them leave and ran his hand over his head.

Several other people still dressed in their costumes piled out of the bar. He checked his phone; it was almost two a.m. He hurried and turned around, heading back into the bar, his heart hammering in his chest as he searched for Kelsey.

Isabella, Leo, and Norah were by the door, putting on their jackets.

"Hey, have you guys seen Kelsey?"

"She's around here somewhere. Maybe check the back. 'Night, Davis," Isabella said.

"Yeah, 'night." He took off in almost a jog, anticipation stirring in his gut.

He reached the bar where Julian was hanging clean glasses upside down buy their stems. The hope began to fizzle. What if she'd slipped out the back door and he hadn't noticed?

"Is Kelsey still here?"

"Yeah, I think she's in the office."

"Thanks."

"No problem. And can you let her know I'm about to lock up," Julian hollered over his shoulder.

Davis pushed through the *Employee Only* door that led to the kitchen and office and searched for Kelsey. He hurried through the kitchen and down the hall, making his way to the office.

When he shouldered into the door and it opened, he glanced around the office, searching through the decorations of fake spiderwebs and pumpkins. He inhaled a sharp breath when he found her, at last. Kelsey was seated at the desk. She'd taken the off the baby blue hat and blonde wig. The blue jacket laid across the desk next to her.

"Kelsey," he said, on an exhale of breath.

Their eyes met and she stood to her feet and rounded the desk. He entered the room with every intention of telling her everything, starting with how he felt about her. That she very well might be the only person in this world who cared about him. Who loved him in a no-strings-attached sort of way. And that he loved her too.

But as he opened his mouth to speak, she advanced toward him, purpose in her walk. When she reached him, she went up on tip toe and cupped his face, her blue eyes darkening with desire, and he couldn't resist her. The past few weeks the craving for her had been hovering just below the surface, waiting to break free.

As he gripped her hips and yanked her into him, she inhaled a sharp breath. "Don't talk. Just kiss me," she whispered like a demand.

When he lowered his mouth to hers, he waited with every ounce of self-control he had left, until at last, she finally gave him release when she kissed him. Her lips parted, opening herself to him and he slipped his tongue inside, exploring and flicking against hers.

She slipped off his hat and ran a hand through his messy hair, driving him wild by her touch and he had to fight to get out of his head that was reminding him *he was kissing Kelsey*.

From this moment on, they'd never be able to go back to what they were before. They'd crossed that imaginary line they'd drawn years ago, and stepped into whatever this new, undefined relationship was. One that involved kissing.

And he wasn't complaining.

He backed her up against the desk and gripped her thighs, lifting her up and setting her on top of it in one quick motion. He stepped in between her legs, opening them with his body and his hands glided up her back before his lips moved to her neck, nibbling, and tasting and she giggled. Her hot breath hummed against his ear, causing him to shiver.

He had learned something new about her, something he didn't think was possible all these years later. Her neck was ticklish. If they had never made it to this moment, he still wouldn't know. And knowing this about her only made the moment shared between them more thrilling. Somehow, he was able to stop his lips from exploring, stop his hands from caressing, stop his hips from grinding and he groaned into her neck as she arched into him, before lifting his head to look at her.

"Are you sure?" he panted.

"I've never wanted anyone more."

At her words, his entire body ignited, and he kissed her hard. He kissed her like he meant it. He kissed her like his very life depended on it. As his fingers went to the buttons on the white blouse, undoing each one with purpose, his eye contact never wavered, never leaving hers. He knew those eyes better than anyone else's. He knew when they were sad, when they were happy, or scared. But this emotion, this lust—he'd never been able to experience it before and it only excited him more.

Kelsey gripped his jacket and yanked it off his shoulders before he slipped his arms out. As she undid the buttons on his dress shirt, he was already tearing hers off. He reached around her back and unhooked her bra. After releasing her breasts, he admired the bare, glistening skin. They were as alluring as he remembered from that night at the hotel. Only tonight, he wouldn't admire them with his eyes alone, he'd touch, lick, and relish them.

When her hands went to his belt, working the buckle, his went to her breasts. She sucked in an audible breath as he took one in each of his hands gently, caressing, kneading, taunting. He brought his mouth down against hers and she nipped his lower lip with her teeth causing further excitement to radiate.

She finally had his belt undone, dragging the zipper down slowly and he stepped out of the oversized costume pants. He needed hers off too. Now.

Lifting her off the desk, he set her down. "Off," he urged.

She undid the baby blue pants agonizingly slow, letting them fall off her hips and pool at her feet on the floor. He admired her with hooded eyes, the usual lust he'd typically feel in this moment with a woman was being overtaken with an adoration and yearning for her. A reminder to take his time with her. To go slow.

Kelsey was special. She deserved a tenderness he planned

to give to her. Hopefully over and over. All night long if she let him.

"Don't even think of going easy on me. It's been a long time," her voice growled.

"That's why I plan to go slow," he admitted, tempted to graze a thumb across her cheek but knowing she hated having her face touched. "I want to give you what you deserve."

"If you're looking for some proper woman, I can assure you, I ain't her. I don't have patience for slow."

With that, she tethered her hands around his neck and leapt into his arms, wrapping her legs around his torso like a spider monkey. Her words and her actions of taking the initiative set him off. He was in complete overdrive.

Forget slow.

He planted her back on top of the desk and it nearly killed him to release her while he removed a condom from the wallet that was still shoved in the front pocket of his pants. She kept firm eye contact with him as he tore the package open with his teeth, her eyes glossing over.

When she hooked a finger at him, and he relented, placing the condom in her hand, he almost came completely undone. Or maybe it was when her warm hand gripped him. The details blurred together into one vast, spectacular moment he prayed would never end.

Davis spread open her legs and stepped in between while she scooted to the edge of the desk, sliding against him. Desire shot through him, his head going dizzy. He kissed the supple skin on her collarbone and kneaded a nipple between his thumb and finger, teasing a sweet moan from her lips.

Unable to drag out this foreplay further, worried he might finish before they'd even began, he thrust inside of her as he gripped her back, fingers digging into her skin. She gasped and the sound made him feel greedy. He wanted to elicit all kinds of sounds from her tonight.

As he rocked his hips, and she bucked against him, they found their rhythm and in between the moments of ecstasy he couldn't help from wonder if they'd been complete idiots by not doing this sooner.

Or, if they were being complete idiots now and were making the biggest mistake ever.

CHAPTER 21
Kelsey

W ho knew Davis's butt was this luscious? This muscular? This perfect.

She'd never given it much thought until a few weeks prior. After she'd seen his rock-hard abs and perfectly sculpted biceps, she'd allowed her mind to wander. Now, there would be no more wondering. She'd not only seen his naked behind, but she had also touched it. And that wasn't even the best part.

As Davis continued to make love to her, rhythmic thrusts helped her to no longer feel the effects of her earlier alcohol intake, allowing her to fully enjoy the moment. With her entire body stimulated, her eyes fluttered closed in pleasure. His touch, his aura, sparked a fervor in her, and each nerve ending hung on the brink of erupting.

In the quiet hum of the presumably empty bar, Kelsey's muscles lost all tension. She whimpered into the flushed skin of Davis's neck as the sweet release wracked her body.

His rapid breathing in her ear, the scruff of his unshaven

beard scratching against her neck, only made the experience that much more rewarding. Their simultaneous pleasure caused another thrill of satisfaction to rattle through her.

"You weren't wrong," Davis said in between ragged breaths.

She swallowed, her heart beating hard against her rib cage. "What's that?"

"You're not a proper woman," he teased, kissing her neck, and evoking a giggle from her again.

"I did warn you."

Davis smiled and took her by the hands, tempting her as he pulled her along with him and walked backward toward the couch.

She eyed him skeptically.

"Do you hear that?" he asked, guiding her down onto the couch. "Everyone is gone, including Julian."

"Silence in the bar is my favorite sound," she admitted.

He climbed on top of her, squeezing her thighs. "Ready to go another round?"

"My my, who's the eager one now?" she asked, grinning as she peered up at him through long eyelashes and reached for him.

Was that even a legitimate question?

He gifted her with a trail of kisses to her collarbone. She pressed her palms against his smooth chest, her hands stilling as she felt the rhythmic beat of his heart. Disbelief filled her, making her head spin.

Had she and Davis Vance just had sex? She'd always known him to be a talented craftsman, but he had other talents she hadn't been privy to until tonight. It felt like he'd opened up to her and shared a secret with her.

She was afraid to move, nearly afraid to breathe as he ran

his hand down her hip, caressing her thigh, because what if this wasn't actually happening? What if this was all in her imagination? Or worse—a dream?

She didn't think she could handle that. Because this was too good. No, scratch that. It was more than good. It was earthquaking, purely blissful pleasure and intimate.

So incredibly intimate.

Wrapping her legs around his waist and her arms around his back, she yanked him even closer. She needed to feel the weight of him pressing into her, feel his skin against hers, have him filling her once again.

CATAPULTING FROM A DEEP SLEEP, KELSEY GROANED, pinching her eyes closed and smashing a hand to her forehead. Her head pounded and her mouth was dry. The result of too many drinks the night before. Too many shots of tequila to be exact. Hadn't she learned not to mix hard alcohol with beer?

Then suddenly she remembered. *Everything*.

Flinging her eyes open, she searched next to her. But Davis wasn't beside her. He wasn't on the couch at all. Or in the office she realized after her eyes took a quick trip around the room.

She pulled the blanket taut around her still naked body. Not wanting to focus on the fact that Davis had left at some point between their second round and now, she distracted herself by locating her scattered clothing around the office. As she did, she paid attention to the fact that her body ached in a deliciously satisfied way it hadn't in quite some time.

Okay, yeah, so she'd been insane to think she could've gone the rest of her life depriving herself of that kind of pleasure. It just wasn't natural.

In the process of dressing in her costume clothes, because lucky her, that's all she had, she also found her phone. She exhaled a breath after checking and finding no unanswered texts or phone calls. She had to be in some bizzarro world because this was probably the first morning she'd awoke to no one needing her. If she had enough time, she'd relish in this tiny —did she dare say it—victory.

But there wasn't enough time.

Kelsey had promised her children she'd take them to Pineridge's Fall Festival. Complete with candy apples, face painting, carnival games, live music, and a few kiddie rides. She was prepared to do it all today.

After the largest cup of coffee, of course.

For the first time in a long time, she felt optimistic. About her future and the bar's future. She had her appointment with a finance specialist at the bank the next morning and she had a feeling it was going to work out in her favor. Call her crazy, but things had to start looking up eventually.

After locking up the bar, Kelsey hurried to her van and drove in the direction of the Daily Grind in desperate need of a caffeine fix before her day could truly begin. Even though she was still dressed in the outdated baby blue suit, she stepped into the local coffee shop proudly. At the same time, she tried to ignore the nagging ache in the pit of her stomach each time her brain reminded her that she woke up alone this morning.

Davis had better have a good explanation.

"Hey, Kelsey," Hannah, the barista greeted her, eyeing her suspiciously. "Nice pants."

"Part of my costume from the Halloween party last night," she explained with a shrug, playing it off.

Everyone in town knew it wasn't unusual for Kelsey to sleep at the bar. Especially if she was working the closing shift.

Better to be safe at the bar than try to drive home sleep deprived after two a.m.

"Hmm...mmm..." Hannah muttered with a knowing smirk.

Kelsey frowned, tilting her head as she stepped to the side and waited for her drink to be made. Why the suspicion? It wasn't like it was obvious she'd finally had sex, was it? Was there some way they could tell? She was being silly. No way could they know.

As the barista slid Kelsey's coffee across the counter, Hannah hurried over and leaned in, glancing around the café, and clearing her throat. "Ya know, a certain Vance twin was in here earlier."

"Yeah? And?" Kelsey talked quieter than normal.

"And...he was still dressed in his costume from last night too," she whispered, hardly able to contain her growing smile.

As a tingle swept up the back of her neck, her ears grew impossibly hot. Normally Kelsey didn't care what anyone thought of her. She'd been the gossip in Pineridge for months after Ricky passed away. But this was different.

Since Davis hadn't been there when she woke up this morning, they hadn't had a chance to discuss what happened the night before. And since they hadn't talked it through, it felt wrong to discuss it with the barista at the Daily Grind first.

"Well, it's not like that's all that strange. It's not like that's something that really needs to be talked about. If you know what I mean?" She had to nip this in the bud before it got out of hand.

"Are you kidding me? If I got lucky with Garrett Vance, you better believe I'd be spreading that news like wildfire," she said.

"Wait...what? But...no," Kelsey tried to get out coherent words.

"Please tell me it was as good as I imagine it would be?"

"Shh," Kelsey shrieked, glancing over both shoulders, and then lowering her voice to a whisper before continuing. "You've got it all wrong—"

"Shut up. Was it not good? Because I've heard he's good but kind of a selfish lover. Is that true? Because I can totally see that."

Kelsey's stomach tightened as Hannah rambled on and she tried to catch her breath so she could set the story straight. Though, did she *want* the town knowing she and Davis hooked up? And she didn't even like the term *hooked up*. Because what they shared last night was more than that. Wasn't it?

Although she hadn't even heard from him so maybe she had this thing all wrong.

Her phone vibrated in her back pocket. She slid it out and glanced at the screen.

MAMA

I need some help at the bakery for a few
hours this morning.

Kelsey groaned. It wasn't a question, but rather a demand.

"C'mon, please give me something." Hannah clasped her hands together.

"I gotta go, thank you for the coffee. And please, keep this between us, would ya?" Kelsey turned and rushed through the door, hoping to not bump into anyone on her way out.

MAIN STREET HAD BEEN COMPLETELY TRANSFORMED AND blocked off to through traffic. It looked as if it had been glittered by the entirety of fall season's favorites. Hay bales lined the sides of the road, pumpkins arranged in pyramids were scattered about. Vendors with booths took up the entire street. Some selling popular fall treats like candy apples and kettle corn, others selling locally brewed beer and hard ciders, and others with their handcrafted goods.

Dressed in layers of a long-sleeved shirt and a black and white flannel and jeans, Kelsey chased after June and Zach while pushing Charlotte in the stroller. They wanted to stop at the face painting booth first, followed by deep fried twinkies, and then a trip on the merry-go-round. Being in a small town where most all the locals knew her, Kelsey still tried to blend in by wearing her sunglasses and an old baseball hat.

It had only been a few hours since she left the café and already she'd received texts from Isabella, Norah, and two other friends all stating they heard the same rumor. She and Garrett hooked up at the Halloween costume party. How had they thought that? Even though Garrett and Davis were dressed in the same costume, how could no one else tell them apart?

And who was it who went to The Daily Grind that morning? Davis or Garrett? She didn't know because she still hadn't heard from Davis.

What was the protocol after having sex with someone? How long were you supposed to wait before you texted or called? She'd been with Ricky so long, she really didn't know. Did you wait a few hours to call? Twenty-four hours? Three to five days?

She and Davis usually stayed in close contact and texted every day. So it felt weird to think she may have to wait a few days until she heard from him. She already didn't like this change to their relationship.

Kelsey hunkered down, sitting on a hay bale while she waited for the kids to have their faces painted. Her phone had been buzzing with incoming texts from Isabella and Norah, but she'd been ignoring them. She wasn't ready to explain. She regretted coming to the Fall Festival. The last thing she wanted was to run into someone who had heard the rumor and wanted to question her.

Because to be honest, she didn't know what to say. If she told the truth—it was Davis, everyone would know her business. But if she allowed the rumor to continue, people would think she slept with Garrett Vance, the biggest player in town. Which was worse?

"All done, Mama," June said, interrupting her thoughts and showing off a unicorn painted on her forehead.

"Aw, sweets, that looks beautiful."

"Can we go on the Ferris wheel now?" June asked.

"As soon as Zach is ready, we'll go."

"Yay!" June grabbed a hold of Charlotte's hands and jumped up and down causing the baby to squeal in delight.

Zach approached her next, showing off his painted Batman mask and looking satisfied with his appearance as well.

"Wow, that looks great, Z. So mysterious," Kelsey said.

"It's not as pretty as mine," June contested.

"It's not supposed to be pretty, it's cool," Zach argued with his sister, his face going stony.

"It's very cool," Kelsey reassured him, standing and double-checking Charlotte was still secure in the stroller's seatbelt.

Sometimes June liked unlatching her, helping her to become the world's tiniest escape artist. But Kelsey didn't have time to worry about Houdini today.

"June wants to go on the Ferris wheel now," Kelsey said, pushing the stroller into the crowded foot traffic on the street.

Zach stopped walking and crossed his arms. "But you said we were getting twinkies next. I want a Twinkie."

"Oh, we're gonna do it all today, don't you worry, Z. But

maybe Twinkie's after the Ferris wheel would be better so you don't get an upset tummy on the ride."

He seemed to consider this for a moment before he started moving again, stomping in his boots. "I want to go two times on the Ferris wheel."

"Fine, two times. We're here all day," she muttered.

The sun peeked out from behind a group of clouds and warmed Kelsey's skin. She welcomed it after Pineridge had seen several days of non-stop rain that week. The fall season only reminded her that winter was coming. And when winter arrived in Pineridge, it was there to stay for an unprecedented amount of time, much like Cousin Eddie in National Lampoon's Christmas Vacation.

As they weaved through the crowd, Kelsey waved at a few acquaintances along the way, exhaling a breath of relief when none of them wanted to stop and chat. They had nearly reached the line for the Ferris wheel when she spotted Isabella and Leo. Her stomach pinched as Isabella's eyes never left hers while she and Leo zigzagged their way toward her.

"Did you lose your phone? I've been texting you all day," Isabella said once she'd finally managed to reach Kelsey.

"No...I...I've just been busy." Widening her eyes and gesturing at the kids, she hoped her friend wasn't too dense to understand her meaning. They couldn't talk about what Izzy so obviously wanted to right now. Not in front of the kids. And sure as heck not in public.

Darn this little town and their gossipy Nosey Nellie's.

"Hi, kids." Isabella bent and smiled, tugging on Charlotte's foot.

June and Zach bombarded Izzy and Leo with hugs but Charlotte eyed Izzy skeptically.

"How about Auntie Izzy buys you tickets so you can ride the Ferris Wheel with Uncle Leo?"

"Yay!" June squealed.

"Okay, but I wanna sit on the end," Zach stated.

"Works for me." Leo nodded at Isabella, and it felt like there was a wordless exchange between them that she wasn't privy to. He kissed Izzy on the cheek and took each of the kid's hands.

"Bye, Mama." June waved over her shoulder.

"You two do not leave Uncle Leo's side, you hear me?" Kelsey shouted.

"I got 'em," Leo assured her.

As soon as the kids were out of earshot, Isabella crossed her arms and spun to face Kelsey, brows up. "Okay, spill the tea. Now."

Kelsey pulled the brim of her hat down lower, checking over her shoulder as she navigated the stroller out of the Ferris wheel line. Isabella followed but didn't look happy about it. But it felt like ears were everywhere.

"What happened with you last night?" Isabella hissed.

"First of all, what makes you think something happened?"

"Seriously? Um maybe because rumors are circulating all over town. Rumors about my bestie and a certain Renovation Dudes star. Hooking up."

"Shh," Kelsey warned.

"Well, you better start talking then."

Hesitating to spill the details of the intimate moment shared between she and Davis from the night before, Kelsey lowered her chin.

Izzy gasped. "It's true!"

"It might be." Kelsey bit her lip.

"You and Garrett? But how? And maybe the biggest question—why?"

Kelsey jerked her head, and her eyes flew up to meet Isabella's. Even her own bestie had the situation all wrong. Even if she didn't come clean with the entire town just yet, she at least owed it to Izzy to tell the truth.

But in her peripheral, she spotted Maddie coming toward her, her eyes cold and her expression tight.

Apparently, Maddie had heard the rumors about Garrett. And worse? She looked like she believed them.

CHAPTER 22

Davis

Woodworking was the only thing to ease Davis's mind. The only thing to distract him. But so far, it wasn't doing the trick today. He'd been in his garage for the last few hours, and currently been sanding the same section of the same board for fifteen minutes. Cooper was keeping his distance, currently sprawled out on the balmy driveway sunning himself.

Going into The Daily Grind to grab a cup of coffee in the morning after leaving O'Henry's had been his biggest mistake. Okay, maybe his *second* biggest mistake. His first, allowing the barista to assume he was Garrett. Now he had no one else to blame about the rumors circling around town.

Only three people knew the truth about what went down the night before. And so far, not one of those three was talking. At least as far as he knew.

He hadn't heard from Kelsey all day. But that didn't surprise him. After he snuck out early in the morning, he didn't expect to hear from her. It was a jerk move. He was well aware, even still, it hadn't stopped him.

That morning, he'd awoken early and took in the sight of Kelsey's beautiful body squished in next to him sleeping. Her hair was wild, and her cheek was pressed to his chest, rising and falling along with his breathing.

But as he gazed at her, completely held captive, his mind spiraled, replaying each moment from the night before. What if she woke up and it was awkward between them? What if she had regrets? What if their night together ruined their future? Because now that they'd crossed the line, their relationship would never be the same again.

To make matters worse, the rumors circling around town had him angry, confused, and no offense to Garret, but down-right disgusted. Garrett—the charmer. Garrett—the ladies' man. Garrett—the player. Garrett—the-best-sex-Kelsey's-ever-had. There was no way Kelsey hadn't heard them too. So why hadn't she set things straight? Or at the very least, texted him.

Davis would've come clean and explained his disappearing act that morning, if he had heard from her. But he still hadn't. So instead, in a means to busy his mind, he dived into a project. Just like he always did. His current project was a little neighborhood library Mrs. Chen had hired him to make. He'd made a few around town. They were simple. A mindless project. Something he needed today.

The sun shined through the open garage door, giving him natural light and warmth. He had the day off from shooting. But they'd be back at it again tomorrow.

The rumble of Garrett's truck rattled the inside of the garage. Davis shook his head. Garrett always needed bigger, better, louder. A few moments later, he strolled up the drive-way. Cooper sat up only long enough to emit a warning bark before recognizing Garrett and returning to his lethargic state.

"Can't even take a day off on your day off," Garrett called, patting Cooper on the head after ducking his six-foot frame underneath the large garage door.

"This is me taking a day off," Davis muttered. He smoothed a hand over the sanded wood before blowing off the sawdust.

Roaming around the garage, Garrett fiddled with Davis's tools. He stayed quiet but it was obvious he had something on his mind. Garrett wasn't one for being subdued.

The longer he restrained, the more agitated it made Davis. How long was he planning to wait to admit he'd heard the rumor? Because he had, hadn't he? That was the reason for him stopping by unannounced?

"Working on another one of those neighborhood libraries?"

"Yep. This one is for Mrs. Chen."

"I don't understand why you subject yourself to such simple work. I've seen you do far more detailed work. You're harboring your talent." Garrett took a seat on a stool underneath the window, sunlight peering in and amplifying the dust on every square inch of surface.

"I'm not harboring my talent," Davis mumbled. "Isn't that what I'm showcasing on the show?"

Garrett shrugged.

"Besides, I like building these. They're mindless. And people appreciate them."

"*I* appreciate what you do on the show. Despite you hating the recognition, you gotta admit the cash flow isn't terrible."

"You're right, it's not," he agreed.

If it wasn't for the show, he wouldn't be able to offer to pay off the debt at O'Henry's. He was financially set for his future, meaning he could do whatever he wanted to do when the show ended. Either stay in business with Garrett without the lights and cameras and fame or do his own thing. Hell, he could afford to build little neighborhood libraries for the rest of his life if he wanted to.

Garrett picked up a paintbrush and ran his thumb against the bristles. "But you are still considering signing if they want to renew our contract, right?"

Davis sighed, placing his hands on his hips. "Is that what you really came over here to talk about?"

Glancing up, Garrett smirked. "Oh little bro, how you know me so well. Or, should I say, how *we* know each other so well?"

Davis waited for the questions, for the accusations. He half expected Garrett to be angry people in town were believing such a rumor.

"So you and Kelsey finally did the deed?" He shook his head, grinning. "I gotta admit, I really didn't think you had it in you."

"Why's that?" Davis asked, instead of denying it. He crossed his arms and leaned against the work counter.

"You guys have been friends for years. I guess I figured if it hadn't happened by now, it was never gonna happen. But it's true?"

Davis nodded. "Last night. At the bar."

"I want to be happy for you, I really do. But please clear up one small detail for me, will you? Why does everyone think *I* slept with her?"

He puffed out a heavy sigh. "My guess is it has something to do with that twin mistaken identity. I went into the coffee shop this morning dressed in my costume from last night. Guess someone assumed I was you."

"Look, normally I wouldn't care if people thought Kelsey and I hooked up, except that I sort of hooked up with someone else last night." Garrett scratched at the back of his head.

Davis tilted his head. "Maddie?"

Garrett winced. "Maybe."

Exhaling a whistle under his breath, Davis ran a rough

palm down his unshaven face. "Not again. You gotta stop messing with that girl. She has real feelings for you, and I think it's damn obvious you don't."

Garrett straightened. "Hey, that's not fair. Maddie is... Maddie...well she's different." He paced.

"Yeah? Because if she's different enough for you to sleep with her not once, but twice, then I think you have real feelings for her. So who are you trying to fool? Me? Her? Yourself?"

"I didn't come here for a lecture." He pointed a finger at his brother. "You're the one whose been hung up on some chick for the last ten years, but you've been too much of a pussy to do anything about it!"

"I have not been hung up on her for ten years."

"Now who's trying to fool who? You talk a lot of talk about me, that I'm managing my grief in an unhealthy way. But you're the one who'd rather let an entire town believe a rumor instead of admitting you've got real feelings for Kelsey."

"It's not that," Davis hollered.

"No, then what is it? Try to make me understand."

He pushed both hands through his messy hair. "Because, what if...what if she regrets it? Sleeping with me?"

"That's crazy. Didn't you guys go for another round this morning? Or at the very least, you talked about it and kissed her goodbye?"

Davis winced. "I left the bar while she was still sleeping."

A grumble exhaled from Garrett before he released a low whistle. "Davey, you've played the ultimate jackass card. Who even are you?"

"I didn't mean to," Davis said, dropping his chin and studying his boots. "It wasn't as if I'd planned to sneak out. I just...freaked out. What if she woke up and regretted everything? I don't think I could've faced that."

"This is Kelsey. She never does anything she doesn't want to do."

Davis nodded. Deep down he knew this. But he was still worried.

"You're just making up excuses. Because you're scared of change."

"You're right," he muttered in agreement.

"Of course I'm right." He patted his brother on the back. "Now forget texting or calling. This is gonna take some groveling. And it has to be done in person."

Davis interlocked his fingers and wrapped them around the back of his neck, staring at the cement floor scattered with a film of sawdust.

"I heard she was at the Harvest Festival. Go find her and talk to her."

It would be easier to text. Easier to call. But Garrett was right, not only did he owe her an explanation, but she also deserved it to be done in person.

It was almost dark by the time Davis made it to the Harvest Festival. Wrapping up the project for Mrs. Chen took longer than he'd expected. Dressed in jeans and a thick fleece jacket along with a beanie, he braved the crisp fall air. Main Street was crowded, and his chest fluttered with concern over if he'd even find Kelsey. He didn't want to give in and text her, but he also wasn't planning on freezing to death over pride.

Illuminated by streetlamps and string lights on each vendor booth, Main Street brought its own warmth to the chilly night. Pineridge had a festival for every single holiday and season. But Davis wasn't big on attending. They were always too crowded.

And why would he willingly wait in a long line for an over-priced beer?

Though he hated to admit, as he strolled further, the glowing lights, the happy faces of the locals, music humming from the stage, and all the fall decorations, it wasn't so bad. A warmth spread through his body. There was something about the community coming together that made him feel blessed to be a part of it. As much as he grumbled about everyone knowing him in town, it really wasn't all that different than before the show aired. In a town this small, everyone pretty much knew each other even if you weren't on TV.

"Hey, that you, Davis?" someone called from behind him.

He spun around. "Hey, Joey. How've ya been?" He back-tracked, hurrying to shake his old pal's hand so Joey wouldn't have to maneuver his wheelchair over.

"I'm good. Can't complain. You?" Joey quirked a brow at him.

"Good." Best to keep it short. There was no telling what Joey had heard since he was married to Vanessa who worked with Hannah at The Daily Grind.

"Man, I loved the work you did on the last episode. Though ever since we watched it, Vanessa has been bugging me for built-in bookcases in our family room. You ever consider quit-ting the show with HGTV and running your own business again? I have lots of things on my honey-do-list." Joey waggled his brows.

Davis chuckled. "Sadly, I think my contract says something about not quitting."

"I don't know why that's sad. Who in their right mind would give up a show on HGTV?" Joey shook his head.

"Yeah, right...I don't know." Davis glanced away, tugging his beanie hat down further. When he did, he spotted Isabella and Leo at the wood carving booth.

"Can I buy you a beer?" Joey asked.

"Um...how about another time," Davis answered, distractedly. "I'll see you around."

"Yeah, see ya."

He jogged over to Isabella and Leo. "Hey, guys. Have you seen Kelsey?"

"Oh, hey, Davis." Isabella eyed him skeptically.

He could only imagine what Kelsey had told her about the night before. Or worse, about the morning.

"We just saw her near the stage. She and the kids were eating dinner with Rita," Leo provided.

"Thanks," Davis said, taking off in the direction of the stage.

"Davis, wait," Isabella called.

He turned and walked backward.

"Is everything okay?"

"I hope so," he said.

One conversation would hopefully clear everything up. They'd been friends too long to throw it away based on one night together.

A local band played a cover of a Zach Bryan song from the makeshift stage. Davis scanned the tables of people watching and listening, and others eating. He spotted Kelsey and her kids with Rita and Howard Hoffman. He weaved through the tables until he reached her. He was still unsure of what he would say.

"Hey," he said, sounding out of breath even though he wasn't.

Kelsey craned her neck, peering up at him. The blue of her eyes shimmered in the gleam of the lights and unease sat heavy in his gut. With one look, he should know the truth of her feelings. But he didn't.

"Davis," she said, tucking her hair behind her ear.

"Davis!" June yelled.

"Did you come to eat dessert with us?" Zach asked. "Mama said we can have another deep-fried Twinkie before we go home."

"Wow, another one? Aren't you a lucky duck?" Davis smiled.

"Hello, darling," Rita greeted him with a friendly smile.

He gave her a nod. "Ma'am. Howard."

Howard Hoffman gave him a fist bump.

"You're welcome to join us," Rita offered.

"Actually, I was hoping I could barrow Kelsey for a second." He rubbed at the back of his neck.

"Um..." Kelsey's gaze flicked from him to her mom and then her kids.

"You know," Rita interrupted, "I have a couple tickets left for the Ferris wheel if you two want to go. Howard and I can keep an eye on the kids."

"Oh, I don't know, Mama."

"Don't you worry, love bug." She leaned in close and whispered but loud enough for Davis to hear. "I haven't had a drink in nearly three days."

"You haven't?"

"Besides, Howard is here."

Chewing her lower lip, Kelsey hesitated.

"You two kids go. Have a good time. Text me when you're finished so you can find us," Rita insisted.

"Okay, fine. Thank you." Kelsey took her time telling the kid's goodbye.

"Thanks, Miss Sanders," Davis said.

Rita smiled up at him. "Darlin', don't thank me yet. That one makes up her own mind. I didn't raise no doormat."

He nodded. He was well aware of Kelsey's tenaciousness. In fact, it was something he'd grown to respect about her. Maybe even love about her.

As they strolled down Main Street, so much space between them an entire football team could fit, Davis stuffed his hands in his pockets. It felt like the eyes of everyone they passed were trained on them. This was exactly what he didn't want. The entire town knowing his business. What would make it in the headlines? What would his producer say?

The lights from the Ferris wheel blared in the distance, feeling like a beacon. Like, if they reached it, they'd be okay. But it was silly. He knew they wouldn't be okay. Not until they talked. And maybe not even then.

The fear of knowing the truth caused his steps to slow, and panic to surge in his chest. What if she confessed to regretting their night together? Or worse, told him they couldn't be friends anymore? He wouldn't be able to handle that.

When it was their turn on the Ferris wheel, they slid onto the seat and pulled the latch closed. With their shoulders grazing, the heat between them spiked, and Davis finally glanced at her. He found her peering up at him, her eyes darkening like midnight causing flashes of memories from the night before to assault him. The way her legs clung to his waist with relentless release. How her fingernails dug into his back and her moans echoed into the night.

CHAPTER 23

Kelsey

Would it be appropriate to jump his bones on the Ferris wheel? Because as he sat next to her, the warmth of his thigh pressed against hers, the way he looked at her like she was...everything—she wanted to tear off his clothes. She needed his lips on hers. She yearned to feel his skin against hers. She ached to have another night with him again.

The heck with appropriate.

"Davis, I—"

"I think we need to talk," he interrupted.

She glanced away, the suggestion they get it on taking a backseat, because she knew they needed to have a conversation. They needed to clear the air. Clear the rumors circulating town. But she wasn't ready.

They were currently on display for the entire town to watch.

As she glanced at the lit-up street below them, she noticed people amongst the crowd gawking at them. And was that a video camera? Was her face going to end up on some tabloid gossip site? Their rendezvous made into some horrendous TikTok gone viral?

She turned into him, trying to block out the Looky-Lou's, and focus on only them.

"Last night..." Davis rubbed at the back of his neck, not looking at her.

"It was fun," she provided for him.

He flashed a look at her.

"To be honest, I haven't had that much fun in I can't even remember how long. It was just what I needed to take my mind off everything. A few drinks, dancing..." her voice trailed, she'd let her mind continue further.

"Right, yeah," he agreed, attention fixated on his hands fidgeting in his lap.

Those hands.

So big. So capable. So talented.

She knew of course, they held the capacity for building beautiful things. But she'd been completely taken by surprise with the power they held when it came to plea-suring a woman. And boy could they ever. She squeezed her thighs together, constraining the craving building between them.

"And you and I?" he blurted.

"You and I, what?" She played dumb.

For how long she could do it, she wasn't sure. But really, she wasn't even sure why anymore. Did it matter what the dumb people in this town thought? Was she going to let Pineridge dictate her love life for her?

Months ago, she didn't think she'd have a love life ever again. So instead of beating around the bush, she should be grabbing this thing by the horns with both hands and announcing victory. She'd skipped over the steps of grief and moved right the heck on.

"And the rumors going around town..." Davis began, and let his words trail off.

And so she finally decided to put him out of his misery. If it even was misery. Because maybe the real reason wasn't being afraid of what people would think of her, maybe the real reason was that Davis didn't actually want her.

Maybe he only wanted one night.

"Right. The dumb rumors." She rolled her eyes. "I don't even know how those began."

"I guess they're partly my fault." He scratched at his chin.

She narrowed her eyes at him.

"After I left O'Henry's this morning—"

"You mean, after you left me. Alone. After we'd spent the night together," she interrupted.

He sighed and his eyes went downcast. "Right. After I left you this morning, I was in my head. But then I told myself to go back in there and have the conversation, no matter how tough it might be. I didn't want you to think I was dipping, so I went to The Daily Grind to pick us up coffee. But when the barista wrote your name on one of the cups and then Garrett's on the other, I panicked." He hunched his shoulders.

"And you didn't bother correcting her."

"I figured if the barista found it so easy to believe that you and Garrett hooked up, maybe I should take it as my sign to stick to my original plan."

She gasped and punched her fist into his arm. "I can't believe you."

"I'm sorry."

"Yeah? For which part? Making me wake up alone? Or letting these rumors about Garrett and I circle around town? Which, Garret by the way? Ewww." She punched him again.

Turning into her, he clutched her hand in his grip and said, "I'm sorry for all of it."

She ducked her chin to her chest and tucked her hair behind her ear. "What are you so afraid of?"

"You...regretting...me."

Her eyes flew up to meet his and her throat thickened.

"You wanting to end our friendship."

She shook her head. "Never. Davis, you're my best friend. Nothing will ever change that."

He caressed the top of her hand, and it sent a shiver dancing up her spine. "Not even last night?"

"Especially not last night. I have no regrets."

"Good." He pushed her hair behind her ear while gazing in her eyes.

The pull between them intensified and all she wanted to do was kiss him. But being out in the open for the public to witness gave her pause.

"What are we going to do about the rumors?"

"Screw the rumors," he said blatantly. "All I care about is us. What are we going to do about us?"

She knew exactly what she wanted to do. Again and again.

She swallowed. "What do you want to do?"

As he placed a hand on her thigh, prompting a sizzle with his touch, he tipped his face closer to hers. "I know what I want to do." His voice was rough and scratchy, reaching low in her belly. "The question is, how much do you care about the audience below us?"

"Have you met me?" she asked, daring him to cross that imaginary friendship line out in public for the entire Pineridge mob to see. Once there were witnesses, they'd never be able to go back to how things were before.

Davis set a hand on her cheek, a thumb grazing her jawline, while his eyes continued to hold hers without breaking away. He leaned closer still until she could feel his breath against her lips. When he finally kissed her, his mouth moved over hers with urgency. It demanded her mouth to open, welcoming his tongue inside to tangle with her own.

She melted into the kiss, melted into him, her hand going to the nape of his neck like it had a mind of its own. As he gripped her hip, she felt needy and desperate to touch every inch of him. One kiss was all it took to steal her intelligence and forget that they weren't alone.

When he withdrew from the kiss, Davis whispered, "Do you think that little show just made the rumors better or worse?"

"I don't know," she answered, a little out of breath. "I don't care."

"Me neither, but what are we gonna do about us?" he asked.

"Honestly? Because I was thinking that later we could pick up where we just left off. Tonight. My place or yours?"

He grinned. "I'm serious. What happened between us... last night...we've never done that before. It's gonna change things."

"Yeah, it will." She nodded along. "It better."

His brows pinched together, and he tilted his head, not following along with her. She was about to put her heart out on the line. As much as she didn't want to admit it, she wanted more out of this friendship. Now that she'd had a taste of how things could be, she craved it.

"You're my best friend, Davis. But now, we could be so much more."

"Is that what you want? I mean, are you even ready for that?"

"Why? Is it not what you want?"

"Of course I want it. You know me. You know I don't sleep around with just anybody. It means something to me. You mean more to me than that."

The Ferris wheel jerked to a stop, and the seats began emptying one by one. It was nearly their turn to get off.

"So what are we saying? Are we actually giving this thing a go? A real chance?" She peered up at him.

"I think we are."

"Good." A dip in her belly caused her to lower her voice. "Because I need something from you that would be super inappropriate to ask for if you hadn't wanted to make a go at this."

Their seat reached the bottom and the bar across their lap unlatched. They stepped off and weaved through the spectators. She leaned into him whispering, "A lot of somethings."

"Sure, anything. What is it?"

She took his hand, yanking him away from the crowd and pushed up to her toes. "I need those talented hands on every square inch of my body," she whispered.

He choked.

She snorted a laugh.

"After all these years, how can you still surprise me?" He pressed his forehead against hers and held his eye contact steady.

Kelsey traced a fingertip along his chiseled jawline. "Oh, just you wait. You have no idea all the ways I can surprise you, Davis Vance." Anticipation wriggled through her just thinking about the next chance she and Davis could be alone.

Kelsey's rendezvous with Davis was interrupted. It was her fault for being optimistic. She should've expected the intrusion, nothing ever went as planned in her life. Especially now that she was a single mother, part bar owner, and the daughter of the town's biggest drunk.

But as the saying goes, the show must go on. She couldn't dwell on the ruined plans. Not when she had an important meeting.

After dropping her kids off at the O'Henry's, Kelsey drove her minivan in the direction of the bank. As the rain pelted the windshield and the wipers swished, she cranked the radio up. The sound of Khalid's voice saturated the inside of the minivan and sent her skin buzzing.

It was difficult to not think of Davis. But at the same time, it was difficult *to* think of him. There was so much riding on this appointment at the bank today. If she got approved for a loan, maybe then she could think of her future. And what it might look like to have Davis in it.

But if the appointment didn't go in her favor, how could she think of her future with any positivity? O'Henry's Bar and Grill wasn't only a part of Ricky, it was a part of *her*. Who would she be without it? She didn't know and she didn't want to find out.

Before stepping inside the bank, Kelsey shook the rain from her umbrella and closed it. As she gazed around inside the small branch, seeing faces she recognized, people she knew, her stomach sank. Maybe she should've drove into Denver. Gone into a bigger bank, one where Benny Benson didn't work, the guy who used to be known as bad-breath-Benny. There was too much history with these folks.

But maybe that would work in her favor. Maybe they'd sympathize with her and grant her the loan, no questions asked, no financial documentation.

Yeah, right.

She approached the information desk where a gal Kelsey had known since grade school sat. When Sue-Ellen spotted her, she instantly rearranged her expression into an over exaggerated sad face.

"Oh, sweetie, how are you?" Sue-Ellen asked.

Kelsey was over the sympathy. She wanted everyone to go back to treating her normally. Not as if she were the most pathetic person in town.

"Fine, thanks. I have a meeting with Benny at noon."

"Let me go see if he's ready for you." Sue-Ellen rose but leaned in close, her long, golden locks draping. "And I just have to say, you're so brave being out and about. Look at you go."

Kelsey lifted her brows. "And what exactly are you referring to?"

"You know?" she whispered, glancing over her shoulders. "After Garrett slept with you and then insisted it wasn't him that it was actually Davis." She shook her head solemnly.

"That's not exactly fact, Sue-Ellen, so maybe you should stop spreading rumors and just do your job."

Sue-Ellen straightened, crossing her arms, and narrowing her eyes. "Maybe you should set the rumors straight then."

And that was it. Kelsey was done. It wasn't in her nature to take crap from anyone. She stood abruptly. "It's not my job to educate you on adult relationships, Sue-Ellen. Why don't you do everyone a favor and mind your own business." She spun around and rushed down the short hallway in search of Benny's office.

When she found him, it wasn't so much an office but a personal space with cubicle walls with glass windows in the top of them, not even a door. However, his name was engraved on a metal plate situated on top of his desk. It read: Benjamin Benson. The professionalism caused a giggle to work its way through her. She couldn't help it. To her, he would always be bad-breath-Benny.

"Kelsey." Benny stood, adjusting his tie at the knot, a phone pressed to his ear.

She had to admit, he'd grown into a decent looking guy.

Close shaven and hair kept short, if you liked that sort of squeaky-clean look. She did not. She preferred her men scruffy, hairy, a little bit messy and unkempt, with a hint of naughtiness below the surface itching to break free.

She forced a smile. "Hey, Benny. I have an appointment at noon."

He blinked at her before speaking into the phone. "Um, yeah, I'm gonna have to call you back." He set the phone down as he took a seat hesitantly.

"Sorry for barging in but Sue-Ellen is an incompetent ass—*assistant*," she corrected at the look of his reluctance.

"It's fine. I was expecting you." He smoothed his tie against his chest. "How have you been?"

She sat down in the worn chair across from him. "Good. And you?"

She wasn't in the mood for pleasantries. He could very well be holding in the knowledge of her future. Of her life.

"I can't complain. Good job. Good health."

She nodded along while pressing her thumbnail into the palm of her opposite hand.

"But you're not here to talk about me. Let's talk about you." He smiled and then moved a folder in front of him, opening it. "It looks like you provided all the required documentations to process the loan request."

She scooted to the edge of the seat.

"And after some serious research and analyzing, I'm sorry to say the bank didn't find enough promise in O'Henry's Bar and Grill to invest."

His words blared loud in her brain, set on repeat; *didn't find enough promise.*

"There must be some mistake. Maybe I filled out the paperwork wrong. If you could just look at it again," her words rushed out.

"You filled everything out correctly. Believe me, I checked and rechecked. And I crunched the numbers myself. I'm sorry." He shut the folder, the sound of it amplified in her ears like a door slamming shut.

"Please, Benny," she said, tears aching in her throat. She felt desperate. "Check again. Ask again. Do something. O'Henry's is the busiest restaurant in town. My sales projections—maybe I did the figuring wrong. Can you look at them again?"

He shook his head solemnly. "I had a feeling you might say that, so I did some digging myself." He pressed his elbows against the desk's surface, resting his chin on his clasped hands. "The overhead to sales ratio just doesn't match."

The realization sunk in slowly. Almost like she was lacking oxygen, unable to catch a breath. She was going to lose everything. Her eyes watered and she considered just breaking down right there in Benny's fake office.

"I'm sorry. I wish there was something I could do. I mean, maybe someone could loan you the money? Your in-laws?"

"No," the word came out garbled but stern. They'd already told her they couldn't afford it.

"What about your mom?"

Kelsey's brows pinched together, and her chest tightened. "What about her?"

He shrugged. "Maybe nothing. But maybe something. I thought you might be stubborn enough to not take no for an answer, so I looked into her business as well." He hunkered down, lowering his voice. "We handle your mom's accounts too. And while her character may be questionable at times, she's never missed a payment. The Sweet Cakes Bakery is a thriving business. If she were to move some things around, she might have enough equity in the business to pay off your debt at O'Henry's."

Despite all her mama's mistakes, she had somehow

managed to hold onto a successful business. Kelsey never expected that her mama would come through for her now. Except that she couldn't risk it. Besides Kelsey and the kids, the bakery was the only thing keeping her mama going. To encourage her to get sober.

"No, I can't," Kelsey finally said. "We have to find another way."

Benny blew out a breath, emitting a stale stench and Kelsey held her own breath. He shook his head. "There isn't another way."

"Benny, I can't lose O'Henry's. I just can't."

She couldn't. But as she sat there in the worn chair in Benny's fake office, feeling helpless, the reality of her situation rested heavy on her shoulders. Ricky had left her without options. Hopelessness ached deep in her chest, her heart sinking lower, and the stubbornness that usually portrayed itself in strength dissipated.

In a way, she felt as if she were back in that place. In the hospital after Ricky's accident. When the doctors told her they'd done all they could to save her husband. She'd still lost him.

Again, the unfairness was raw, and the helplessness was massive. She felt paralyzed. She was going to lose everything.

CHAPTER 24
Davis

Sex sells.

His producer wasn't wrong. And Davis wasn't an idiot. He knew that statement to be true. There was a reason why Victoria's Secret was a multibillion-dollar company. Though he'd maintained his dignity by not unbuttoning his t-shirt and letting the chest hair fly, word had gotten around about his recent so-called promiscuous behavior.

While at first, the rumors circulating had been of Garrett sleeping with Kelsey, those had since been put to bed and the new one that had risen was the truth; he had slept with Kelsey. The news that Davis had been a brooding hero all along, a secret "hot guy", as the tabloids were referencing him, had somehow increased ratings on the last episode of Renovation Dudes that had aired.

Having the attention on him was not something Davis appreciated. But it seemed to bother Garrett, and that kind of made Davis enjoy it even more. Garrett thrived on attention and now that he wasn't getting it, he'd been on edge. Since they'd began preparation on the last episode of the year, the Christmas one, Garrett had been pouting.

The Christmas episode was a kitchen and nook remodel. They had already filmed the demolition, laying down the engineered hardwood floors and replacing the cabinets. Today, they would film him and Garrett installing the countertops and the oversized farmhouse sink.

While Garrett had been grumpy all day, Davis had tried to remain focused. He was hoping they'd get the install done quickly and that filming went smoothly so he could see Kelsey afterwards. It had been four days since their Halloween hookup and each day since, something had interrupted them from spending any time together.

He'd been thinking of nothing other than getting her alone once again. This time, he'd take his time. He'd explore, savor, absorb every inch of her.

Kelsey had been down since her meeting at the bank. Them turning down her request to invest in O'Henry's had sent her spiraling. He wanted to help, wave his own offer in her face, but he didn't want to be *that* guy.

Kelsey didn't want a knight in shining armor. But she did want a partner. That was something he could be. Both in life and in business. If she'd just let him. He needed to wait for the right moment to present it to her. If he could just get her alone, maybe he could show her this could be the answer for both.

Davis had already told Garrett about his offer to buy O'Henry's Bar and Grill and his brother had been giving him the cold shoulder ever since. Maybe he should've waited to tell him because if Kelsey turned down his offer, there wouldn't have been a point in telling Garrett. And he wouldn't be acting like a giant toddler right now, only talking to him when it came to the show.

The whole thing was stupid anyway, Davis knew Kelsey

and he knew she would say no. But at the same time, he also knew she was running out of options. And time.

What would she do? Accept the offer from the out-of-town investor? Because at least if she accepted his offer, he was local. He wouldn't be interested in changing things or making decisions without her. They'd be a team.

Today, there were too many cameras pointed in their direction and lights surrounding the twins while they worked. Because no matter what the show's producer or Garrett tried to tell him, to Davis, this was still work. They had been hired to do a job. It was really the only thing keeping him going. That, and of course the signed contract.

Some days he could forget that he and Garrett had a popular home improvement show on HGTV. On the non-filming days, they could work in silence for hours. They'd put on music and occasionally sing along. Garrett was laidback, not trying to impress the viewers. Those were the best days.

But as the lights blared, ricocheting against the glossy quartz countertop, and heating his body temperature a thousand degrees, it made it difficult to concentrate. Not to mention there was an overabundance of people there than normal. He despised shooting days.

If Garrett flashed his smolder look for the camera one more time, Davis would poke his own eyes out so he wouldn't have to witness it any longer.

"Today is an exciting day," Garrett was saying to the camera, "Davis and I are on the last step before staging and revealing the renovation to the Larson's. I don't know about you, Davis," he glanced in his direction momentarily before facing the camera again, "but reveal day is my favorite day." Big smolder into the other camera, a different angle. Or according to Garrett, his best angle.

"Definitely mine too. I can't wait to see the reaction on the

Larson's faces. But first, you guys gotta go and let Garrett and I get back to work." Davis approached the camera directly in front of him with his palm held up until he covered it completely. He inwardly groaned. Did he mention how much he hated shooting days?

"Whoa, whoa, okay, but don't go anywhere just yet. Because today Davis and I are installing the quartz countertops and then mounting the sink." Garrett said.

Davis shuffled toward the garage door, waving a hand over his shoulder as he went. "Fine, why don't you come along with us. But you'd better hurry. The family is expected home in six hours and we're running out of time." Davis rolled his eyes.

"Cut!" The producer shouted and everyone froze awaiting the next direction. "Let's run that again. And Davis, maybe try not rolling your eyes in front of the camera."

"Sorry," he grumbled out the apology. Because he wasn't sorry. This script was awful. Did viewers actually believe reality TV was real and unscripted? If they did, they were idiots.

"Action," the producer called.

Davis returned to his position and ran his line again, this time being sure to restrain his eye roll until after he'd turned around and pushed into the garage. The countertop slabs had all been premeasured and precut and waited in the garage, ready for a quick install, partially while being filmed.

Cooper had been hiding out, resting on his dog bed in the corner. Davis gave him a quick pat to the head, mostly because it was in the script but also because having Cooper on set with him kept this whole thing manageable. Davis kept his head low while taking an end of one of the countertop slabs and Garrett continued with his lines.

"Now, the Larson's chose a quartz countertop. And I have to say, I think that's a solid choice. Quartz is not only nonporous, but it's solid, making it one of the most durable counter-tops, isn't that right?"

"That's right, Garrett. So, let's get to it, shall we?" He gestured his chin toward Garrett.

Cooper barked.

"Cut!" The producer called out.

"Sorry," Davis apologized for Cooper, but he chuckled to himself. Clearly Coop didn't want to be there anymore than he did.

RITA'S CAR WAS PARKED IN KELSEY'S DRIVEWAY. WORST case scenario, she was passed out on Kelsey's sofa again and he'd shown up in time to drive her home. Best case, Rita was passed out on her sofa again and he'd still get his moment alone with Kelsey. Davis parked his truck on the street in front of Kelsey's house. She wasn't expecting him, but he needed to see her. She was down. He hadn't even had to talk to her to know. He could sense it in their texts.

Even if she just needed a friend and just wanted to talk, he had to be there for her. Like he always had been. Their relationship shifting into new territory wouldn't change the fact that they were still best friends.

He knocked on the door softly. It was late and if the kids were sleeping, he couldn't risk waking them. When the door creaked open, and Rita stood there the hope died in his chest.

"Oh, hey, Miss Sanders." He pushed a hand through his unruly hair.

She smiled at him. "Davis, hello. Come on in." She stepped aside so he could pass.

He ducked inside, finding the house quiet and still, glowing by a lamp in the corner of the living room. It was warm and inviting and the scent of spices streamed from the kitchen.

"I'm glad you're here. God knows my love bug could use a boost."

"She's still pretty down, huh?" He peered wistfully up the stairs where the bedrooms were.

Rita nodded before turning and walking into the living room. "I wish she'd just let me help her. But you know Kelsey. It's gotta be her way."

"Yeah," he muttered, following her.

Rita wrapped a scarf around her neck and began dressing in her coat. "Listen, I got the kiddos down for the night but, I'm gonna scoot."

"Is Kelsey still up?"

"She might be. I told her a nice bath might do her some good."

If she was already sleeping, he wouldn't be able to present his offer to her. But he could crawl into bed with her like he'd done in the past when she was sad after Isabella had left for college. They'd lay in bed for an entire day sometimes watching comedies and only crawling out to go to the bathroom and get more food. Maybe this time would be different. Maybe he could wrap her in his arms and hold her all night.

Taking a hold of his arm, Rita leaned in and pressed a kiss to Davis's cheek. "Night, sweetie. You take good care of my girl." She winked at him.

There was a lot conveyed in that wink. An insinuation he recognized. He felt a flutter in his chest and along with it, heat crept up his neck.

Oh, he could think of many ways to take care of Kelsey. His imagination went wild while his creativity kicked into gear. And along with it, his hankering for her.

After Rita had slipped out the door, he flipped the lock and tiptoed up the stairs, side stepping the toys strewn around. He found her bedroom door cracked open, a nightstand lamp illuminating the space. But her bed was empty, still perfectly made from the morning.

The bathroom door was closed, and the light peered from underneath. He stepped to the door and rapped on it quietly and waited.

"I'm almost done, Mama. It's okay for you to just go on home," Kelsey hollered through the door.

Davis cleared his throat. "Uh...it's Davis."

There was a lengthy pause, followed by the sound of water splashing.

"Davis?"

"Uh...yeah. Your mom let me in."

Silence.

"Do you want me to go?"

"No."

No? Well what was he supposed to do?

"Did you want me to just wait downstairs...or?"

Or what? He wasn't implying...or maybe he was.

"Or you could come in."

He twisted the knob, his heart hammering in his chest. But when he opened the door, for some reason even though he knew what to expect, he was still surprised by the sight of Kelsey in the bathtub.

"Sorry, for just coming by..."

She gave him a half smile. "I'm glad you did."

"You doing okay?"

"Not really." She pursed her lips.

"Anything I can do to help?"

"You could get your butt into this tub."

Was she for real? Because if she was, he could probably

have his clothes stripped off in 2.5 seconds. But he didn't want to come across as presumptuous.

"You sure?"

"Are you kidding? Of course I'm sure. Get in."

He undid his belt, unzipped his jeans, and shimmied out of them. As he did, he glanced up, catching her watching him. She didn't look away which turned him on even more. When he gathered his t-shirt at the hem and yanked it over his head, she bit her lip, her eyes dark.

When he tugged his boxer briefs off his hips, stepping out of them, his chest filled with anticipation. He climbed into the tub and the hot water stung his feet. As he sat down across from her, the bubbles surrounded them both.

A sweet smile pulled at her lips. "I'm glad you came."

"I was beginning to wonder if we were ever gonna get a moment alone together again or if that one time was a fluke." He scratched at his chin. "Not that I'm assuming...that tonight...we...you know?"

She snorted a laugh. "We better," she stated so matter of factly.

Stretching his long legs out, he wrapped them around the outsides of her body. When he leaned in closer and reached his arms around her, she released a long sigh. The feel of her wet, smooth skin as his hands ran down her back set fire through his veins.

"I missed you," he whispered.

"You missed me or..." she teased.

"You. Definitely you. But...I've been anticipating this. Or nearly this. This, right here, right now, is better than I could've imagined."

"Show me," she encouraged.

Was he hearing her correctly? He felt like he was in a dream. Or like he was watching this happen to someone else.

Because it couldn't be reality for him to be this lucky. To be in a bath with Kelsey. She was too good for him. Too beautiful. And yet she wanted *him*.

He took her face in his hand and pressed a soft kiss to her lips. Or at least he intended it to be soft. But when she parted her lips for him, he couldn't resist. As he flicked his tongue inside and intertwined it vigorously with hers, heat pooled in his groin.

She clasped her legs around his waist, pressing her entire front against his. His head went dizzy, and he wanted to take her then and now. She thrust her hips into him, signaling she was wanting this as much as him.

But somewhere in the back of his mind, he remembered he was going to take things slow this time. He was going to take his time and memorize everything about her body. Each dip and curve, and every freckle.

He pulled away from their kisses that made his head spin, and made him delirious, and buried his face into her neck. She giggled and shoved him away. But then pulled him back to her, pushing her fingers through his hair and yanking his head down to her breasts.

It was the perfect opportunity, an invitation, a request to pay attention to the beauty before him. He swept his tongue across her skin, and she gasped. Arousing her felt like an honor. She ran her fingers through his hair and breathed harder, faster. And then he lifted his chin, returning his mouth to hers.

Davis slipped an eager hand in between her legs, running his palm up and down the inside of her thighs. Her moans gave him the urgency to continue. It was agonizing for him as well. Taking things slow with her was harder than he imagined it would be.

With each movement, she arched into him impatiently. She skimmed her tongue over his ear and slid a hand down his chest. He shuddered at her touch, both wanting and needing her to never stop.

At last, he gripped her backside, and she helped guide him. She clutched his shoulders and gasped. She moved with him, and together they rode it out. This yearning, this lust, this hunger. He simultaneously wished it would never end and at the same time, anticipated the end. He wanted her to come undone in his arms, in the light, to see the look in her eyes, the way she appeared when she lost all control at his touch.

"Woman, you're driving me wild. Are you about ready to finish?"

"Are *you* ready?" she challenged back, a teasing smile on her lips.

He grinned. "Kels, I've been ready."

She clung to him tighter, her chest pressed against him, and he held back. But he didn't have to wait long. Her breathing quickened, and she gasped, until finally, she fell completely apart, shattered, in the best and most unbelievable way possible. And right before his eyes. He reveled in it, soaking up every second of it.

And as a lazy smile spread across her lips, he wanted to do it again. And again.

So they did.

Finally in her bed, they cuddled in close underneath the warmth of the covers, her wrapped in his arms, her head against his chest. He twirled circles with his fingertip across the bare skin of her arm. Her breathing slowed and he inhaled her scent. Clean from the bath but also his scent on her. The thought only made him want her all over again. It made him feel clingy and needy.

Davis had to push away the worry that while he was in this relationship one hundred percent, she might not be. He was the first person she'd slept with since Ricky. What if he was the in-between guy? The one before the next serious relationship? Imagining her with someone else caused his skin to heat. He had to know if she was all in or not. Before he drove himself insane with fear.

Awakening to the still pitch blackness of the night, Kelsey nudged him until his eyes opened fully. It was not his idea of a good morning. But then he caught the panic on her expression in the slice of light from the moon shining into the room.

"What's wrong?" He sat up, scrubbing a hand over his face.

"You need to go." She scurried off the bed, rushing around.

"Now?" He checked the time on his phone that laid on the nightstand. "But it's barely five in the morning."

She tossed his clothes at him. "I know. I'm sorry. But the baby will be up soon which means the other two will be soon to follow. You shouldn't be here when they get up."

"Oh, right." If she'd started with that, maybe he wouldn't have been so concerned she was filled with regret after their night together.

"Hurry," she whispered.

He slid out of the bed, half asleep and stepped into his cold jeans, a shiver jolting through him.

She flipped on the nightstand lamp, exposing her still naked body. As she raced toward the closet, he got the perfect view of her bare backside.

Okay, he was wide awake now.

As he yanked his t-shirt over his head and stuffed his arms into his jacket, he checked her out while she stepped into a pair of shorts and pulled on a sweatshirt.

She spun around to face him.

"Ready?"

"Sorry, I was busy enjoying the view," he teased.

A smile tugged at the corner of her mouth as she dipped her chin. "There's no time for gawking. You have to get out. Now." She went to him and shoved him in the back, steering him in the direction of the bedroom door.

He tiptoed down the stairs in his stocking feet, snatching his boots off the floor. She didn't wait for him to put them on, she opened the front door and shoved him out. The crisp early morning fall air stung his skin.

But she wouldn't get rid of him that easily. He whirled around, dropping the boots to the dewy porch. He grabbed her backside, one delicious cheek fitting perfectly in each palm, and lifted her up. She wrapped her legs around him and he brought his mouth to hers, giving her a kiss he was hoping she wouldn't forget anytime soon.

He returned her to her feet, pressing one more kiss to her lips before picking up his boots and crunching through the leaves toward his truck, an extra bounce to his step.

CHAPTER 25
Kelsey

Waking up next to the hard, warm body hadn't been on Kelsey's agenda today, but it sure wasn't a terrible way to start the day. Yet imagining the shock on her kid's faces meant she couldn't enjoy the moment for long. When she first got a glimpse of his firm pec so close to her cheek she dared to move, worried if she did, she'd wake up from this dream. Because her and Davis spending the night together surely had to be a dream.

She and Davis were best friends. They didn't sleep together. And they definitely didn't take baths together. Nope. She was sure she'd dreamt the entire affair.

Except it hadn't been a dream.

The high from her night spent with him would have to take her through the day. She had to go meet her mama at Sweet Cakes, and the encounter had her feeling stressed out.

Her mama had sent her a text that morning asking her to stop by the bakery to discuss something urgent. Kelsey had to bribe the kids with treats at the bakery to get them to hustle.

They paraded into Sweet Cakes, dressed and teeth and hair brushed, but looking not too happy. There had been at least two feuds on the drive over and Kelsey's house was only a few minutes from the bakery. She didn't have the patience for it and part of her was a bit thrilled they were extra ornery today since she'd be dropping them off with the O'Henry's soon.

But the thrill was short lived when she saw her mama's expression and instantly apprehension stirred in her gut.

"I want a cookie," June whined.

"No, cake. A cake pop," Zach demanded.

Charlotte fussed and wiggled to break free from Kelsey's arms.

"How about June gets a cookie and Zach gets a cake pop? Everyone wins."

"Yes!" June jumped.

"Tell your gran what you want and I'll put Charlotte in a high chair at the big table in the corner that faces the TV."

Her mama winked at Kelsey before tending to the children. "Hi, loves, you come in the back with Gran and pick out what you want."

Kelsey fastened Charlotte into a highchair while the baby resisted, working up a fit that would be a doozy. Quickly, Kelsey flipped the TV on and the noise and moving images on the screen was enough to distract Charlotte long enough for Kelsey to set an applesauce pouch in front of her. Hopefully it would buy her some time before her mama came to the rescue with cookies.

Kelsey checked her phone in her rare spare moment of downtime. She found a few new texts from Isabella and Davis. A tingle zipped through her as a memory from that morning flickered through her mind.

Hard pecs, solid biceps, and firm abs. Tempting and so

close, like a front row seat to a concert. Except they were close enough to touch.

"All right, here we are," Mama said in singsong with Kelsey's two littles following behind her like they were baby ducklings.

Her mama set a plate of mini cookies in the center of the table. Both Zach and June had a cake pop in their hands. It would appear that not only were the kids going to the O'Henry's a bit fussy, but they were also going sugared up. The only thing working in their favor, the kids would most likely crash in about two hours and take a good nap for them.

"You three enjoy your treats and behave while your mama and Gran have a chat," Kelsey said as she backed away from the table hesitantly.

She and her mama slipped behind the display case where her mama leaned a hip into the counter.

"So? What is it?" Kelsey hopped onto the counter.

Her mama chewed on her lip, tugging the sleeves of her sweater over her fingers, and fidgeting with it.

"Mama? You better spill it right now before I start thinking the worst."

"There's two things."

Kelsey exhaled. Okay, two things. Maybe if they were two small things, that would be okay. If they were two big things, someone better be ready to scrape her demise off the floor and put her back together because honestly, she didn't think she was strong enough to handle anything else.

"Okay maybe it's more like three things," her mama admitted.

"Mama," she spoke firmly.

"I don't think it's a big secret that Howard...err...Mr. Hoffman and I have been spending a lot of time together lately.

And...well...the two of us have decided to make a real go at this."

Shock overtook Kelsey's ability to form words. Howard Hoffman and her mama were dating? Since when? Sure, she'd been aware of his presence more often as of late and he'd been helping her out a lot lately. Like the times he had come to her rescue the past month. But the thought of the two of them dating had her feeling uneasy.

"C'mon, love bug, say something," her mama coaxed.

Kelsey's eyes burned. "I don't know what to say."

"For starters, you could say you're happy for me. I haven't felt this way about a man in, well, maybe never."

Unable to help herself, Kelsey's eyes widened, disbelief settling in. "You expect me to believe that?"

Crossing her arms, her mama's eyes flittered away. "Yes. I do. And I was hoping you'd be happy for me."

"I guess it's just hard for me to process. You've dated...actually no, you've hooked up with more men than anyone I know. Howard is a nice man. Please don't do this to him."

"Don't do what? Date him?"

"Sleep with him and then dump him like he's yesterday's garbage."

Her jaw set. "I wouldn't do that."

"Really? Because I've seen you do it before. Several times." Kelsey hopped off the counter.

"This is different."

She looked at her mama, really looked at her. While her fingers fidgeted inside the sweater sleeves, her face revealed a genuineness Kelsey didn't see often.

"Are you serious? You really like him?"

"Oh, I don't know if *like* is the right word." She dipped her chin. "I might love him."

The release of her mama's words hit Kelsey in the chest and bloomed. "Love?"

Her mama glanced up revealing glossy eyes. She nodded, a smile forming on her lips.

"Wow. This is big."

"It really is. I wanted to tell you before it got too serious. But, love bug, I think it's too late because we're already discussing the future."

"The future?"

"I told you, we're both pretty smitten. There's just one problem," her mama admitted.

"What's that?"

"Before we can even plan a future together, I need to get my act together. I need to get sober. Once and for all. So, Howard has convinced me to go to rehab." She smiled wide.

Rehab? Kelsey had been hoping, praying, begging her mama for years to get help for her addiction. Now, some guy comes along, and she decides to do it for *him*? Don't get her wrong, she desperately wanted her mama to get sober. But she needed to do it for the right reasons. If she and Howard broke up, wouldn't it send her into a relapse?

"Aren't you gonna say something?" her mama asked.

"Are you going to rehab because you think you need it or because Howard thinks you need it?"

"I don't understand. I tell you I'm going to rehab, something you've been harassing me about since you were a kid, and you're gonna question my motives?"

"Yeah, that's right. Because you need to do it for you. Not for some man."

"He's not just *some* man, I told you that."

"Mama, I've begged you to go. For years. And you wouldn't. I guess I'm just having a hard time with the fact that I wasn't enough of a reason to go."

Her mama reached for her, but Kelsey took a shaky step backward. "Oh, love bug. You know that's not true. I just wasn't ready. My past...your daddy..."

"I just find it ironic is all," Kelsey interrupted. Her heart thumped hard against her rib cage. She felt desperate to get away. "Look, thanks for the treats for the kids, but I gotta get going."

Rushing out from behind the counter, Kelsey headed toward the table her kids were seated at.

"Please don't leave yet. There's more I'd like to discuss." Her mama followed her.

Kelsey whipped around to face her, rubbing her temples with her fingertips. "Mama, I'm happy you want to get help. And...I guess it doesn't matter the reason. I just want you to get better."

"Thank you."

"But as much as I'd like to take a trip down memory lane with you, I can't right now. My plate is full."

"That was part of what I wanted to discuss."

Kelsey's brows pinched together.

"Since I'll be checking into a rehab facility in Denver, I'm going to need someone to run this place while I'm gone."

"What about Cheryl?"

"You know I love Cheryl, she's a fantastic assistant. But she's not management material. Not like you are."

The compliment warmed and expanded in Kelsey's chest. But hadn't she just told her mama her plate was too full right now? She was currently fighting for her restaurant. Fighting for her children's legacy. Fighting for her job.

"I appreciate it, Mama, but I just don't have the time."

"I was thinking, since you won't be working at O'Henry's anymore, maybe you'd consider managing the bakery."

"You actually think I'm going to lose the bar?"

"I mean, you told me yourself you can't afford to recover from the relapse in payments."

"But I'm still trying. I haven't given up. Even if everyone else has." Kelsey unlatched Charlotte from her highchair. "C'mon, kids, clean up your mess. We need to go."

"But I haven't eaten my cookie yet," Zach whined.

"Take it with you," Kelsey muttered.

"Hey, if you've come up with a way to save it, by all means, I'm for it. You know I'll support you. I was just trying to help," her mama said.

Kelsey propped Charlotte on her hip and stared at her mama through glossy eyes. "You want to help? Why not offer to back me up at the restaurant? Use the investment on the bakery to put toward O'Henry's."

Her mama blinked at her, folding her lips in between her teeth.

Julia tugged at her grans hand. "Bye, Gran. Thanks for the yummy treats."

"Bye, bye, sweets. Anytime." Her mama hugged and kissed the children quickly before finally making eye contact with Kelsey who was waiting for a response. *Any* response.

She'd never even wanted to ask her mama for help. Risking the bakery was a last resort. It was the only thing her mama had going for her. But she was desperate. This was DEFCON 5. This was it.

"Mama, you know I wouldn't ask if I didn't believe in the bar."

"It's not that," her mama said, glancing at her feet. "The bakery is barely staying afloat."

An ache throbbed in her throat at the lie, at the betrayal. Kelsey knew the bakery was in good enough financial status for her mama to take on another loan to help her. And yet, she'd lied to her. Why was her mama lying?

"You know I would help if I could."

Tears stung at the corners of her eyes. She blinked, urging them not to form. Swallowing the lump of disappointment, she nodded and encouraged her children toward the door.

"Fine," she finally managed to say.

"Please say you'll at least keep an open mind about managing the bakery?" her mama said.

How could she think Kelsey would agree to helping her at the bakery while her own business was slipping through her fingers? Maybe because she'd always helped her mama. She'd always been the reliable daughter.

Maybe not anymore.

"Thanks again for the treats," Kelsey said as she and the children shuffled out the door and into the chilly fall day.

She had zero intention of managing the bakery. She didn't need to think about it. In fact, she had no intention of working at the bakery ever again. For years, Kelsey had been there, cleaning up her mama's messes. Filling in for her when she'd been too drunk to complete orders, too hung over to open the bakery, too sick to order inventory.

While Kelsey's own life was rocked to the core and she'd lost her husband, her mama couldn't even pull herself together enough to get sober to help her. Instead, she'd slipped deeper into her addiction, forcing Kelsey to juggle her time between the bar and the bakery. Not to mention she'd had to shuffle the kids back and forth between her in-laws and the bar.

That last thought had her heart aching as she pulled her van into the driveway at her in-laws. As the days passed, and she found herself nowhere closer to saving the restaurant, she couldn't help but wonder if it was a lost cause. Maybe the O'Henry's were right. Maybe letting the bar go was her best option. There would be no more shuffling the kids around. No more late nights.

But as much as Kelsey let the idea permeate in her mind, the more the pit in her stomach grew. Losing the restaurant didn't feel like an option. Even if everyone else around her thought it was her only one.

She'd find a way to prove them wrong. She had to.

CHAPTER 26

Davis

If he thought about it too long, he'd screw it up. But Davis couldn't get over the fact that Kelsey was in his bed. It was the first time she'd spent the night at his place. And he could really get used to it.

There was no better feeling than waking up next to her. If he'd known life with her could be this good, he would've asked her out years ago. Instead, after Isabella had left for college in New York, Davis knew Kelsey needed a friend. So that's what he'd been to her. He'd never regretted that decision.

Okay that was a lie.

There was one time, after they'd been friends for a few years and before Ricky entered the equation. Though he supposed Ricky had always been in the equation. In high school he'd hung out with Kelsey, Isabella, and Leo. It was surprising the two hadn't gotten together then. But Kelsey had said she and Ricky argued like crazy.

Tracing a finger up the bare skin of her arm, he pushed thoughts of the past, of Ricky to the back of his mind. He wanted to live in the present. Because the present day was like a dream. No, better than a dream. It was like heaven.

The only thing looming over his head was the offer he still hadn't presented to her. He planned on doing so. Soon. But it was a delicate subject and he'd have to do it at just the right moment. And the morning after an epic night of sex was probably not the right moment.

Kelsey's eyes fluttered open and a sleepy smile drew on her lips. He hoped it was a satisfied smile. After their night spent exploring every single inch of one another's bodies, he felt confident it was.

"Good morning," she murmured.

Unintentionally, he was instantly aroused. That's what she did to him. With a look, a smile, a single word spoken. He was crazed. He felt greedy for her.

"Morning," he growled, gripping her hip, and tugging her against him.

She snorted a laugh. "Well, someone woke up eager," she teased, setting a hand on his chest.

"Nah, just happy."

When she peered into his eyes, it sent an electrifying hunger for her. He leaned in and kissed her hard, ravenously, as he ran his hand down her back.

He broke the kiss, pressing his lips to her jawline, then her neck. She twirled her fingers through his hair.

"Are you?" she asked.

He withdrew, gazing down at her. "Am I what?"

"Happy?"

Davis's eyes took her in for a long moment, his palm sliding onto her face, stroking her jawline. He admired the slight bump in the bridge of her nose and the near invisible freckles sweeping across her cheekbones that were left over from summer. Dragging the pad of his thumb over her lower lip, he inspected the faint scar just beneath, a result of a tooth laceration after falling at a concert with him years ago.

"Deliriously," he said, a smile tugging at his lips.

Her own smile appeared, her eyes shining, and she snuggled in closer to him.

"And what about you?" He dared the question, so afraid, he realized too late, of her answer.

She'd been married to Ricky for eight years. They'd been split up in a devastatingly unfair way. Her opening up to him in the ways she had in the past few weeks had been so unexpected. The talk of her happiness now, with him, was a delicate topic he'd been too afraid to examine out loud with her.

Her fingers drew circles on his neck, twirling in his hair while she gazed at him. "Honestly, I didn't think happiness would ever exist for me again. But your friendship gave me hope that it was a possibility. Your love gave me the freedom to dream again. You did that."

"Nah," blush burned in his cheeks. "You did that. It was all you, Kels," her name rolled off his tongue easily.

"C'mon, at least take some of the credit, while I'm giving it to you," she bantered.

"I mean, I'll take it. Some of it," he corrected. "But you make it easy to love you."

She blinked at him. "You love me?"

"Are you kidding? I've loved you since you forced yourself into my life and demanded a friendship with me all those years ago," he teased.

Her eyes closed and her chin dipped. "Oh, right."

Placing his finger underneath her chin, he raised it, willing her to look at him. She opened her glossy eyes.

"But now I love you in a new, unique way that I never thought I'd be lucky enough to. This time, instead of forcing yourself, you've welcomed me into this new, intimate part of your life and I'm soaking it up and trying to savor it. I'm definitely not worthy, but regardless, I love every part of you."

Kelsey's eyes watered and she gripped his neck, drawing his face close to hers. "Darn it, Davis, you know I hate being vulnerable. It makes me feel so...exposed."

He shrugged a shoulder, his hand gliding against the smooth curve of her lower back. "I mean, you are naked."

She snorted a laugh before saying, "So help me God, I love you, Davis Vance."

The pressure that was previously building in his chest released, and he kissed her smiling lips. He clutched her around the back and in one swift motion, rolled her on top of him. With her warm body pressing against him, he could think of nothing else other than showing her exactly how much he loved her. Again, and again. He'd spend the entire day trying to convince her if that's what it took.

The vibrating of his phone as it skittered across his nightstand sounded distant and he tried to block it out while he spread languid kisses down Kelsey's neck. She writhed on top of him, and he felt like he'd won the lottery with this woman. How had he gotten so lucky?

But the damn phone vibrated again. She pushed herself up, so she was straddling him. He gazed at her with pure appreciation. He truly was one lucky S.O.B. He wanted to stare at this view all day.

"Make the buzzing stop," she grumbled, stretching across him, and reaching for his phone.

This position of hers was so achingly perfect and tempting, he snatched her up in his arms.

She giggled and handed him the phone. "It's Garrett. Sounds urgent."

He took the phone and read the missed texts from Garrett

and groaned. They were shooting today. He'd completely forgotten. And he was already an hour late.

Not only had he missed Garrett's texts, but his producer's texts as well.

"What is it?" she asked, stroking a teasing finger down his chest.

As much as he didn't want to make her stop, he had to. "I forgot about the shoot today."

"Are you serious?" She smacked him in the gut.

"Hey! What happened to the loving touches?"

Climbing off him, she groaned. "You forgot they were filming? Like for your show? Your last show of the season?"

"Yeah." He scooted to the edge of the bed and threw his legs over.

She picked up her pile of clothing from the chair in the corner of his room. "How do you forget something that important?"

"Believe me, you've been quite distracting this morning. Do you know what you look like?" he teased, grinning.

She crumpled his t-shirt and tossed it at him. "Whatever. But if we're going to do this, like have a real relationship, we need to tell each other things. Maybe we should share calendars or something?"

"Okay, I can do that."

Share calendars. Now there was a thought. One he found he didn't mind.

They'd advanced several spaces in this relationship game just this morning. They admitted they were happy. They had both confessed they loved each other. And now, they were in a real relationship.

Kelsey shimmied into her jeans and hell, he could get used to this too. Watching her get dressed. Watching her get undressed was even better, but he'd take this too.

He smirked at her before turning around and strutting into the bathroom. He sent a quick text to Garrett and then splashed cold water on his face, hopeful it would be enough to cool him down.

Davis squeezed toothpaste on his toothbrush before shoving it into his mouth and stepping out of the bathroom. He wanted to take advantage of every opportunity he had to gaze at her before she left his house. And he needed a promise from her that they'd see one another that night. It would be the only thing to get him through his last day of shooting.

But when he entered the bedroom, he found Kelsey sitting on the chair in the corner, concentrating on the papers in her hands. She glanced up, brows raised and confusion smearing her expression.

"What is this?" She held the papers out to him.

His jaw went slack, and the toothbrush dangled from his mouth and threatened to plunge to the floor. He caught it just in time, taking it out of his mouth. There wasn't time to come up with an excuse. He needed to rip off the Band-Aid.

"An offer? Partners for the bar?"

He nodded. "I was waiting for the right moment to discuss that." He approached her, rounding the bed cautiously. The look on her face told him, there would never be a right moment.

"Like when? After we slept together?"

The hurt shining in her eyes penetrated his soul. It sucked the breath from his lungs and stole the words from his mouth.

"The date on these papers is two weeks ago. In the last two weeks you couldn't find the time to bring this up?"

"I'm sorry, okay? But it never felt like the right time. Was I supposed to bring it up when the Pineridge rumor mill thought you slept with my brother? Or when a sleaze ball out-of-town investor offered to buy you out? Or when you were finally opening up to me? Maybe, when you were dealing with your alcoholic mother?"

"That's not fair. Don't try to put this on me." She snatched her gray sweater from the top of his dresser and yanked it on over her tank top.

His chest lurched as he felt her urgency to flee. He took a hold of her hand, stilling her. "You're right. And I'm not meaning to. I should've talked to you right away. But our relationship shifted so quickly. When we crossed that line of friendship, I wasn't sure how to approach this."

"That's just it, Davis. We may have crossed the line of friendship, but that doesn't mean we stop being friends. I hoped that meant our friendship would deepen. Instead, it's like the sex gave you brain fog." She wrenched her hand from his holding and rushed past him and out of the bedroom.

"Would you wait a minute? You don't even know what the offer is." He chased after her, his undone belt dangling as he went down the hall.

She whipped around and he nearly bumped into her. He stumbled to a stop.

"What's the offer?" She stared him down, her eyes brimming with challenge. The confidence he always admired about her was present but taking on a different meaning now.

"My plan was never to change anything. You'll get to run the bar however you want. You still make the decisions. I'll be like a silent partner."

Tears welled up in her eyes as she stared into his for a moment, her lips pinched together. Until finally, she asked, "Why?"

"Why? Because I want to help."

His words were like a blow to her chest. It was as if she deflated before his very eyes. Her shoulders caved in, her tears fell, and her chin dropped. He waited for her reply for what felt like forever; the seconds ticking by agonizingly slow.

When she finally spoke, her voice came out scratchy. "While your offer is generous, it's too generous and I'm afraid I can't accept."

"C'mon, Kels, stop being stubborn," he said, but realized too late he should've only said that in his head.

"When I asked you *why*, maybe if you would've said, because you believe in the bar and you think it will be a good investment, then maybe I would've seriously considered your offer. But doing it because you want to help me—" she paused and her body looked smaller, more fragile somehow— "isn't a good enough reason."

"You're right. I didn't mean that. Or at least not *just* that. Look, when the contract is done with Renovation Dudes, I want to do something different. And I want an excuse if they try to extend the contract. Investing in O'Henry's could help us both."

It was too little too late. But he had to at least try.

"I have to go," she said, turning around and heading to the front door.

He continued to follow her. "You're running out of time."

She shoved her feet into her Chuck Taylor's, lacing them quickly. "Don't you think I know that?"

"You'd rather lose the bar altogether than agree to my offer?"

"I don't know."

"You don't know?"

His phone continued to vibrate in his back pocket, and he ignored it.

She stepped outside and he followed in his bare feet. "If I do accept your offer..." she paused, and motioned between them, "this is gonna end. I can't do both. I *won't* do both."

His chest tightened, and he fought for air. "Fine. Then forget the contract. I choose this. I choose us," he finally said, attempting to swoop her into his arms but she resisted him.

"I need some time."

As much as he didn't want to respect her wishes, he had to. He'd been patient, waiting for her to heal after losing Ricky and waiting for her to open herself up to him. He'd have to wait for this too.

Taking a step backward, he nodded.

"I'll see you later." She turned and hurried down the walkway toward her minivan.

He watched her go, his chest aching.

Which mistake had been the biggest? Coming up with the offer to begin with or not presenting it to her?

And was he doing this just for her? The bar seemed to be thriving. But did that mean he wanted to invest in it? He didn't know the first thing about running a restaurant. He knew wood. He knew home designing.

Maybe Kelsey was right, maybe he'd acted on impulse and this decision was a bad idea.

CHAPTER 27

Kelsey

An afternoon with her bestie was exactly what Kelsey needed. Isabella and Leo had invited her and the kids over to roast marshmallows and make s'mores. When she arrived at their home off the mountainous road, and next to part of the river that ran through town, June and Zach ran ahead of her.

Kelsey trudged across the soggy terrain while Charlotte clung to her neck, just like she always did until she'd had some time to warm up to her surroundings. By the time she reached the firepit, Leo was already helping her kids stuff marshmallows on the end of poker sticks. Charlotte gave a squeal when she noticed the fire.

"I can see my children have made themselves right at home," Kelsey muttered, giving them a look of warning.

"Don't worry, they used their manners," Izzy assured her.

"They better have." Kelsey adjusted Charlotte on her hip, but the little one wasn't quite ready to be put down just yet.

"Mama, look, Auntie Izzy said I can have two mallows," June said, flashing a delighted smile.

"Lovely, is that so?" Kelsey replied.

"You can have two marshmallows too, if you want?" Izzy held them out like a peace offering.

She snatched one from her palm, rolling her eyes playfully at Izzy as she gave it to Charlotte. When the baby kicked her legs, Kelsey set her down and watched while she happily took a giant bite of the marshmallow.

"Charlotte, wanna cookie?" Leo knelt in front of Charlotte, handing her a graham cracker and she grinned as she accepted it.

"And that's how it's done," Leo said.

Izzy waved him off. "Stop bragging. Once she's old enough to appreciate shopping, who do you think she'll be coming to?"

"Hopefully you, because I won't have the money to support that addiction," Kelsey said.

But her joke fell flat.

Charlotte took off, a treat in each pudgy fist as she scaled the Adirondack chairs with her arms. Kelsey followed quickly behind her. Since she was almost walking, she couldn't let her out of her sight.

"I can keep an eye on her, if you wanna make a s'more," Leo offered.

"You sure?"

But the two of them were already on the move. With June and Zach across the fire, roasting their marshmallows, Kelsey took a minute to breath. She sat on one of the Adirondack chairs, admiring the craftsman quality.

Izzy handed her a poker stick with a marshmallow already stuffed onto the end. She accepted with a grateful smile before holding it close to the hot, fiery coals at the base of the fire. It was beautiful out here. Away from the tight-knit community of Pineridge, more accurately, away from the gossip.

There was a sense of peace, hearing the bubbling of the river at the shore where Izzy's yard ended. The giggles of her children sent warmth radiating in her chest that swallowed the chill in the air. The aspens were showing off their autumn colors, boasting in yellows, golds, and reds. Their fallen leaves underfoot wouldn't stay that way long. Not with three small children who were skilled at making piles and jumping into nature's confetti.

"Have you given it more thought? What you're gonna do?" Izzy asked as she laid a blanket over Kelsey's lap.

"About which thing, exactly?"

"All of it, I guess," Izzy admitted, twirling her own poker stick in the fire.

As Kelsey stared at the red coals, mesmerized by the glow as it flickered, she said, "I think it's time."

Whipping her head in Kelsey's direction, Izzy said, "Time for what?"

"Time to let O'Henry's go."

Instead of questioning her decision, Izzy remained quiet. They both sat in silence for a long moment, focused on the blazing fire. It didn't last long, the kids were chasing Leo around the yard, throwing handfuls of leaves at him and laughing hysterically.

Kelsey pinched the nearly burnt marshmallow as she slid it off the stick. She blew at it in between saying, "I'm ready for something different."

"You're not gonna give in and help your mama out at the bakery, are you?"

"Not on your life," Kelsey muttered. "You know I love her, but it's also time she grows up too. If Cheryl can't handle the bakery while she's at rehab, then she'll have to close until she's back."

When Izzy didn't respond, Kelsey glanced over her shoulder at her where she sat next to her. When she did, she found her gazing at her, her eyes bright and glossy. Suddenly self-conscious, Kelsey tucked her hair behind her ear with her free, non-sticky hand.

"What?"

"It's nothing...just...I'm proud of you."

A blush of heat swept across her cheeks. "Alright, stop it."

"Stop what?"

"Saying it is one thing, doing it is something entirely different." She took a bite of the gooey marshmallow before deciding it would be less messy if she popped the entire thing in her mouth.

"Have you ever thought of being a photographer's assistant?" Izzy waggled her brows.

Still chewing, Kelsey smirked and finally said, "Something tells me Leo and I working together would be a bad idea. We're both too headstrong for that."

Izzy laughed and nodded in agreement.

"Something will feel right. Until then," Kelsey said, watching her kids, nostalgia building in her chest, "I'll enjoy my time with my kids."

Isabella patted Kelsey's knee. "I think that's a great idea."

AFTER SHE PAID JULIAN AND SOPHIA THEIR LAST paychecks, Izzy, Leo, Norah, and Maddie helped Kelsey pack up what was hers in the bar. She'd debated asking Davis to help. Mostly because she simply wanted to see him. She missed him. But it was true what she'd said, she needed space. She needed time.

"I think that's the last of the boxes from the kitchen," Leo said, hands on his hips and slick sweat on his brow, despite it being under forty degrees outside.

"Thanks," she said, glancing around the empty dining area of the bar, and trying not to focus on one area too long.

There were memories all over this place. From her childhood, her teenage years when she, Leo, Ricky, and Izzy hung out here, from her adult years as she supported Ricky's dream. Even the past year she'd worked here tirelessly.

The anguish built in her chest and tears threatened at the corners of her eyes. But she wouldn't cry here. She'd wait, until she was alone. Ben and Jerry's would be getting an earful tonight, that was for sure.

"I think all that's left is the office. And you mentioned you wanted to pack that up on your own," Isabella said.

Right. The office.

Not only had it been Ricky's office, but then hers. She'd never spent much time in there until after Ricky had passed. Mostly, she only came to O'Henry's so the kids could see their daddy before bed, or she'd pick up dinner and take it to her in-laws.

"It's mostly packed up. It will just take me a minute."

"Take your time," Maddie said.

Kelsey bit her bottom lip and nodded before turning and heading to the back of the restaurant. Inside the office, she'd already cleaned up the Halloween decorations, wrapped up the kids' photos, and taken down Ricky's posters from the walls.

The old green tool bag sat on the desk, and she dragged a finger across the worn material, her heart racing. Tears welled in the corners of her eyes, and she blinked them back. Lifting the heavy bag, she set it into a box and closed the flaps.

Her eyes took a trip around the small space, taking in every nook and cranny, trying to memorize the room in its entirety. When her gaze found the couch, her mind was bombarded with the memory of her and Davis making love there. The loss of him hit her out of nowhere. She'd been prepared to miss Ricky, but this curveball surprised her.

Her chest filled and tightened as her heartbeat thudded louder and faster. While she did miss her late husband and the life they shared together, she'd already grieved him. Now, she felt as if she was grieving the friendship with Davis. She yearned for him, and what they'd been. She craved him and what they could be.

She had to hold onto hope that he hadn't given up on her, because she wasn't ready to give up on them. She'd lost too much. But him, and their friendship, she wasn't willing to let go of either. If she'd learned anything through the process of losing Ricky and now O'Henry's, it was that life was too short. You had to grab onto what you wanted and not let go.

When Kelsey had found the job listing online at Tapp's Brewery as an assistant brewmaster, her stomach had fluttered with excitement. Learning how to brew beer had always been an interest of hers. She'd told Ricky it would save them money in the long run if they supplied their own, but he'd always shot down the idea.

Sure, she lacked the skills and experience for the job, but everyone had to start somewhere. And she'd had a longstanding relationship with the current brewmaster, along with the owner of Tapp's Brewery.

She didn't want pity. But at this point in her life, she wasn't opposed to groveling. This new career could be the best thing for her. But she wouldn't know unless she tried.

Dressed in heels, her black leather leggings—*thank you,*

Spanx—and a blue sweater, she entered Tapp's Brewery with her head held high. Even though her ankles wobbled, she hadn't worn heels in quite some time, she felt confident.

Her phone buzzed in her purse. She wanted to ignore it. But when you were a mom, you didn't have that luxury.

She pulled out her phone, and a smile tugged at her lips after seeing her mom's name on the screen.

MAMA

Hey, love bug. Just checking if you were still planning on coming to family weekend?

Of course. The kids are really excited to see you!

MAMA

I can't wait. I miss you all!

Only a few more weeks and you'll be done. I'm so proud of you, Mama!

MAMA

Love you! See you in a few days.

Despite Kai Johnson's boyish face, he had a body resemblance to The Rock, with similar Samoan tribal tattoos on his chest and arm. He grew up in Pineridge and after he finished college in Oregon, he returned with a business degree and opened Tapp's Brewery. He and Kelsey had never been super close as he was a few years younger than her, but they'd done business together and that meant something.

She hoped.

Standing inside the brewery's restaurant, Kelsey glanced around, admiring the space. It was bare, though with a rustic Pineridge vibe she could appreciate. The door to Kai's office opened and she straightened.

"Kelsey?" Kai scratched at his chin. "You're here to interview for the assistant brewmaster position?"

She nodded and raised her hands at her sides. "Yep. Surprise."

He chuckled nervously. "Yeah, surprised is right. I mean... don't get me wrong, I'm stoked you're here, I just never thought you'd be interested."

"Well, not only have I been serving beer for nearly a year. I was in business with you and a number of other breweries, which required me to sample all the different brews." She talked fast. Or maybe it only sounded fast to her own ears.

He adjusted the trucker hat on his head with the large Tapp's Brewery logo across the front in bold threaded lettering. "Okay, yeah, I feel you. Why don't you come with me, I wanna show you something. It's been a while since you've been in the brew pit."

"Oh, uh...sure...I just thought..." she paused, hiking a thumb over her shoulder as she hurried to keep up with his stride, "we would go into your office for the interview."

"You already sold yourself, you're overqualified for an interview."

She wasn't really sure what that meant, but excitement thrummed in her chest. Kai took her into the brew pit, where giant, shiny vats lined up against one side of the wall. All her senses were on heightened alert and her skin tingled.

"First, I want you to taste the newest brew we've been working on. Then I'll introduce you to our brewmaster."

"Okay," she answered with a giddiness she'd never felt before.

"The brewery is going through a lot of changes. New assistant brewmaster," he said, gesturing to her and causing her pulse to pick up, "New brews, new investors, and new marketing. I'm excited about where it's headed, and who we have on our team. While I'm hoping to expand, I won't jeopardize the local vibe at Tapp's. We're here in Pineridge for a reason. And we're here to stay."

She loved everything she was hearing. This was exactly what she loved about Tapp's, about Pineridge. But she couldn't find words to respond.

He continued, "That's why, as soon as I saw you in here, I knew you were the one for the job."

"Are you telling me, I have the job? Just like that?" Her brows lifted.

"If you're for real, and you want it, it's yours."

Relief poured through her veins, but also excitement. The more she'd thought about this opportunity as a possibility, the more she realized how bad she wanted it.

"Are you kidding? Of course I want it."

Kai grinned. "Good. I was hoping that's what you'd say."

CHAPTER 28

Davis

After the producer called— "That's a wrap!"—Davis felt the thundering applause in his chest. The emotions that burned in his eyes surprised him if he was being honest. With the finish line to the end of the season of Renovation Dudes always in his vision but seeming far from reach, it was hard to believe it was finally over.

Garrett wrapped him up in a hug, smacking his back and uttering a *congrats* in his ear.

He said it back to his twin, the relief thick in his throat. "Congrats. We did it."

Rearing back, but still holding his shoulders, Garrett said, "See, was that so bad?"

Bad wasn't the right word. But at least he'd managed to last through the season without quitting. Admittedly, he enjoyed some of the episodes, and not just the work and designing. Being alongside his brother during all the tapings gave him a comfort he wouldn't have had otherwise. Now that it was over, he realized the show itself wasn't all that bad.

"I'm glad we got to do this together," Davis admitted.

With hopefulness in his eyes, Garrett said, "If you're up for it, something tells me we're going to be offered to sign a new contract."

They hadn't spoken about Davis wanting to go in as partners with Kelsey since the day at Sweet Cakes. After word got around town she'd decided to sell, Davis didn't see a point in discussing it again. But as far as the contract with HGTV, that was still up in the air.

Davis glanced down, studying his boots as they shuffled back and forth. "I can't make any promises."

"That's fine." Garrett held up his palms in surrender. "Take the six-week break before we start taping the next season to relax. The new contract won't come until spring anyway...if it does come."

Franklin stepped in between them then, interrupting, "Oh believe me, it will come. Our ratings on the last episode were through the roof. Whatever this new charisma is with you, Davis, it's working."

Franklin could thank Kelsey and the rumors circling around town for his new *"charisma"*. Though since their argument at his place over two weeks ago, they hadn't seen one another or spoken. He'd given her a week of silence before he tried, sending her a text apologizing, and letting her know he missed her. It had taken her two days to respond with a text that simply said, *I'm still not ready.*

"The crew is heading to Tapp's Brewery to celebrate," Garrett said, an arm still hooked around Davis's neck.

He had seen the *closed* sign in the front window of O'Henry's almost a week ago. The sight of the vacant parking lot gave him chills. The realization also hit him hard—Kelsey hadn't asked him for his help or his advice. Just the very idea that they were drifting apart felt suffocating.

"Count me in," Davis said.

"All right." Garrett fist bumped him.

Getting out of the house would do him some good. While he could tell Cooper enjoyed him being home, cuddling on the couch with him while he sipped spiked hot cider and watched stupid romcoms missing Kelsey, it was growing embarrassingly ridiculous.

INSIDE AN ABANDONED AND REMODELED INDUSTRIAL building, Tapp's Brewery had a local, relaxed atmosphere. It was simple and that's what Davis appreciated most about it. A chill vibe and unornamented, made it the kind of place that would make any resident of Pineridge, no matter their income bracket, feel at ease.

While their beer menu was extensive, their food menu was simple. It made ordering quick, easy, and painless. He felt relaxed and all the usual tension in his shoulders and gut released.

When he saw Kai Johnson, the owner of Tapp's enter the restaurant, he strolled over to him to say hello.

"Hey, Kai?" he called just as Kai was about to leave and enter the brewery side of the building.

Kai spun around and circled back. "Davis Vance. What's up, brother?" He gave Davis a fist bump.

"How's life?" Davis crossed his arms, gripping his forearms.

"Groovy. Can't complain." Kai tipped his hat. "What about you? The show? Is it over yet?"

"Just wrapped up tonight."

"Awesome, I'll catch you on my TV then." He held out his hand.

"Yeah, sounds good." Davis found himself in some strange

secret handshake he wasn't privy on the details of but managed to make it through.

As Kai strutted away, he called over his shoulder, "If you need a job in your downtime, come see me."

Heat flushed through Davis's body in an instant. "Wait... are you serious?"

Kai eyed him curiously. "I mean, brother, not really. I don't have a job; my last opening has already been filled. But I am looking for a partner. Think you might be interested?"

Davis tilted his head, his skin tingling as a thrill shot through him. *Kai was looking for a partner?* Something like this felt like a once in a lifetime opportunity. And maybe the exact thing he'd been craving.

"Hell, yeah."

Kai's thin lips pulled into a wide smile. "Well, all right then. Man, I don't know how I keep getting so lucky. First Kelsey, then you."

All at once, it felt as if his heart slammed against his chest and the air sucked from his lungs.

"Kelsey?" her name came out like an exhale.

"Yeah." Kai frowned at him. "I thought you two were inseparable. You didn't know?"

Davis shook his head solemnly while mixed emotions ran through him.

"She's in the brewpit. C'mon." Kai waved him inside the door that led to the brewing area.

His legs felt like wet noodles as he walked. She'd made it clear she wanted space and didn't want to see him. And yet, he had a strong desire to see *her*.

When he turned a corner, Davis saw her. She stood on the ladder in front of one of the giant kettles as the steam rose and poured hops into the boiling brew. With a determined expression on her face, Davis felt a shot of adrenaline pulse through him.

Kai nudged him in the side. "Meet Tapp's newest partner and brewmaster. She's a natural."

She looked it.

She was beautiful.

Davis had admired her as a mother, and a bar owner, as a daughter, and as a friend. But in that moment, as he stared at her doing something she was passionate about, it shook something loose inside of him. This was to her like woodworking was for him. It looked as if it calmed her. And he wanted to stand there and watch her for the rest of the day.

But after she closed the kettle and turned around on the top of the ladder, she saw him and the two locked eyes. He sucked in a breath, and she froze. For what felt like forever, they held eye contact neither giving away how they might be feeling. Until finally, she gave him one nod with her chin, her lips curving into a smile, the one he fell asleep imagining every night. And then she climbed down the ladder and went in the opposite direction.

Kai cleared his throat.

Davis swallowed and tore his eyes off her.

"When can we discuss this partnership?" he asked eagerly.

"Celebrate and party first, business later," Kai assured him.

With purpose in his steps, and hope in his heart, he followed Kai back into the restaurant to find Garrett and the Renovation Dude's crew.

THE FALL SEASON HAD NEARLY ENDED, AND DAVIS HADN'T taken his canoe out to the lake once since it began. Between

Renovation Dudes, the side projects, and helping Kelsey, he'd been busier than usual. Cooper ran up ahead as Davis dragged the canoe across the terrain and to the embankment.

"Some help you are," he called to the useless dog. This was why people had friends. Someone to take one end of the canoe so you didn't look like a dumbass dragging it for hundreds of feet by yourself.

Cooper stepped into the lake before turning around and immediately hightailing it back to meet Davis on the lake's edge.

Davis chuckled. "What were you thinking, boy? I told you it would be cold?" He heaved the canoe a bit further before dropping it onto the sand and releasing a strangled breath.

Cooper did zoomies and Davis just shook his head, watching the aging dog. Apparently, this ride was long overdue. He bent and pushed the canoe into the water, stopping when one end remained in the sand.

He whistled to Cooper. "All right, Coop. Get in." The dog did as he was told, jumping into the canoe and it rocked back and forth. "Sit," Davis commanded.

After Cooper sat, Davis pushed the canoe, launching it into the water and then he quickly hopped in. He sat on the seat as it jolted back and forth before slowly coming to rest. Davis wrapped a plaid, fleece blanket around Cooper and the dog panted in appreciation. Or at least, that's what Davis assumed was his emotion. He'd surely freeze his giblets off out here.

Davis covered his own lap with a blanket and then zipped his jacket up. Tugging his beanie down further, fighting off the biting breeze, he shuddered. Davis picked up an oar and began paddling them out deeper.

Through the thin fog, he spotted another canoe further in the distance and a small fishing boat. But other than that, the lake was scarce today. It was quiet and peaceful, and it was exactly what he needed.

His phone buzzed in the front pocket of his jeans. He ignored it and continued paddling. But when it buzzed again, he groaned, and yanked it out of his pocket.

GARRETT

Need to talk.

Meet me at Tapp's.

Tapp's Brewery had become Garrett's new hangout since O'Henry's closed. Thinking of O'Henry's only made him think about Kelsey. And he couldn't let his mind go there.

The past few weeks his senses had been on overload. The commotion during filming, sticking to their deadlines, Franklin, and that stupid memo that pretty much backfired on him. Because at the end of the season, after the rumor fiasco, Davis hadn't had to work his sex appeal after all. Turned out, some women—a lot of women actually—liked the nice, sweet guy who also was labeled as someone's best-sex-they'd-ever-had.

Davis didn't care anymore about any of it. All he was grateful for was that the season had wrapped up and he had six weeks off. It would hopefully give him the time to decide if he'd sign a new contract with HGTV or not. Since Kelsey hadn't taken him up on his offer, and Kai had presented him with the opportunity at Tapp's, it felt like the universe was pointing him in a new direction.

Kelsey took up a lot of space in his head these days. All the ways he'd messed up. All the ways he should've tried to make it better. He didn't only miss her and the love making, he missed her friendship. She was his person, the one he went to for everything. Without her, he felt lost.

What sounded like thunder boomed in his ears and Cooper

barked, startling him, and shaking him free from his Kelsey brain-fog. "Okay, boy, you ready to go back?"

The dog wagged his tail and panted.

Davis maneuvered the canoe and as he started for the shore, he noticed dark, ominous, clouds filled the sky. That much gloom meant it was about to downpour. Davis paddled faster.

The raindrops fell moments later, thudding onto the lake and ricocheting off the canoe. Shit. They were still several yards away. Cooper bounded toward him, hunkering down when he reached him, and whimpered near his boots.

"It's okay, boy. We're almost home," he lied. But Cooper wouldn't know the difference.

Davis glanced over both shoulders, searching for the other boats he saw earlier, but the fog had thickened across the darkened sky, and he could hardly see behind him. He returned his attention ahead, drove the oar into the water, deeper, faster. His heart raced, the adrenaline pumped, and he continued to whisper loudly to Cooper, if nothing else than to assure himself.

"We're okay, Coop. Almost there. Almost home. We got this."

At last, the shore came into view. But before he allowed himself release from the fear, he squinted and pushed the oar faster. The rainfall was filling the canoe rapidly and even though he could almost hop out on the shore, he held his breath.

Until, finally, the canoe slid up onto the sand and thudded to a stop. Davis whistled to Cooper, and he jumped out, the dog on his heels. With all his strength, he heaved the canoe out of the water and then slipped, falling back on his butt into the hard sand.

For now, the canoe would be fine left there. He and Cooper

made a run for his truck, the tension in his shoulders finally easing. His mind flashed first, to an image of the life jackets that were in his garage. Next, to an image of he and Cooper abandoning the submerged canoe and swimming back to the shore. Then, to an image of Kelsey, grieving the death of another lover.

He tripped up the embankment and he caught himself from falling completely, landing on his knees. Cooper stopped beside him and barked incessantly. "Cooper," Davis hollered over the torrent, his breathing accelerated, and his chest rising and falling rapidly. "It's okay. We're okay."

But Cooper continued to bark. A shadowy figure appeared in the distance through the somber fog. Davis sucked in a breath.

A voice cut through the noisy rainstorm. "Davis?"

He could scarcely hear it, but it was enough for him to decipher. He'd always be able to recognize his best friend's voice. His heart pounded and his entire body tingled.

"Davis?" she called again.

"Kels?" he responded, climbing back onto his feet, his legs wobbly.

When she finally came into clear view, his heart lurched in his chest. She stopped and he picked up his pace once again, rushing toward her. In that moment, he was so afraid he wouldn't make it to her in time before something like lightning struck one of them down. He would not allow anything to separate them again. Not stupid disagreements, or pride, and certainly not the weather.

CHAPTER 29
Kelsey

The rain came down in sheets, making her vision obscured. But she could recognize Davis's silhouette easily. Even more so, she could identify the sound of his voice.

With her heart beating fast, the pulse ticking in her neck, she picked up her pace, hurrying across the soggy terrain. The closer she got to him, the more desperate she felt to reach him.

Until at last, she did. Stopping in front of him, she pushed back her drenched hair while she frantically scanned his body, checking for what, she wasn't sure. That he was in one piece? That he was safe and not injured?

His clothes were soaked, rain dripped from his hair, and he'd never looked more enticing than he did at that moment. The outline of his sculpted chest as it rose and fell was amplified in the wet flannel. Her blaring and rapid heartbeat made her feel alive, and not only her hormones.

"What are you doing out here?" Davis shouted above the booming rainfall.

"Me?" she replied. "I was looking for you. What are you doing out here?"

"You shouldn't be here. It's not safe."

She licked the rain from her lips. "It's not safe for you either," she insisted.

Cooper barked.

She glanced at him momentarily. He was soaked, but besides that and clearly being worried, he looked okay too.

"You need to hurry up and get out of here. You're drenched." He took her hand and tugged her with him.

But she wrenched her hand from his grip. "It's too late. I can't get any wetter at this point."

He tilted his head, studying her. "Well, what do you plan on doing? Standing out here in the rainstorm all night?"

"If that's what it takes," she stated.

"What it takes?"

Cooper circled them, releasing a string of barks.

"I'm sorry," she finally shouted.

He frowned. "Sorry? What are you sorry for?"

She took a tentative step toward him. "Oh, c'mon, are you gonna make me say it?"

Confusion still overtook his expression. "Yeah, I guess I am."

"Fine, stubborn ass," she muttered, wiping a hand across her wet mouth.

"*Me* stubborn ass? Who pushed who away? Who hasn't even wanted to talk?"

"I'm sorry for pushing you away, okay? For not accepting your help...and...for letting you go." She tucked her hair behind her ears.

A wide smile pulled at his lips and he shook his head. "There. Was that so hard?"

She smirked. "You better say you're sorry for letting me go

too, or I'm turning right around and leaving you out here. I don't even care if you get struck by lightning."

He reached for her then, snatching her hand and yanking her into his arms in one swift move. She sucked in a breath, her chest pressed against his, the unforgiving downpour not letting up and giving them any reprieve.

But all wet, and in the dimness of the late afternoon, Davis looked at her seductively, his dark eyes flaring. She could see his craving for her, feel it deep in her bones, and the ache for him grew between her thighs. A trembling racked her body from the iciness of the rain as it soaked her.

"I'm sorry," he said again, his breath the only warmth to touch her skin and it caused a shiver to shoot through her.

Despite the longing for him, she said, teasingly, "I didn't quite hear you, what was that?"

"I'm sorry," he shouted.

She snorted a laugh, rising to tiptoe and tethering her arms around his neck.

"I shouldn't have let you go." He squeezed her to him, tighter. "You're the best thing to ever happen to me. You and the kids. You guys are the best things in my life. Kels, I not only love our friendship, but I love our sexship."

She choked on a laugh. "Our what?"

"I don't know," he said with a chuckle. "It sounded better in my head. Our lovemakingship?" he tried again. "Fine, our rela-tionship. I just love all the ships. I love spending time with you, and I love you."

Tears burned at her eyes. That was enough for her. It was more than enough.

She drew his head down to her, their lips grazing before she whispered loudly like a confession, "I love us too...I love you."

Even though her clothes were soaked through, and her skin was cold down to her bones, when Davis finally pressed his wet lips against her own, it was like he set a fire there. It burned in the most satisfying way possible. He ravished her mouth as her lips parted, inviting his tongue inside to tangle with hers.

It was heated and sensual all at once and as her body reacted to the sultry kiss, shuddering from both pleasure and the cold. His hands held onto her back, keeping her pressed tightly against him. He lowered his head and bestowed kisses to her slick neck. She wanted him. She hungered for him.

"I was so worried about you," she said, breathlessly into his ear. "What if...what if something had happened to you?"

He lifted his chin, brushing the scruff of his cheek against hers, squeezing her body even more snug. "Shh...I'm okay, I'm okay," he whispered.

"I can't lose you," her words choked out.

"You won't," he replied, pressing his lips to hers and kissing her again and again.

"You can't know that."

He reared back, raising her chin with his finger. "You're right. But what I can promise you, for as long as I live, you'll have me."

In Kelsey's experience, she should worry about that. But instead, his words comforted her, gifting her with an ease her anxieties and her heart needed.

"And you'll have me," she replied.

He kissed her again, sweetly, gently. For a moment, she had forgotten about the rainstorm, about Cooper bounding through mud and barking, and about her freezing body that was now shaking.

"Let's get you out of the cold," he said.

"Maybe...y-you...can think of a w-way...to warm me up," she said, her teeth chattering.

As they began their trek back to the small gravel parking

lot, his gaze traveled down the length of her, his brows furrowing. "Why are you dressed up?"

"There was a...p-party at Tapp's. When I saw Garrett there and he told me he h-hadn't heard from you, I got w-worried. I j-just knew you were out here being s-stupid in this bad storm."

"You were worried about me?" he gave her a teasing smile.

She rolled her eyes. "Don't p-push it." Her teeth chattered and she'd never been so happy to reach Garrett's truck. Her hand shook as she yanked on the handle and hurried inside.

He chuckled and let Cooper into the cab of the truck before climbing in himself. "What was the party for?"

"It was for me...and you."

His brows lifted. "Me?"

"When were you going to tell me about Tapp's?"

"When were *you*?"

She pursed her lips. "Fine. Call it even?"

He smirked. "Looks like the two of us ended up as partners after all."

They made eye contact and she nodded. "Looks like it."

He pulled a hoodie out of the console of the truck and handed it to her. "Here, put this on. It will be big on you, but at least it's dry."

She unwrapped it and gazed at the *Tapp's Brewery* logo on the front. "It's perfect."

He simply shrugged. "Perks of owning a business."

"*Our* business," she said.

"I like the sound of that."

"Besides being partners in business though, we're already the best kind of partners. Friends and lovers."

He rested his hand on her thigh, eliciting a shiver from her that racked her entire body. His eyes darkened and he grinned. "I can't decide which I like best."

She leaned across the center console, her lips drawing near his, teasing him. "Maybe I can help you decide," she whispered.

"It might take some time to convince me," his voice growled just before he drew her in for another kiss.

She pulled back slightly, her gaze moving over his face. "That's okay, I've got time."

He grazed her cheek with his thumb. "As in...the rest of your life?"

Her eyes watered again. "Davis Vance, are you asking me what I think you're asking me?

He chuckled. "I guess I am."

"While we're both drenched and freezing, and I've got mascara running down my face? Because you better not be."

Resting his other hand on her face, he brushed some of the black makeup off her cheek. "You're beautiful. Besides, you've never cared about all that nonsense."

A wide smile pulled at her lips, and she swallowed the rising lump in her throat, her watering eyes dancing over his. "We've never even officially dated. And I don't know if I ever want to get married again. But...there's no one else for me but you."

"Who said anything about marriage? I just want you to spend the rest of your life with me, Kels."

She laughed and nodded and before she could get any words out, he pulled her in closer and smashed his lips against hers; sealing their commitment with a kiss.

Acknowledgments

First, I'd like to thank God for giving me the gift of writing, for giving me grace where it's needed, and giving me the strength to pursue this author life.

Which leads me to the next person who's responsible for encouraging me to pursue this often times, wild dream—my husband, Jeremy. This book was by far the hardest for me and you never stopped believing I could finish it. You support me in many ways, and I definitely wouldn't have any published books if it weren't for you. I love you and thank God each day for you!

Thank you to my kids, Jensen, Jaidyn, and Jace, for accepting this dream of mine as a part of life, and as my career. You all have supported and encouraged me in different ways, and I love you so much. I see the way you each have taken to your own passions and are beginning to pursue your own dreams and I couldn't be prouder to be your mom.

To the talented artist, Stephanie Henigen, (@stephsbook-therapy) who designed the perfect cover characters for Davis and Kelsey. Thank you for collaborating with me in creating this beautiful series. And thank you for making the cutest book boyfriend bookmarks!

Thank you to my parents who gave me wings and roots. I miss you every day, Dad. To my in-laws who continue to support me, I'm so blessed by you.

There's no way I would've finished this book without a few important people. My CP's, betas, and alpha readers, Bethany

Dodson, Lissa Ruck, Ashley King, and Katherine Quinn. My words are not enough to say thank you. But I hope you know how truly wonderful each of you are. I'll take you on this journey with me always.

To my siblings, thanks for teaching me about life and love and forgiveness. Love you all.

To those of you who came along at some point during my journey, whether you've been here all along or have shown your support recently—thank you. To the ones who have joined in for cover reveals, and entered giveaways, who have tagged me in, (positive) reviews, who have commented, liked, re-posted, shared my Instagram stories: Thank you! It's people like you who deserve the praise. There are so many authors who have welcomed me, taken me under their wing, gave me a seat at the table, and accepted me. Even as I navigate both traditional and indie publishing. I hope I can return the love you have shown me. Authors like, Torie Jean, Zoe Shae, to name a few.

And last but certainly not least, to my readers, reviewers, and bookstagrammers—if you've stuck with me through this book, I thank you from the bottom of my heat. This was by far my toughest book. Some are just like that, and this was one of those for me. Between writer's block, a cross-country move, losing our dog, Samson, a change in editors part way through, losing my dad, and taking back the rights and re-publishing this myself, it was tough to get through. There were several times I questioned if I'd ever finish. But my passion for writing and telling love stories continued to reveal itself, and very special people kept reminding me that I could do it. They pushed me when I didn't want to be pushed, they believed in me when I didn't believe in myself, they reminded me why I started writing to begin with. So, I did not quit. I completed it. I did the dang thing!

About the Author

 Starla DeKruyf writes swoony love stories with a happily ever after. Her love of romance novels began when she borrowed her friend's copy of Tiger Eyes by Judy Blume and kept it hidden from her mom. When she's not working the day job or hanging out with her family, you can find her jamming out to her book playlists and writing her next swoony romance, usually by hand. She lives in Spring, Texas, with her husband, three children, and a rescue pup.

Pineridge series—book 1:

Eight Days of Christmas

Pineridge series—book 3:

A Little Bit Yours

Juniper Ridge series—book 1:

A Pumpkin Patch and A Fling

A Standalone Romantic Comedy:

The Heart Rehab Experiment

www.ingramcontent.com/pod-product-compliance
Lightning Source LLC
Chambersburg PA
CBHW011413310726
48972CB00011B/2960